She was the target.

If Logan hadn't been with her, she might've died... But he and Boomer *had* been. He'd probably saved her life, but he was injured because of that. All these thoughts tumbled over each other. "Oh, God," she whispered, and stepped into Logan's comforting arms. When they enfolded her, she broke down sobbing. Of all her concerns, she voiced the one that made most sense to her troubled mind. "You're hurt. You got hurt because of me," she said in a quavering voice.

Logan held Ariana as she cried. He never would've imagined this strong, determined woman capable of tears, let alone falling apart as she was. Knowing that others would be joining them soon, he encouraged her to pull herself together. He recognized how fragile she was—and that caused a whole maelstrom of emotions to break loose inside him, not the least of which was a reminder of why he'd avoided relationships his entire life.

Dear Reader,

It seems like yesterday that I placed my fingers on the keyboard to start writing *When the Right One Comes Along*, the first book in my K-9 Trilogy. It's hard to believe this third book is now complete, too.

I've spent a considerable amount of time over the past year and a half with Cal, Jessica and Scout; Rick, Madison, Sniff and Nitro; and finally Logan, Ariana and Boomer. I've enjoyed discovering these characters' stories, and their heartbreaks and happily-ever-afters.

When I Found You is a work of fiction. Although it refers to the leaked results of Homeland Security's inspector general's 2015 covert testing of the Transportation Safety Administration's (TSA's) operations and technology, I want to draw special attention to the difficult and demanding job that TSA's frontline workforce performs. I would also like to recognize the San Diego Harbor Police, who have responsibility for providing law-enforcement services at San Diego International Airport. Although in the story I assigned this responsibility to the San Diego Police Department, the Harbor Police's Explosives Detection K-9 Team is currently the only TSA-certified explosives-detection team south of Los Angeles. I hope they will forgive me for the liberties I have taken in the name of fiction.

I hope you enjoy *When I Found You*, and maybe you'll miss these characters a little, the way I do. I've provided some discussion questions on my website, in case you'd like to use this story for your book club.

As always, I would love to hear from you! You can connect with me at www.kate-james.com, www.Facebook.com/katejamesbooks, @katejamesbooks or at PO Box 446, Schomberg, ON, L0G 1T0, Canada.

Kate

HEARTWARMING

When I Found You

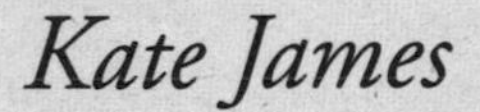

Recycling programs for this product may not exist in your area.

ISBN-13: 978-0-373-36797-9

When I Found You

This edition published by arrangement with Harlequin Books S.A.

For questions and comments about the quality of this book, please contact us at CustomerService@Harlequin.com.

Printed in U.S.A.

Kate James spent much of her childhood abroad before attending university in Canada. She built a successful business career, but her passion has always been literature. As a result, Kate turned her energy to her love of the written word. Kate's goal is to entertain her readers with engaging stories featuring strong, likable characters. Kate has been honored with numerous awards for her writing. She and her husband, Ken, enjoy traveling and the outdoors with their beloved Labrador retrievers.

Books by Kate James

Harlequin Heartwarming

A Child's Christmas
The Truth About Hope

The K-9 Trilogy

When the Right One Comes Along
When Love Matters Most

To my parents, for selflessly providing me with the opportunities and encouragement to pursue my dreams.

To the men and women who dedicate their lives to law enforcement—they deserve our unwavering support and gratitude.

Acknowledgments

My editor and I considered a number of titles for this book, but none seemed just right. So we asked readers. I was thrilled to see the tremendous enthusiasm demonstrated by many people. As it turned out, we didn't have just one winner but four: Summer Halls, Laurie Iglesias, June Smalls and Jill Weatherholt. Thank you, ladies!

I would also like to extend my appreciation to Maria Reeves for allowing me to "borrow" the name of her beloved yellow Labrador retriever, Darwin, for the newest four-legged member of the San Diego Police Department's K-9 Unit. Darwin and his handler, Shannon Clemens, might have their own story one day!

Thank you, once again, to Constable Jim Hilton and York Regional Police (Ontario, Canada). Constable Hilton, a member of YRP's canine unit, was invaluable to my research for this trilogy.

Finally, none of my books would be what they are without the contribution of my fabulous editor, Paula Eykelhof. Thank you, Paula, for all that you do! Thanks also to Victoria Curran, senior editor, for challenging me and all the Harlequin Heartwarming authors to tell the very best stories we can.

CHAPTER ONE

"THE PILOT'S BRINGING the plane back?" Ariana Atkins, chief of security and asset protection for the San Diego International Airport, swiveled away from her desk and stared at her senior security manager.

"Yeah. The plane is on its way," Max Golding responded. He was leaning against Ariana's door frame, a hand tucked into the pocket of his stylish dress pants. "You know as well as I do, it's the pilot's call."

"Two vacation-going women bound for Barbados overindulge in their duty-free alcohol purchase, are drunk before the plane is out of our airspace, get into a fight on board, and the pilot declares it a security risk and decides to turn the aircraft around? Have I got that right?"

"That sums it up." Max straightened. "I was told the flight crew had trouble calming them down."

He moved to Ariana's desk, fiddled with her mouse and called up the security camera footage he'd emailed her of the women at the gate.

"They were inebriated before they boarded! The gate crew shouldn't have let them on that flight."

"I can't argue with you about that. The San Diego Police Department is sending a team to meet the plane."

This was news to Ariana. "Why? We can handle two drunken women ourselves with the SDPD officers assigned to the airport."

Max shrugged. "I would've thought so, but one of the charming young ladies uttered a threat against the crew and passengers. She said, and I quote, that she'd blow them all to kingdom come."

Ariana rolled her eyes to the ceiling. "Great. Just great." That added weight to the pilot's decision to bring the plane back.

As far-fetched as it was that one of the women involved in the altercation might have a bomb on board, the United States Transportation Security Administration required that all such incidents be taken seriously.

They'd have to hold the plane away from the terminal building until they had confirmation that there were no explosive devices on board. Only then could it taxi to a gate.

Her stomach rumbled and she glanced at her watch. She'd missed lunch. It wasn't likely that she'd be having dinner anytime soon either.

"I can handle this, Ariana, if you want to go home." Obviously Max had heard her stomach, too. "You've averaged ten-hour days all week. You deserve some downtime."

She rose, grabbed her jacket from the back of her chair. "Thanks, but I'm okay. We've all been putting in long hours since the budget cuts. Besides, we could be dealing with a lot worse than two drunken women and a planeload of understandably disgruntled passengers."

"True." Max's iPhone pinged several times in quick succession. He checked the incoming messages. "Game time. The plane has landed, and two members of the SDPD K-9 Unit are on their way and authorized for the airfield. Oh, did I mention the plane has a fighter jet escort?" he said over his shoulder as he exited her office.

Ariana groaned at the absurdity of that. She followed Max out and locked her door. "I trust they're doing it as a training exercise rather than out of a belief that it's a matter of national security. And to make our day even brighter, we can look forward to spending time with Brody," she pointed out, referring to SDPD K-9 Unit officer Tom Brody, who was the airport's primary contact when dealing with bomb-related threats or drills. Brody's explosives detection canine partner, Nitro, was as efficient and effective as they came. Despite her phobia of dogs, Ariana had a far greater level of unease with Brody.

"No, we won't," Max interrupted her musings.

"Sorry. What?"

"We won't be seeing Brody again. He's no longer with the police department." Max's grin was bright and white, a sharp contrast against his dark complexion. "You hadn't heard?" he asked as they jogged down the escalator.

She shook her head. "What happened?"

"The department is trying to keep it quiet, but I was told he'd been on the take from one of the Mexican drug cartels. In addition to his other endearing qualities, he reportedly had a gambling addiction he had to feed. Even worse, there was something about a personal vendetta against one of his colleagues." Max's smile dimmed. "From what I understand, it's sordid stuff. If the allegations are substantiated and he's convicted, he'll do a long stretch of time."

Ariana let out a hiss of disgust. How on earth did guys like that get on the police force when they'd rejected her because of a simple heart murmur? She understood the rationale intellectually—but emotionally it festered. "Who are they sending instead?" she asked.

The smile was back on Max's face. "The captain of the K-9 Unit, Logan O'Connor. The renowned Jagger himself!" he added, bringing up the captain's police department nickname.

Oddly, Ariana had never met the captain during the year she'd been in her job. It wouldn't take much to be an improvement over Brody, but she'd heard O'Connor was a first-rate cop and an admirable leader. She was about to find out if that was true.

LOGAN O'CONNOR WAS feeling mean as a badger. He was on his way to the San Diego airport to deal with an absurd situation involving a couple of inebriated women uttering a bomb threat on a plane. And he was doing it after a long day, following another mostly sleepless night. To add to his annoyance, this was a call that Tom Brody should've been taking, if he hadn't been suspended from the department. Logan shook his head, as much in frustration as to clear his groggy brain.

He couldn't spend many more nights consoling Becca over her broken heart, or he would lose his sanity. Sometimes relationships just weren't meant to be.

No wonder he preferred the single life—easy and commitment-free. The promise he'd made to himself because of his mother was important, but so was avoiding complications.

What he wouldn't have given to spend last

night in his own bed. Instead, he'd sat with Becca on her sofa. When she'd ultimately cried herself out and drifted into a troubled sleep, he'd carried her to her bed. Then, as the first tentative streaks of pink and orange had stained the sky, he and Boomer, his explosives detection canine partner, had left Becca's apartment to return to his own house.

By the time he'd changed, gulped down a strong cup of black coffee, ate a stale muffin and made it to work, he was just in time for the start of his shift.

When he'd finally left the division, the call came in about the situation at the airport. Thanks to Brody's transgressions, Logan was now the only explosives detection handler on the K-9 Unit. Instead of going home, he was heading to the airport to inspect a plane that almost certainly didn't contain any explosive devices. At least it would be an opportunity for him to observe rookie K-9 officer Shannon Clemens—whom he was still assessing for a specialization—to see if she had a feel for explosives detection.

Logan stopped his SDPD-issue Ford Explorer at the security gate leading to the airport's infield and lowered his window. He showed his badge to the security guard. He saw Shannon pull up behind him, and the guard inspected her credentials, too. While he waited for the gate arm to be raised, he rubbed his forehead in an attempt to relieve the dull ache that pulsed there.

The gate arm rose and Logan followed the pavement markings to the aircraft's designated holding area. He'd been advised the plane had just landed and that security was already there, along with the SDPD officers currently on duty at the airport.

Nearing the location, he saw two airport vehicles and an SDPD cruiser. Three civilian males and a female were standing by the cars, along with two policemen. Logan's attention was immediately drawn to the statuesque brunette in the middle of the group. She was slim, and dressed in narrow-legged navy pants, a matching jacket and practical, low-heeled shoes. Her dark hair—and she seemed to have plenty of it—was coiled in a bun at the nape of her neck.

He parked beside the cruiser and released Boomer from the back of his vehicle. Affixing the dog's leash to his collar, he waited for Shannon to park and do the same with her dog, Darwin.

As they approached the group, Logan could see that the woman had light blue eyes, a dramatic contrast to the olive skin and dark hair. He noted the strong cheekbones, arched eyebrows and full, unpainted lips. Along with the stunning looks, she appeared capable. From the confident stance and the air of authority, he could readily see she was in charge. Based on that and the fact that she was the only female in the group, he guessed she was Ariana Atkins, head of security for the airport. He hadn't met her before, but he'd heard she was good…and tough. They'd neglected to mention she was beautiful, too.

The three men gathered around her must have been members of her team. The cops he recognized as being from the airport contingent of his division.

Logan greeted the officers first, then extended a hand to Ariana. Although she offered hers, her gaze swung to Boomer and she seemed to withdraw from him.

Well, what do you know? She doesn't like dogs.

"Boomer, sit, stay," Logan commanded. "Ms. Atkins. I'm Captain Logan O'Connor." When he released her hand, she moved slightly to her left and away from where Boomer sat sedately.

Logan introduced Shannon and the two dogs, and also shook hands with the members of Ariana's team.

"Thank you for coming, Captain, Officer Clemens," Ariana said, keeping a cautious eye on the dogs.

When Boomer opened his mouth to pant, Ariana took two small, hurried steps back.

"Ah, here's the plane in question," she noted, looking over Logan's shoulder.

They watched the Boeing 767 wide-body, twin-engine jet taxi slowly into place. A deafening roar briefly drowned out all other noise as a fighter jet soared overhead. Incredulous, Logan turned to Ariana. "A fighter jet escort?"

She shrugged. "Probably a training exercise."

"That would make sense." Logan was having trouble keeping his eyes off her. It was more than her appearance. There was an indefinable quality about her that appealed to him. He forced himself to concentrate on the situation that had brought him to the airport. "Nothing came up on the two women involved when we ran them."

Ariana nodded. "That corroborates what we know. Not surprising. The two women are barely out of college and this, we're told, was supposed to be a celebration of the start of their so-called independence."

"Heck of a way to start."

"I hope their field of study wasn't law. This little fiasco is likely to leave a smear on their record."

Logan noticed the slight curving of Ariana's lips and returned the smile. He was feeling distinctly better than when he'd arrived. Damn, she was beautiful. In addition, she was clearly smart and had a sense of humor. She was the whole package.

He directed his concentration to the approaching plane. It shimmered in the dry heat rolling in waves off the asphalt. He couldn't resist a sideways glance at Ariana. Her body was angled toward the aircraft. Loose strands of dark chestnut-brown hair fanned around her face. The sharp line of her cheekbone, small straight nose and what he could only think of as pouty lips, drawn in a straight line as she watched the plane advance, made for a profile as striking as her face head-on.

Focus, O'Connor. You're here to do a job.

Ariana's phone signaled an incoming call. She stepped away, had a brief conversation and walked back.

"They're ready for us. We'll get the mobile staircase in place. Those buses—" She motioned to their right. "They're for the passengers, to take them to the terminal building once you're finished with them."

Another car pulled up as she was speaking. It was marked with the United States Homeland Security crest and the words *Transportation Security Administration*. A tall, slim man with a slight hunch to his shoulders and thinning blond hair got out and approached them.

"This is Federal Security Director Angus Stewart," Ariana said. "FSD Stewart, meet Captain

O'Connor and Officer Clemens of the SDPD K-9 Unit."

"FSD Stewart," Logan acknowledged the other man, mildly surprised by the lack of strength in his handshake and the clamminess of his palm. He had an immediate dislike for the TSA director. Judging by Ariana's body language, she wasn't a big fan either. "You don't have explosives detection dogs at this airport?" Logan asked to confirm.

"No. We mostly rely on electronics trace detection technology."

Logan wasn't about to get into a debate with Stewart about the relative merits of the two methods of detection. The data showed that dogs were far superior in terms of accuracy and cost effectiveness.

"The report stated that the women were already inebriated when they boarded. Why were they let on the plane to begin with?" Stewart asked.

"Good question, and one I would like the answer to, as well," Ariana responded.

"If someone had done their job, it could've saved us all a lot of hassle."

The cat's-eye shape of Ariana's lids, which hinted at some exotic heritage, narrowed as she held Stewart's gaze. "FSD Stewart," she began in a voice that could have doused a raging fire.

"Of course you're aware that passenger boarding is the responsibility of the airline."

Prickly, Logan thought, but somehow that just made her more intriguing.

"Yeah, I'm aware of that. If the women were that drunk, shouldn't the people doing the boarding have called security?"

Her light blue irises were icy as a glacier, but she remained silent. Logan had the odd sensation of wanting to squirm even though her steady-eyed scrutiny wasn't directed at him.

"They didn't call security nor did they report it to their own management, correct?" Stewart persisted. "They just took the path of least resistance and let the women board."

"That's right."

"This is a ridiculous and unnecessary use of our time due to sloppy procedures," Stewart sneered.

Despite the improvement in Logan's disposition, the headache that had been brewing behind his temples began to throb. He longed for his bed. He shifted from one leg to the other. "Yeah, I can understand your frustration," he cut in. "You must have a lot on your plate, implementing all those recommendations from the Inspector General's office." He resented Angus's jabs at Ariana. He put it down to how tired and irritable he was that the nasty comeback was out of his mouth before he realized it. He'd implicitly referenced the colossal failure of the TSA in a covert testing of its practices conducted by Homeland Security's Office of the Inspector General a year ago. The classified results had been leaked and were very much in the public domain. Included in the recommendations was one for the TSA to introduce more dogs, especially at larger airports. Angus must not have gotten the memo.

Angus's sharp intake of breath told Logan he'd hit the mark. He noted that Ariana's expression remained inscrutable, but her eyes sparkled. She mouthed the words "thank you."

He acknowledged it with a slight incline of his head and, when Angus wasn't looking, a quick grin.

They waited as the mobile staircase was moved into position.

"If everyone is ready, we can start the deplaning," Logan said and glanced at Stewart for confirmation. The FSD didn't seem eager to take charge. TSA had jurisdiction, but without detection dogs there was little they could do in this situation. "Okay, then." Logan turned to Ariana. "Two hundred and six passengers and crew in total, correct?"

"Yes."

"Boomer and I'll check them for explosives

before they board the buses. Officer Clemens and Darwin will assist. Once the passengers are all off, we'll sweep the aircraft."

"I'll need you to take the two women involved to the division," Logan addressed the other cops. "Ms. Atkins," he turned to her again.

"Ariana is fine."

"All right, Ariana. I would appreciate it if members of your team could hold all passengers until we're done with the aircraft."

She nodded. "Of course."

"Anything you'd like to add?" Logan asked Stewart.

"No. Let's get this done," he grumbled.

Man, no wonder TSA had problems, Logan thought as the passengers started to disembark.

Although Darwin was still in training, Logan had Shannon do the primary check of passengers with her dog. It was good experience under low-risk conditions.

They deplaned thc two women first. The other passengers followed, their irritation apparent. Who could blame them? They were losing valuable vacation time.

Logan did his best to ignore the pounding in his head, and to be polite and pleasant as he and Boomer did a brief secondary check. When all passengers had disembarked, he and Boomer, aided by Shannon and Darwin, went to work on the aircraft itself. An hour later, and with the headache hammering so hard behind his eyes it made it almost impossible for him to see, Logan led Boomer down the stairs, Shannon and Darwin right behind him.

"Good job, Shannon." He bent down to scratch Darwin's ear. "You did great, too," he praised the dog. "I'll see you tomorrow to debrief," he said to Shannon.

"I can go back to the division with you now, if you'd like."

Logan couldn't fault her for enthusiasm, but going back to the division was the last thing he wanted to do. "Thanks for offering, but there's no need. We can cover it tomorrow."

"Great. Thanks." Shannon said her goodbyes and headed back to her SUV with Darwin.

As Logan and Boomer walked back to where Ariana, Max and the others waited, all eyes were on him, but it was Ariana's gaze he held. It surprised him that he felt a powerful tug of attraction despite his blinding headache. "The aircraft's clear," he announced, trying not to stare at her. "There was no sign of explosives on board. Not unexpected."

Ariana glanced at Boomer, but held her position. "No, it's not," she agreed, her gaze lingering a moment longer on the dog. "You've taken the women into custody?"

Logan nodded, and just that slight movement made his head feel as if it was about to explode. "Yeah. They should be on their way to the division by now." He glanced around, noting that Stewart and his car were gone, too. "What happened to the FSD?"

"He had more pressing matters to attend to."

There was that hint of a smile again. Logan wished he was feeling better so he could've taken some time to get to know her. That wasn't happening today, though. "Nice to meet you. Thank you for your cooperation," he mumbled and started to move toward his vehicle.

"That's it?" Ariana called after him. "Officer Brody usually stayed on site to discuss the incident with us."

Logan turned back. He nearly winced from the sharp pain that cleaved through this head. "I'll write up a report at the division. You'll have a copy tomorrow." Answering his phone when it vibrated, he trudged off with Boomer beside him.

ARIANA STOOD WITH the other members of her team and watched Logan's retreating back. He was tall and fit, as would be expected for his job. The short-cropped black hair and the way he moved would have told her "cop" even if she didn't already know it. She hadn't expected to like him, but she did. He'd scored major points with her when he'd taken that shot at the FSD. Two other area airports were part of Angus's responsibilities along with San Diego International. The average failure rate for the covert testing of the three was actually higher than the abysmal national average of 95 percent. And, Angus loved to criticize *her*.

Ariana liked the spirit Logan had displayed. Not many people would go toe-to-toe with a Transportation Security Administration director. Yet he appeared weary as he walked away. Uncharacteristic, from what she'd heard about him.

She felt a flutter in her belly, and this time it wasn't caused by her unease with the dog trotting along beside him.

She hadn't intended to eavesdrop on his telephone conversation, but since her attention was focused on him, she unintentionally overheard his side of it.

"Look, Becca, I'm sorry I left while you were sleeping this morning, but I can't be with you 24/7. I have a job, for Pete's sake! You've got to..."

He was too far for Ariana to hear anything else. She found herself unexpectedly—and unreasonably—annoyed at what sounded like the cop having walked out on his girlfriend. Or was she bothered by the fact that he *had* a girlfriend?

Ridiculous!

She might have found him attractive, with that rough and rugged, macho thing he had going on, but she wasn't interested in him…or anyone. Her career came first. She'd been in her job for barely a year, and in the airport industry that was nothing. In addition, she'd always avoided relationships in the workplace. Logan might not be employed by the airport, but it was close enough. Also, based on what she'd heard, he was seeing someone.

"Well, that was an incredible waste of time and money."

Ariana spun around to face Dave Langdon, one of the supervisors in her department. A former SDPD officer, he'd worked at the airport for over ten years, first as a security guard and the last four as a supervisor. Dave was one of the people who consistently made her feel like a newbie. Conversely, she'd questioned time and time again why Dave had been kept on as long as he had. He might have experience, but his work ethic was lacking and she couldn't find a kinder phrase to describe him than "mean-spirited." She knew he'd applied for her job, and it didn't surprise her that he'd been passed over.

"Do you have a problem with the FAA protocols, Dave?" she retorted, referring to the Federal Aviation Administration.

"Nah. It's just a lot of trouble for two drunken women. You know how the airport's CEO and the board are all about keeping expenses down these days. This'll cost us *and* the airline."

"What would you have done differently?" Ariana asked, her voice cool and professional. It wasn't her style to challenge an employee in front of others.

Dave had defied her authority before. It had never been overt enough for her to call him on it officially, but it had been an undercurrent since she'd been in her position. Now he was sounding a lot like FSD Stewart and doing it in front of two other members of her team, who stood silent and watching.

"It always has to be your way, doesn't it? Those of us who've been on the job would do it differently." He stalked off before she could respond.

And there it was again. That disdainful tone he used with the innuendo that he was better than she was, because he'd been a police officer. She didn't think Dave had any way of knowing about her failure to get on the force because of her health condition, but he seemed to like dropping those little barbs. She'd worry about that later.

Seeing the outrage on Max's face, she gave him a look that left no doubt that she didn't want to talk about Dave. The other security officer, a young man she'd hired recently, was obviously uneasy with what he'd heard, if the pink tips of his ears and the fact that he was preoccupied with studying his shoes were indications. She couldn't be concerned about his reaction either. Right now, she still had work to do.

Dave hadn't been far off in his "waste of time and money" comment, she thought as she drove back to the terminal building with Max. She'd already squandered at least five hours of her own time getting the report writing and follow-up done. Considerable departmental resources had also been expended. Since the cuts, she didn't have a lot of room in her budget.

She understood that as nonsensical as it might seem to have brought the plane back, the pilot had no real choice once a threat had been made, despite the considerable expense to the airline and the airport. She hoped the women had learned an important lesson.

It had been a shock, although not an unpleasant one, to learn that Officer Tom Brody was gone from the police department.

She wondered again how a guy like Brody had been able to get on the force in the first place.

Ariana's thoughts veered back to Logan as she unlocked her office. She was glad that she wouldn't have to see Brody again, although she wasn't convinced that SDPD K-9 Unit captain

Logan O'Connor would be easier to deal with, for entirely different reasons.

As much as Ariana tried to concentrate while she worked on her report, Logan kept creeping back into her thoughts. It was obvious that he knew what he was doing, and it would be difficult to find fault with him professionally from what she'd seen. And on a personal level? When Logan smiled, he was hard to resist. But what was all that she'd overheard about him sneaking out on his girlfriend in the middle of the night?

She was attracted to him, no question, but he was definitely off-limits.

With her mind wandering, Ariana lost track of where she'd been in her report to her boss. She had to finish it before she could go home. She refocused, and ten minutes later she clicked Send. The email, with her report attached, was on its way to Calvin Murdoch, the airport's chief executive officer.

The final task of her day complete, she felt as if she'd crashed into a wall. She hated to think of the mood she'd be in tomorrow, if she didn't get home and recharge.

CHAPTER TWO

ALL LOGAN WANTED to do was fall into bed and get some sleep. He didn't care that it wasn't even nine yet. As soon as he took the turn onto his street, he knew that wasn't going to happen. Becca's red Mustang was parked in his driveway. As he got closer, he could see her sitting on the bottom step of his porch, legs crossed, elbows on her knees, her chin resting on her fisted hands.

Although she had a key to his place, she must have forgotten it.

She looked sad and forlorn. He couldn't hold back the sigh, but thankfully it escaped before he'd gotten out of his SUV. As soon as he let Boomer jump out of the back, the dog bounded over to Becca, enthusiastically nuzzling and licking her. She shoved Boomer's head away and wiped her face with the back of her hand.

Logan leaned against his truck and folded his arms across his chest. He'd figured if anyone could cheer Becca up, it would've been Boomer. Yet she just kept pushing him away. He resolved the impasse by climbing into her lap—no easy feat for an eighty-five-pound dog. Boomer whimpered and rested his head on Becca's shoulder. Finally giving in, Becca wrapped her arms around the dog and buried her head in his glossy fur.

Almost instantaneously, her body convulsed with sobs.

Logan sighed again, and dropped down on the step, draping his arm around her.

"Men…are…horrid," she managed between sniffles.

It was the same refrain Logan had been hearing for days now. He turned his head toward her. "Yes, we are. It's a burden we have to bear."

Becca jerked her head up, bumping his chin. Logan let out a muffled "ouch."

"No, I didn't mean *you*," she protested.

He tested his jaw, and rubbed it to ease the discomfort. He'd always known she had a hard head, but this was the first time he'd felt the brunt of it physically. "I'm a man, aren't I?"

She gave him a watery smile. "Brothers, especially good ones like you, don't fall into that category."

He was relieved to see the smile, as feeble as it might have been. It was the first he'd seen from her in days, since she'd broken up with that punk Winslow after she'd caught him cheating on her. Becca had done the right thing, but Logan hated to see her hurt. So much so, he was tempted to have a *chat* with Winslow—what kind of a name was Winslow anyway? "There are lots of women who might disagree with you," he joked, hoping to keep her spirits up.

"What do *they* know?" she said, and her smile firmed.

Sleep was overrated, Logan decided. Becca had been his top priority since they'd lost their parents. Since then, it had been just him and his kid sister.

He wished he could've spared Becca the heartbreak of a first love gone wrong. As he couldn't, the least he could do was support her and help her through it. "How about I throw some burgers on the grill and you make the salad?"

"It's got to be nine o'clock by now," Becca said with a hiccup.

"At least. Have you had dinner?"

She averted her gaze. "No."

"Lunch?"

"I had a bowl of ice cream."

Logan rose. "There you go. I'm making us dinner. I'll even toss the salad myself."

He held his hand out to her. When she placed hers into his, he tugged her to her feet, eliciting an annoyed whine from Boomer as he was dumped unceremoniously from her lap.

"C'mon," he said and whistled for Boomer to follow.

DESPITE THE LATE NIGHT, Ariana was at work at seven the following morning, as usual. She didn't get as much done the evening before as she'd hoped, because her thoughts kept drifting back to the events of the day and a tall, attractive cop. Although she could appreciate looks, they weren't of highest importance on her list, so she didn't understand why she couldn't seem to stop thinking about Logan.

She was walking through the passenger concourse when her phone rang. Seeing Max's name and number on the caller ID, she answered without slowing her pace. "What's up?"

She could tell right away that there was a problem, from the tone of his voice.

"We had another security breach early this morning. A passenger wandered out of the secure international departure lounge into the domestic area."

"How did that happen?" Ariana asked, switching her phone to her other ear.

"The door had been left propped open."

"What? That can't be right."

"Sadly it is."

"But that's a secure door. Only about twenty of us can open it." Ariana moved to the edge of the corridor and stopped. "Do we know who left the door open?"

"We checked the video footage. It was Dave Langdon. For whatever reason, he hung around the airport last night. He wasn't on duty, but he didn't go home after our incident yesterday. He must've slept in the office and gone out to the airfield early this morning. On his way back, he passed through from the international to the domestic area and left the door open. We have him on camera."

"What was he doing on the airfield?"

"You'd have to ask him. My guess would be he went out to have a smoke. Can you believe it? All for the sake of saving himself a couple hundred yards of walking?"

Ariana did a slow turn to face the wall. "You've got to bc joking. Even if he was stupid enough to do that, why didn't the door alarm go off?" She knew it was programmed to do so.

"We're trying to determine that."

"Get me the video file. I want to see it as soon as possible. Check his restricted area identity card record for the entire evening, too, would you?"

"Sure. Why?"

"If he accessed any other secure areas while off duty, I want to know about it."

"Okay."

"And the passenger? What happened to him?"

"It seemed to be an honest mistake. We took him through security again and to his proper departure lounge. He's probably boarding his flight now."

"Was there anyone else impacted?" Ariana was hoping not, given the earliness of the hour. If other passengers were involved, in addition to inconveniencing them, it could have caused flight delays.

"Fortunately not."

"All right. Let's discuss it once I've had a chance to watch the video. And I want to see Dave, if he's here." This could be the last strike for Dave Langdon, if in fact he had left that door open. "Wait, are you in your office now?"

"I am."

"And you've got the video file cued up?"

"Yeah."

"I'm closer to your office than mine." Max was in the terminal, near the screening areas, for rapid response if needed. Her space was in the administration section. "I'll see you in a few minutes."

Ariana holstered her phone. Since the day she'd started, she'd been trying to tighten security at the airport. If she'd learned one thing from her time working for a private security company before she'd joined San Diego International, policies and protocols had to be tight, effective and strictly adhered to. Not that her predecessor had been lax, but times had changed, and she'd been steadily making improvements to the extent her budget allowed. The TSA covert testing outcome had been a wake-up call. Yet every time she felt she took a step forward, there seemed to be something else that dragged her back. She bought two coffees on her way to Max's office. Handing one to him as she entered, she placed the other on the corner of his desk. "Show me."

Max held his chair out for her and started the video clip. Dave's face wasn't visible, but his movements, general body type and the clothing he wore—the same he'd had on that day—left little doubt that it was him. And if that wasn't damning enough, Max confirmed that Dave had used his access card to open the door.

When the video segment ended, Ariana rose. Leaning against Max's desk, she took a sip of her coffee. "Dave's not stupid. He'd realize we'd know it was him. Does he *want* to get fired?"

Max shrugged. "I can't answer that. I've never been able to figure the guy out."

"Is he in the building?"

"Last time I checked before you got here, yeah."

"Get him to my office in fifteen minutes. I need to talk to Human Resources first."

IT WAS A crazy morning for Ariana. As much as she disliked Dave Langdon's attitude, she hated firing people more. Human Resources had supported her decision and the deed was done. Dave had tried to deny that it was him. He'd claimed that he'd stayed at the airport overnight because he and his wife had had an argument that morning, and she'd kicked him out. He claimed that he'd slept in the office and hadn't been walking around. That it must've been someone else who'd lifted his card and accessed the secure area.

He made the point that he'd changed, as she could see for herself, so the clothes he'd worn yesterday had been stuffed into his locker. He suggested someone could have taken them. When he'd realized that she wasn't buying it, that she was really going to terminate him, he'd become belligerent and threatening. So much so that she reminded him she could have him escorted off airport property immediately. In the end, she persuaded him that wouldn't be in his best interest, and allowed him to save face.

She let him pack up his belongings, and Max walked him out.

The rest of the day hadn't gone much better for Ariana. It seemed to be one niggling problem after another. It was well past six when she finally left.

Ariana let herself into her apartment, tossed her bag and keys on the hall table, and pulled the restraining band from her ponytail. She dragged her fingers through the length of her hair, slipped out of her shoes and placed them neatly inside the hall closet.

By the time she'd finished, her cat had sauntered over. She bent down and stroked her tortoiseshell-and-white coat. "Hey, Sabrina. How was your day? Better than mine, huh?" she murmured.

Taking her briefcase and placing it on the dining room table, she walked into the kitchen, pulled a Coke Zero out of the fridge and took a drink straight from the can. A second long drink went a considerable way to soothing her parched throat.

Soda can in hand, she walked back to the dining room and set up her laptop.

Her apartment had two bedrooms. The smaller one was configured as an office, but she seldom used it. If she had to work, which she did most nights, she preferred to do it with a view of the ocean, visible through the dining room window.

As her computer booted up, she made herself a large spinach salad for dinner and hunkered down with her laptop to catch up on her emails and various other mundane matters that she hadn't gotten to during the day. If she had time, she wanted to review her risk map, to decide which area she would next target for improvement.

With a long-suffering meow, Sabrina threaded between her ankles a few times. Ariana couldn't resist picking her up and taking comfort from cuddling her for a few minutes. When she placed Sabrina back on the ground, the cat leaped onto a chair, curled up and in minutes was snoring contentedly.

Ariana kept working for as long as she felt she was being productive, crawling into bed near midnight.

It seemed she'd just rested her head on the pillow when her alarm went off at five thirty. With bleary eyes and a sluggish body, she got ready for work and wished for a quieter day.

Thankfully, it turned out to be uneventful. Ariana did some follow-up on the incident involving the two drunken women and initiated the hiring process to find Dave's replacement. On the plus side, she had the opportunity to tour a group of schoolchildren through the airport's emergency operations center. By late afternoon, she had her second wind and was feeling energized rather than drained. She was engrossed in a proposal Max had presented to her for upgrading their security cameras in the parking garages. An enhanced video management system was her current focus.

The knock on her door frame caused her to jump, and she pressed a hand to her racing heart. Spinning her chair around, she felt her heart rate accelerate further.

Logan stood in the doorway, dressed in indigo jeans and a pale blue polo shirt. She glanced down quickly to see if Boomer was with him. Not seeing the dog, she shifted her gaze back to Logan. He had one arm causally braced against the jamb, the stance emphasizing the muscles in his arm and torso. His dark hair glistened under the harsh fluorescent lights of the corridor. He had a smile on his lips and in his eyes. And those intense blue eyes mesmerized her.

"I'm sorry to startle you," he said, drawing her out of her reverie.

Realizing her hand was still on her chest, she lowered it. "Oh, it's not your fault. I was reviewing a report and must've been absorbed in it." She felt her lips curve in response to his smile.

"I was here debriefing with the officers on site," Logan said. "We were discussing new operating procedures in view of what happened the day before yesterday. I wanted to fill you in and see if there were any new developments on your end."

She shook her head. "No. We've closed the file on that incident. Have the two women been charged?"

"Oh, yeah!" He gave her that appealing smile. "So do you have a few minutes or do you need to get back to your report?"

She glanced at her watch.

"We can do it some other time," he suggested. "If you're busy right now."

Ariana realized she didn't want him to go, and it wasn't just professional curiosity as to what the SDPD's new procedures were. "No, that's okay. I'm ready to call it a day. Come in."

Logan dropped his arm and took a step forward, but paused, his eyes crinkling at the corners. "Since you're calling it a day, why don't we get out of here? I'll buy you a coffee or, better yet, a drink. We could probably both use one."

Ariana was about to agree. Then his conversation with his girlfriend, Becca, came to mind. She opened her mouth to decline.

"We can discuss the procedures," he said quickly before she could respond, and cast his gaze around her small, sparsely furnished office. "But in a more comfortable environment.

If you don't already have plans, I'll throw in dinner to sweeten the pot."

There was that smile again. Ariana laughed. "No need for dinner, but okay to getting out of here." It was going to be a business discussion, that's all. She routinely had coffee or lunch with men in the course of her duties—her profession was male-dominated. Why would it be any different with Logan? Whether he had a girlfriend or not was irrelevant. The butterflies in her stomach aside, it was going to be nothing more than business. "Let's go have a coffee," she said.

CHAPTER THREE

BY THE TIME they reached Ariana's car, Logan had somehow convinced her to have a drink with him instead. He suggested Buster's Beach House Bar.

Ariana had never been there, but Logan must have frequented the place, if the number of people who said hello or had a quick word with him were any indication.

He motioned for her to precede him to the back of the room, and she slid into a corner booth. A waitress appeared almost before he sat down.

"Hey, Carly," Logan greeted her.

"Good to see you, Jagger. The usual?" she askcd and gave him a flirtatious smile. It made Ariana wonder about the relationship Logan and the waitress had. She felt guilty about her curiosity as soon as Carly turned an equally warm and welcoming smile on her. "And for you?"

Ariana found herself smiling back. "What's his usual?"

"Corona, with a slice of lime, straight from the bottle."

"I'll have the same but with a glass. Thanks."

"Sure thing," Carly said, placing two cardboard coasters on the scarred wooden table.

"I was wrong," Logan said after Carly left.

"Wrong about what?"

"I would've bet a month's salary that you'd be a wine drinker. A white—smooth and well-chilled."

Ariana laughed. "You're not wrong. I've been known to have a glass of chardonnay or sauvignon blanc now and again. Working in the field that I do, beer has become an acquired taste. Hanging around so many men, I've learned to enjoy a frosty glass of Corona as much as a glass of wine. So, tell me, how'd you get the nickname Jagger?"

Logan cleared his throat and his eyes darted around the room. He seemed uncomfortable with her question and appeared relieved when the waitress returned.

"Appreciate it, Carly," he said, when she placed the bottles and glass, along with a small bowl of nuts, in front of them.

"I like adaptability in a person," he said with a chuckle when they were alone again, gesturing to her beer.

Obviously he wanted to change the subject.

He raised his bottle and clinked it to Ariana's glass, then took a long, slow sip. "What made you choose security as a career?" he asked.

"I thought you wanted to discuss your new procedures."

"I do. It doesn't mean we can't get to know each other a little first. With Brody gone, we're likely to be working together again." He flashed her a smile.

Ariana placed her glass back on the coaster, reached for a candied nut, popped it in her mouth. Okay, they could play it his way. She was curious about him, too. "It matters to me to make a difference. Keeping people safe is important."

"And why the airport?"

She tilted her head. "I've been fascinated by airplanes since I was a kid. My father was an engineer. He went to school in England, where his father was from. I learned about mechanics and laws of physics from an early age, but to this day I remain in awe of the fact that we can get a nearly four-hundred-thousand-pound, one-hundred-and-fifty- or sixty-foot wingspan piece of machinery, loaded with people and cargo, into the air, and it stays there over great distances." She laughed. "Silly, I know, but flying fascinates me."

"I never thought of it that way." He watched her for a few moments. "If you don't mind me saying, you don't look British."

"My grandfather was English. My grandmother, Brazilian."

His long, contemplative gaze caused all sorts of odd sensations inside her.

"That explains it," he said, and surprised her by touching the back of her hand. "And it explains the color of your hair. But where does the eye color come from? Your father?"

She chuckled. "My mother's side. She's blonde and blue-eyed, as mostly everyone is on her side of the family. American for generations, but her ancestry is Swedish."

"That's an interesting combination. Do your parents live in California?"

"No. They moved back to England a couple of years ago. Enough about me," she interjected before he could ask her more questions. She didn't want him digging any deeper, even though she found it effortless to talk to him. "What about you? Why did you become a cop?"

"I wanted to make a difference," he said with an easy smile, echoing her own words. "I wanted to contribute in a positive way to people's lives. And it runs in my family. Both my father and grandfather were lifers on the job. My father was the chief of police for Burbank."

She thought his eyes were clouded with sorrow for a moment.

"My parents, my mother in particular, might

have wanted for a different career for me," he continued. "Maybe a doctor or a lawyer, but that wasn't happening. I wanted to be a cop as far back as I can remember."

His comment made her think of her own childhood dream of becoming a police officer, but she pushed it aside. "If you're from Burbank, what brought you to San Diego?"

He raised a shoulder, let it drop again. "My dad was a hero. A figure larger than life. As much as I loved and admired him, I didn't want to live in his shadow. I also wanted to know that I'd be making it on my own. Not because of who he was, what he'd accomplished or how highly people regarded him. I wanted it to be on my own merits. I wanted to build my own career."

Ariana watched him carefully, searching for any sign of bitterness or envy, but all she saw was pride and admiration. To her, that said a lot about Logan, and it was all good. She saw a decency and a depth she hadn't expected.

"Speaking of making a difference," Ariana said with a smile. "What will happen to the women on Flight 396?"

Logan grunted. "Yeah, we made a *big* difference there! They've been charged, as I said. Public mischief. It'll probably be reduced to a misdemeanor. Even before they sobered up, they were both bawling. It only got worse when their parents showed up." The laughter was gone. "They won't soon forget it. Nor should they." He reached out, brushed his hand over hers again. "But it gave me a chance to meet you."

His proximity and especially his touch triggered those sensations again. She absorbed the warmth that had come into his cool blue eyes. "There is that," she said softly, and meant it, but she leaned back, subtly sliding her hand out from under his.

Logan reached for his bottle and took another drink. "So, will there be civil consequences for the women? They inconvenienced nearly two hundred other passengers, and the cost to the airline, the airport, not to mention the military for the fighter jet escort…" He rolled his eyes at that. "The expense has got to be substantial."

Ariana didn't know what to make of the feelings he was stirring up inside her and tried to remind herself of all the reasons why she wasn't interested in him. With effort, she concentrated on the question he'd posed. "Yes, there are significant costs associated with the incident, but I don't think there'll be any legal action. The airline might do some posturing, mostly as a deterrent to other would-be troublemakers. They'll have to cover costs associated with rebooking passengers who might've missed connecting flights to some of the outer islands and, if need be, overnight accommodations as well as the expense of bringing the plane back. Pursuing a claim against the women would cost them more money than they could hope to recover." She shrugged. "The military escort? I have no idea how much that would've cost. We got confirmation that they used the incident as a training exercise, as we suspected. For the airport..." She smiled again. "It's all in a day's work for us. What about the police department?"

"All in a day's work, too. For us, the real issue is that while we're dealing with something like that, we're not out there addressing real threats to the public. With our limited resources, it's about trade-offs. We prioritize based on risk—likelihood and potential outcome. Though the likelihood of an explosive device being aboard that plane was deemed negligible, we couldn't ignore it. That means we weren't dealing with other matters."

"I get that. There are never enough resources to do all that needs doing," she murmured. She was thinking of her own department as much as the police.

"You're right."

Sipping her beer, she looked around. She watched a young couple sitting near the middle of the room and frowned.

"Hey, you with me here?"

Ariana shifted her gaze back to Logan and let out a short laugh. "Sorry. I can't help it. It's sort of a game I play, whenever I have a quiet moment in a public place."

"What kind of game?"

This time the discomfort came through in her chuckle. "Since I was a kid, when I first decided I wanted to…" she'd been about to say "be a cop," but caught herself "…to work in my field, I've tried profiling people. Maybe that's the wrong word. I don't mean like what law enforcement organizations do. Just reading people better, I suppose. I took a course in college, too. I do it mostly to amuse myself. It does come in handy at times in my field, though, as you can imagine. Studies have shown that profiling airport passengers based on their behaviors can be an effective adjunct to security screening. I like to watch people and try to figure out what they're all about."

She saw his eyes track to the couple she'd been observing. He motioned with his bottle toward them. "So, what's their story?"

"Oh, I don't think I want to do this. Certainly not with you!" She felt the heat on her cheeks and glanced away.

"Okay, how about I go first?"

That made her smile. "All right."

He took a few moments to study the couple. She did the same and noted again how the man seemed to be attentive and interested, until the woman's head was turned. Then his eyes landed on or followed the nearest female.

"They're married, maybe five years," Logan began. "No kids. He's a midlevel manager. She's probably in PR or advertising and earns more than he does. She loves him, although the shine has dulled over the years. He begrudges her some for being the higher-income earner, and he has a straying eye. Although he probably hasn't cheated on her yet, it's only a matter of time. He feels he's entitled and believes he needs to do it to make himself feel more of a man."

Her startled laugh erupted, and she put a hand over her mouth.

Logan turned incredulous eyes on Ariana. "You find that funny? That he'll probably cheat on his wife?"

"No. No. That part is sad. It's what you said about them. All of it."

Logan smiled. "Are you laughing because you think it's ludicrous or because you know I'm right?"

"The latter," she said, still chuckling. "You're good at this game!"

"So you agree?"

"Mostly. All the tells are there. The husband's roving eye when she's not paying attention. The fact that he handed her the bill when the waiter brought it, and so on."

Logan nodded. "Now it's your turn."

Ariana scanned the room. She wanted to pick carefully to be as on the mark as he had been. Not only because of her competitive nature. Maybe it was silly, but it mattered that she gained his respect.

She was considering the man who'd just entered the bar when Logan motioned to the new arrival. "How about him?"

She scrutinized the tall Hispanic man standing with his back to them. "Okay," she said. She had more or less settled on him already.

He was chatting with the occupants of a booth close to the entrance. His dark hair was longish, nearly reaching his collar. His clothes, although casual, were of good quality. Expensive. His stance and manner were confident. He was highly aware of his surroundings. When he turned his head, she could see he was attractive, but there was a dangerous—not quite tame—aura about him.

He was wearing a light windbreaker. She was experienced enough to recognize that he more than likely had a concealed weapon under it. Her smile faded and she shot a tense glance at Logan. He was watching her, heedless of the man, amusement dancing in his eyes.

Ariana leaned in. Her voice was low, her tone serious. "The man you picked? Don't look!" she whispered as Logan's gaze started to drift toward the man. It snapped back to her, and he had a considering expression on his face.

"He's confident, self-aware," she continued in an insistent whisper. "He's not easily intimidated or one to shy away from confrontation. In some cases, he might welcome it. He seems dangerous and resigned…somehow fatalistic. He comes off as laid-back, relaxed, yet he's intense and perceptive. He's got money. Probably quite a lot, but he doesn't flaunt it. My guess is he's involved in the drug trade. Likely a drug dealer for a cartel out of Tijuana," she concluded.

Logan started to smile and shifted his eyes again. She placed her hand hurriedly on top of his. "No. *Don't look*," she repeated urgently. "He's carrying. I'm certain of it." She glanced at the man. "Okay. He's facing the other way. You can look now."

Logan did, slowly and discreetly. Nonchalantly he took another drink, keeping his eyes in the general direction of the man they were discussing. Ariana saw the moment the man's eyes met Logan's. A look she couldn't decipher passed between the two of them.

She saw the narrowing of Logan's eyes, the tightening of his lips. A knot formed in her stomach. She wondered if the new arrival was known to Logan.

Ariana could only gape when Logan placed his bottle on the coaster, pointed a finger at the man and beckoned him to approach.

"What are you doing?" Ariana murmured uneasily.

Brows furrowed, he glanced at her briefly. "You'll see. Just stay calm," he added.

Ariana gazed back at the man as he sauntered up to their table. He aimed assessing eyes on her before meeting Logan's gaze. "You want something?" he asked.

"I do. Yes," Logan replied, leaning back in his chair.

Ariana's heart was thundering. This close, she was more convinced that the man was carrying a gun. There was an element of fearlessness, almost recklessness, about him. She looked around quickly. The bar had filled while they'd been there. It was packed. There were people everywhere. What was Logan thinking, confronting a potentially dangerous criminal in a busy public place? If either of them drew a weapon, there were bound to be casualties.

"Keep your hands where I can see them," Logan said in a tone that broached no argument, almost as if he'd read her thoughts.

Ariana nearly missed seeing the man's mouth

twitch, as if he was enjoying the confrontation that was unfolding between him and Logan. Could there have been something else going on here? Something she wasn't aware of? Before she could explore that thought, the man slapped his palms on the table. "Good enough for you?" he asked with an amused drawl.

He found this funny? Not a good sign.

"Now, using your left hand only, empty your pockets," Logan instructed. He tapped a finger on the tabletop in front of Ariana. "Put your possessions right there."

What was Logan doing? Ariana wondered in alarm. Had he lost his mind? He hadn't even identified himself as a cop. She had no time to deliberate further, as the man—surprisingly—did exactly what he'd been asked. It appeared he *was* enjoying himself, and that made no sense. Her earlier thought returned. Could this be a joke?

She watched the man draw objects out of his coat pocket first. A package of gum, a San Diego Padres ticket stub, a set of keys on a chain, a separate key on a Harley Davidson motorcycle key chain. When he reached for the front pocket of his jeans, Logan shot a hand out. "Easy now. Do it slowly."

The man angled his head, seeming to be holding back a smile. He reached into his right front pocket with his left hand and slowly drew out its contents. Palming whatever he had in there, he held his hand out and let it hover over the table. He watched Logan expectantly.

Logan gestured to the small pile in front of Ariana. "Go ahead," he encouraged.

The man spread his fingers.

Holding her breath, Ariana watched as the object clattered onto the table's surface.

She was staring at a San Diego Police Department badge.

With narrowed eyes, she looked up at Logan.

"Ariana, meet Sergeant Rick Vasquez," Logan said. "Rick, this is Ariana Atkins, head of security at the San Diego airport." He motioned for Rick to take a seat.

Rick extended a hand to Ariana, which she shook briefly. He then sat in the chair next to Logan.

"Rick's a member of the K-9 Unit," Logan explained. "He specializes in narcotics. He's now working with Tom Brody's former canine partner, Nitro, and is retraining him for narcotics detection. Their job is to thwart the drug trafficking that takes place across the San Ysidro border between Mexico and the United States."

Although Ariana had started to suspect it might have been a joke and could see the humor in it, she felt a little foolish. Logan must have realized it, as a tinge of red crept up his cheeks.

"You did great!" Logan assured her. "If Rick *seems* like a cartel operative, it's with good reason. He's supposed to. His job often requires him to go undercover."

Logan held up his hands. "I'm sorry. Really. If it makes you feel better, you were right on with your assessment. You read Rick exactly the way a person is supposed to."

There was no harm done. If Ariana had been in Logan's shoes, she probably would have done the same thing. She smiled.

Rick appeared contrite, as well. "I was an accidental participant, but I apologize, too. As much as I'd love to stay, have a beer with you and find out what this was all about, I get the sense that I'm a third wheel." He pushed out of his chair and grinned at Logan. "I'm going to leave you to each other." Turning his smile on Ariana, he held out a hand to her again. "It's nice to meet you. I hope our paths cross again, under more... conventional circumstances." He rested a hand on Logan's shoulder. "We'll catch up tomorrow, Jagger."

After Rick left, Logan gave Ariana a conciliatory smile. "I shouldn't have tricked you like that. When I saw you zero in on Rick, it was just too tempting. Besides, you were right on the money. Rick *has* to be good enough to fool the cartel bosses—his life depends on it. If he can fool the cartel, he should be able to convince most people, including those in law enforcement."

Logan had a point. If Rick didn't have good cover dealing with the cartels, it *could* cost him his life. She glanced down at the glass in her hand, and felt the fatigue she'd been trying to stave off all day intensify. She sensed Logan's eyes on her and looked up.

"You all right? I really didn't mean to offend you."

"It's not that. I'm just tired. It's been a long couple of days."

"Yeah, it has. We both could use an early night." Logan pulled a twenty-dollar bill from his wallet, much more than what two beers would've cost, and placed it on the table. He waved to Carly as they walked through the crowded room.

Nearing the door, Ariana suddenly turned, causing him to bump into her. This close up, his eyes were even bluer than she'd thought.

"Did you forget something?"

"Uh…we never discussed your new operating procedures."

Logan chuckled and held the door open for her. "Good point. Rather than having you think it was a ploy to get you to go out with me, how do you feel about having dinner with me sometime soon to discuss them, so I can prove we really *do* have new procedures?" he asked when they'd stopped beside her car.

Ariana had enjoyed herself. Logan wasn't at all what she'd expected. She was on the verge of saying yes when she remembered Becca.

She sensed Logan's interest in her was more than professional and she was drawn to him—something that didn't happen often. But if he had a girlfriend, she didn't want to encourage him. A dinner with Logan would be more than strictly business.

She couldn't say yes, but she couldn't say no either, lost in those eyes of his again. "I'll let you know," she said, noncommittally.

As he said good-night and was about to leave, a thought occurred to her. "Was it?" she asked.

Logan paused. "Was what?"

"Was the idea of discussing your procedures a ploy? To get me to have a drink with you?"

He held her gaze for a long moment, and she could readily see his charm.

"That would've been conniving of me, wouldn't it? And very unprofessional." With a quick show of white teeth and a jaunty salute, he strode away toward his own vehicle.

CHAPTER FOUR

ARIANA WASN'T ONE of those people who could function with little sleep over an extended period of time. She wasn't a morning person either, regardless of the hours she kept at work. *Refreshed* and *buoyant* weren't generally words she would apply to herself early in the morning, especially after only five hours of sleep. Yet this morning she was unarguably both!

And she was thinking of Logan O'Connor.

Maybe Logan's relationship with Becca, whoever she was, wasn't serious. He wouldn't have asked her out, would he, if it was? Logan seemed decent and ethical. Or maybe she'd misinterpreted, and his suggestion to have dinner was entirely business-related. Had it been wishful thinking on her part? She *was* interested in him, although she had her reasons for why she *shouldn't* be. Somehow, she couldn't seem to recall exactly why some of those reasons had seemed so important.

She tried to remember the last time she'd had

a serious relationship. It was before she started working at the airport.

She tried to put Logan out of her mind as she showered and dressed. Suddenly feeling lonely, she reminded herself to call her parents.

The day was uneventful and passed quickly, as did the following two. Ariana took the opportunity to catch up on routine reports and paperwork, and to get her team started on the tender for the enhanced video management system. Their technicians hadn't been able to determine why the door that Dave Langdon had left open hadn't set off an alarm, so she asked Max to get quotes to inspect all held-open and intrusion alarms at the airport. She hadn't budgeted for it, but she'd have to find the money somehow.

That morning, Ariana received a call from her predecessor, George Dennison. They'd stayed in contact since his retirement. She still thought of him as a mentor, and she appreciated that he was always available if she wanted to bounce ideas off him or simply catch up. She regretted not having told George about the problems she had been experiencing with Dave, as George was stunned and dismayed when she informed him she'd terminated him.

She knew George had always prided himself on his team. Even so, it surprised her when he said he'd never had the slightest issue with Dave.

That led Ariana to wonder if it was something lacking in her leadership style. George had been the one who encouraged her to apply for the position when he'd decided to retire. She hoped he wasn't questioning his wisdom about that, but she was too busy to dwell on it for long.

Periodically throughout the day her thoughts returned to Logan. Would he call her to follow up on his invitation to dinner? Or was he expecting her to contact him? A couple of times she nearly picked up the phone, but she either talked herself out of it or was distracted.

By Friday afternoon, she was nearly up to date with work. If she put in a half day on Saturday, she'd be completely caught up.

At the light tap on her door frame, Ariana glanced up from the incident reports she was scrolling through on her computer. Cynthia, her executive assistant, stood in the doorway.

"It's after six," Cyn told her. "Why don't you pack it in for the evening?"

Ariana smiled. "I will, but I want to go through the rest of today's reports first."

"The reports will be waiting for you Monday. Knowing you, you'll get back to them tomorrow morning anyway. There's nothing noteworthy. I already checked. Max and I, and some of the supervisors, are going to grab a drink at The Runway," she said, referring to the popular bar in one of the hotels close to the airport. “We’d really like it if you joined us. It’s been a while since you’ve come out for an after-work drink.”

Ariana pushed back her hair and tucked it behind her ears. “Thanks for the invite, but I should finish the reports.” She pointed to a stack of file folders on her desk. “The work is piling up.”

Cyn came into the office and stopped in front of Ariana’s desk. “It would mean a lot if you came along. Everyone’s worried about you.”

That’s exactly what Ariana didn’t want. The department was under enough pressure right now with all the cost-cutting that had been going on. Not wanting to burden her team, she’d been carrying the brunt of it. She knew they looked to her to set the tone. If she avoided them, it would only make matters worse. Cyn was right.

Ariana offered a weak smile. “You always know what to say, don’t you?”

She’d get everything done, even if it meant continuing to work at nights and on weekends, but they didn’t have to know that. She’d lead by example and show her team that all was well.

Even if it wasn’t entirely true.

“You’re right, Cyn. Thanks. I’ll meet you at The Runway in thirty minutes or so,” Ariana said and turned back to her computer screen.

"Nope."

Ariana glanced up with surprise.

"If I leave you here, despite your best intentions, it'll be a lot more than half an hour before you're out the door. By then you'll probably have changed your mind about joining us. Come now."

Ariana sighed. She couldn't argue with Cyn. They'd been working together for as long as she'd been at the airport, and Cyn knew her well. "Fine," she conceded.

"Great!" A smile sprcad across Cyn's face. "I'll buy you your first drink."

"You don't have to do that."

Cyn shrugged. "I might as well. A couple of the guys bet me you wouldn't show. I knew you would. There's a twenty in it for me—times two." She flaunted the smile again. "So, I might as well share the spoils with you. I'll go freshen up, come back and get you. That'll give you ten minutes to finish up."

Ariana watched Cyn stroll out of her office. Her assistant's parting comments were a wake-up call for her. Her team was betting against her—even if just related to social matters—and she couldn't let that happen. As a leader, she needed to be present, calm and steady. She thought again about her discussion with George and wondered if she could have done anything differently with Dave.

She'd have to thank Cyn, she decided, as she sent off the authorization to proceed with the upgrade of the video management system in the parking area and shut down her computer. She pulled her handbag out of her bottom drawer, changed her practical work flats for a pair of high-heeled pumps and was running her brush through her hair when Cyn returned.

For Cyn, freshening up meant reapplying her makeup, undoing the updo she'd had her golden-blond hair in, and adding a slick coat of bright red lipstick. She'd also removed her off-white jacket, exposing the siren-red sleeveless dress she wore beneath.

"All set?" Cyn asked.

"Absolutely. And thanks," Ariana added softly.

The Runway was busy, as it usually was on a Friday night. They bypassed the entrance to the restaurant on their way to the lounge and squeezed by the throng gathered by the bar.

Ariana watched with amusement as heads turned their way, the men no doubt giving the undeniably beautiful Cyn appreciative glances.

The crowd was eclectic as always, a mixture of traveling business executives on layover, airport workers, law enforcement types assigned to the airport, construction tradesmen, and women either there to mingle with the men or—Ariana knew plenty about the seedier side of executive travel—those working and hoping to meet a john.

She was relieved when they made it through the worst of the congestion and incredibly loud noise, and she spotted the table that their group had commandeered.

Max rose and waved to them from across the room. It warmed Ariana to see the genuine pleasure on the faces of her team members when they saw her. She smiled and waved back. As they wound their way between the tables, Ariana's attention was drawn by loud cheers from a group to the left. She recognized a couple of faces and frowned. Logan's coal-black hair and brilliant blue eyes were unmistakable. Also at the table was the other cop…Sergeant Rick Vasquez. The one she'd met at Buster's Beach House Bar. There was another man with them. Judging by the haircut and demeanor, she assumed he was a cop, too, but one she'd not seen at the airport. The three cops were surrounded by a bevy of attractive women. The two on either side of Logan were the most striking of the group. A slender, elegant blonde sat on his right, and the most stunning redhead Ariana had ever seen was on his left.

Just as she and Cyn reached their table, out of the corner of her eye, Ariana noticed Logan push out of his chair, nearly toppling it, and draw the redhead out of hers and into his arms. The redhead wasn't petite by any means, but Logan lifted her off her feet as if she weighed no more than a feather. He spun her around before giving her a smacking kiss on the lips.

"Now, why can't I have luck like that with women?" Max murmured into Ariana's ear as he pulled a chair out for her, thankfully not giving her direct view of the table where Logan was. "That guy earns the right to his nickname."

After greeting everyone, Ariana tried hard to keep her gaze from wandering back to Logan and gave Max a questioning look. "What do you mean?"

Max chuckled. "You haven't heard about how he got his nickname?"

She shook her head, not wanting to admit that she'd been curious about it.

"You do know O'Connor's nickname is Jagger, right?"

She nodded. "As in Mick Jagger? Thank you," she said to the waitress when she was handed a glass of white wine.

"I took the liberty of ordering for you when Cyn texted me that you were on your way." Max raised his bottle of beer to her glass and tapped it with a clink. "Good to see you out. As I was saying, yes, as in the Rolling Stones."

"He sings?" she asked, incredulously.

Max laughed, barely managing not to spit beer on everyone around the table, and caused heads to turn his way. "No. He earned his nickname because of his moves with women. Mick Jagger is famously successful with them." Max made a subtle gesture with his bottle toward Logan. "It seems the captain shares that trait."

The image of Logan lifting the gorgeous redhead into the air and placing his lips on hers was vivid in Ariana's mind. Against her better judgment, she peered around Cyn, seated on her other side, and cast a furtive glance at Logan. He was sitting down again and leaning back in his chair, a huge grin on his face. He had an arm draped around the back of each of the chairs occupied by the redhead and the blonde. When his hand squeezed the redhead's shoulder and he whispered something to her, her rich and sensual laugh could be heard clearly. As Ariana watched, the redhead leaned in and rested her head against Logan's shoulder briefly before glancing at Rick.

Was the redhead Becca? Ariana experienced an unusual sensation watching the vignette. Trying to put a name to the feeling, she astonished herself. *Jealousy?* She was feeling *jealous*, watching the cop she barely knew with a woman! "Well, more power to him," she grumbled in response to Max's statement. "As long as he does his job and does it well for us, what he does with his personal time is no concern of ours."

LOGAN WAS THRILLED for Rick and Madison. His sergeant and the K-9 Unit's veterinarian had just announced their engagement. If that wasn't enough happy news, Cal Palmer, one of his best K-9 officers, and his wife, Jessica, were expecting their first child together, to join Cal's daughter, Haley, from his first marriage, and Cal and Jessica's adopted daughter, Kayla. They had a *lot* to celebrate. When Rick had announced the engagement, Logan had been the first to sweep Madison up into his arms and congratulate her, before he gave a hearty bear hug to Rick, too.

He glanced at the blonde on his right. He wouldn't have known Jessica was pregnant if they hadn't announced it, despite the pregnancy being nearly four months along. His colleagues across the table, Rick and Cal, were both wildly in love with their women. Logan couldn't have been happier for them. Their impromptu celebration included Shannon Clemens, the newest addition to the K-9 Unit, and the unit's administrative assistant, Beth. Madison had invited two of her colleagues from the Mission Bay Veterinary Clinic: Heather, their office manager, and

Jane, one of the other veterinarians who used to work with the SDPD dogs until Madison had come along. As Logan listened to what Heather was saying, he noticed a table behind her, at the far end of the room.

She sat tall and erect, long dark auburn hair hanging more than halfway to her waist. Her back was to him and partially blocked from his view, but there was no mistaking the thick, pin-straight hair or the quarter profile he glimpsed. He'd just been thinking about how lucky his friends and colleagues were to have found such special women: intelligent, warm, caring and—never one to underestimate the importance of it—beautiful, and Ariana had popped into his thoughts. He'd meant to call her, but then one thing after another had come up. Or, if he was honest, he'd avoided it because he was wary of the emotions she'd stirred in him in the short time he'd known her.

As if he'd conjured her, she was sitting not more than a hundred feet from him. He saw her flick her hair back and laugh.

Logan tried but was unable to keep his eyes from repeatedly drifting back to her. When she rose, said what appeared to be goodbyes and slung the strap of her handbag over her shoulder, he stood, too, as if drawn by a magnet.

"Enjoy the rest of the evening," Logan said to the table in general.

"Leaving so soon?" Rick inquired. "I figured my engagement might be worth a few more rounds at least."

Logan chuckled. "Believe me, we'll have *many* more rounds for an occasion as monumental as this. Besides, I'm driving tonight." He glanced toward the front of the room, and saw Ariana winding her way through the crowd around the bar. He noted more than a few admiring glances cast her way and what he assumed were pickup lines, as well. "Uh...I just remembered something I have to do."

He kissed Madison's cheek and shook Rick's hand. "I'm very happy for you two." He offered congratulations to Jessica and Cal a final time. With a wave to everyone else at the table, he hurried out of the lounge.

Logan was glad he'd decided to follow Ariana when he saw that someone else had the same idea. Except Logan was convinced that the other guy's intentions were less honorable than his, based on the way he was leering. The guy was definitely headed toward Ariana and her car, when Logan dropped a firm hand on his shoulder. "I don't think so, pal," he stated in a no-nonsense tone.

"Hey! What the heck?" The man tried to

shove Logan's hand away and took a drunken swing at him.

"I wouldn't try that again, if I were you." Logan hung on to him by the back of his shirt and pulled his badge out of his pocket with his other hand. "Go back in the bar and have one of your buddies take you home. You're in no shape to drive."

The realization that he was tangling with a cop must have permeated the guy's alcohol-sodden brain. He mumbled an apology, made two attempts to yank his shirt back into place and, with his head hung and shoulders slumped, hightailed it back into The Runway.

The incident had given Ariana time to get into her car and start backing out, evidently oblivious to the little drama that had unfolded. That annoyed Logan. What kind of a security professional was she, parking in a remote, unlit area of the lot, and so unaware of her surroundings that she didn't realize that an inebriated jerk had followed her? He didn't want to think what could've happened, if he hadn't been there to intervene.

Logan's mood was decidedly sour by the time he stalked up to Ariana's car and stood in front of it. He could see the surprise register on her face. He stomped over to her window and signaled for her to lower it.

He didn't let her get a word in before he spoke. "You should know better than to park in the farthest and darkest corner of the lot. What were you thinking?" He hadn't realized how much it bothered him to contemplate that drunk harassing her.

He couldn't explain the protectiveness he felt toward her. It wasn't akin to what he felt for Becca, because there was nothing sister-like about his feelings for Ariana.

"It's nice to see you, too, Captain," Ariana said with a forced smile and syrupy-sweet voice. "Are you here to deliver the safety tip of the evening?"

"No." He'd followed her on impulse and was glad he had. "Did you..." He trailed off, ignoring the curious expression on her face. There was no point enlightening her about what had happened. He was starting to think logically again. Being around Ariana seemed to frazzle his brain. She wasn't careless. She'd arrived late, after him. The bar and the parking lot were both already full when he got there. She'd probably taken the only spot available.

"Did I what?" she prompted.

"Uh..." He recalled the reason he *had* followed her out. "Will you have dinner or a drink with me?"

She laughed. Light and airy. It wasn't the first

time he'd heard her laugh, but it appealed to him in a way he couldn't explain.

She gestured toward the building. "I just had a drink, and, *Captain...*" she put distinct emphasis on his title "...one drink is my limit if I'm driving."

It was his turn to chuckle. He rested a hand on her window frame. "I didn't mean right now."

An odd expression flitted across her face. "Of course not. Is there a new development I should be aware of?"

Logan didn't know if she was being coy or had forgotten about their discussion. He never had this much trouble asking a woman out on a date. Despite her laugh, she seemed reserved and, well, standoffish. He had no idea what had changed. He'd thought they'd hit it off the night they'd gone to Buster's. "No. Not for business. Just a chance to spend some time together...get to know each other better," he clarified.

Her eyes darkened and a vertical line formed between her brows. She swung her gaze toward the entrance to The Runway before meeting his again. "I think you have enough company to keep you entertained, Captain."

He wasn't sure what she meant, but this time her use of his title sounded derogatory.

"C'mon. Have dinner with me." He offered

his best smile. "There're always the policies to discuss."

"Thanks, but I'm busy."

"I haven't suggested a night yet."

"Right. Well, *that* night that you'd be suggesting, I have plans."

He had to draw his hand away quickly as she raised the window. If he hadn't taken a step back, she might've run over his foot, too, as she pulled away and out of the lot.

Logan heard a hearty laugh and turned toward its source.

Cal stood some twenty feet away, his arm around his wife. Jessica was grinning ear-to-ear.

"Crash and burn! I don't think I've seen you strike out before, Jagger," Cal remarked.

Logan knew the reputation he had at the division. He didn't know how he'd earned it. He was no more a player than most single cops. Although he avoided romantic entanglements, he tried to never hurt a woman he was seeing. That was more than could be said for some of the others. Having a witness to his strikeout with Ariana was mildly embarrassing, but there wasn't much he could do about it. "It's not the first time, nor do I expect it'll be the last," he said pleasantly. Waving good-night to Cal and Jess, he headed to his own vehicle.

It irked him more than he cared to admit that

the beautiful security executive had brushed him off. There was no denying his attraction to her. When they'd ended their evening at Buster's, she wouldn't commit to dinner but he was certain the appeal hadn't been one-sided.

Logan shrugged. Probably for the best if it didn't go anywhere. At least until he either finished training Shannon or hired a replacement for Brody.

And of course, there was the whole reason why he avoided getting serious with women and why he'd procrastinated calling Ariana. Despite how happy his close friends were in their relationships, he'd seen up close, with his mother, what being married to a cop could do to a person.

His attraction to Ariana was unlike anything he could remember experiencing before, and he wasn't prepared to risk thinking long term.

CHAPTER FIVE

MONDAY MORNING IN the terminal building, on her way to her office, Ariana grabbed a coffee—strong with a splash of milk. She placed the cup on her desk, her bag beside it. Sitting down, she turned to slide her laptop into its docking station and stared in surprise at the plain white envelope propped up against her monitor. It hadn't been there when she'd left Friday night. Few people had access to her office: a cleaner, her duty supervisor, Max, Cyn and herself.

A quick scan of her office revealed nothing else was out of place. She nearly reached in her drawer to pull out a pair of blue latex gloves, to put them on before she handled the envelope.

She chuckled at herself. It was undoubtedly a corporate memo that had been delivered to her door and the cleaning lady had brought it in. Overreacting was an occupational hazard in her field, always expecting the unexpected from simple situations. As the saying went, you planned for the worst and hoped for the best.

Ariana slit the envelope open, pulled out the single sheet of paper and unfolded it.

Reading the typed message, she felt a rush of adrenaline.

She snatched up the phone, began dialing, then stopped. It was before seven in the morning, and Cyn wouldn't be in for an hour. She called her duty supervisor instead. "Get me the video footage for the hall outside my office, would you please, Trevor?"

"Of course. What time frame would you like?"

Ariana gave him the duration between when she'd left the office Friday evening and when she'd arrived just now.

"Anything you want me to check for?"

She considered his offer and decided that, under the circumstances, she wanted to do it herself. "No, thanks. Just get me the file as soon as you can."

"Right away, boss."

She quickly composed and sent out an incident notification. The message would reach the appropriate parties at all the devices they had registered in the system. She added Logan to the distribution list, because he wasn't registered in the system as one of the normal recipients. After hitting Send, she tried FSD Stewart's cell number. When it went straight to voice mail, she didn't bother leaving a message. The emergency notification system would already have done that.

Ariana's next call was to the San Diego Police Department and Logan. Last Friday morning she'd been thinking about him, and contemplating calling him to take him up on his suggestion about dinner. What a difference a couple of days made. More accurately, what a difference it made learning about his reputation and witnessing firsthand how he'd earned it.

She assumed it would be Logan, working in collaboration with the federal authorities, who'd be looking into the letter she was holding. He was the key contact regarding the investigation of the two women on the Barbados-bound flight; it made sense he'd be assigned for this latest development, too. The officers stationed at the airport would be supporting the investigation, but Logan would probably be the lead for the SDPD. Unable to reach him, she left an urgent message for him to get back to her. She called the division's dispatch and advised them, too. Her final call was to her boss, Calvin Murdoch, the airport's CEO.

If genuine, this had the potential for being a significant occurrence. In keeping with protocol, he needed to be informed that she was initiating their critical incident response plan.

Calvin would have to be available for key decisions on her recommendation, such as a possible ground stop, diversion of aircraft and—if it came down to it—an evacuation of the airport or portions of it. He didn't answer his cell and wasn't in his office so she asked his executive assistant, Marlene Harris, to have him call her as soon as possible.

When Cyn poked her head into her office, Ariana was glad that her assistant had arrived early. "We have a situation. I need you to get Molly for me," she said, referring to the vice president of communications for the airport.

Cyn gave her a questioning look but didn't say a word. She knew that Ariana would fill her in when she had the time and if appropriate. Ariana said silent thanks, as she had on many occasions over the past year, that she had someone of Cyn's qualifications and caliber to support her.

When Ariana's cell phone rang, Cyn left the office and discreetly closed the door behind her. Seeing the blocked number, Ariana assumed it was Logan responding to her messages.

She was correct.

"Thanks for getting back to me so quickly," she said.

"I only wish you'd called to tell me you changed

your mind about dinner. But I know why you did. I saw the incident notification."

"Good. That'll save some time." She went on to explain the details of the situation.

"I'm on my way," he said as soon as she finished. "I'll brief the officers on site and have them meet us at your office. Have you spoken to FSD Stewart yet?"

"Not yet. He's on the notification list. I tried calling him, too. I'll mobilize the multiagency security committee in the meantime. I'll get anyone presently at the airport to meet us. What's your ETA?"

"I should be there in less than twenty minutes. Once you've got everyone together, start without me. We don't know if the threat is credible, but we can't afford to take any chances."

As soon as Ariana hung up, she called Angus again. San Diego was the largest of the airports he was responsible for, but it was still no surprise he wasn't on site. Contacting Max, she gave him clear instructions. She paused to take a call from Calvin and filled him in on what was happening.

Cyn tapped on her door. "Molly's not in. I have her on the phone. Can you take her call now?"

Ariana nodded. As she was finishing briefing Molly, Trevor, her supervisor on duty, arrived. Not bothering with the docking station, she inserted the USB drive he handed her into the port on her laptop.

Trevor rested a forearm on the back of her chair and leaned in to watch the screen with her. “What are we looking for?”

“Someone accessing my office over the weekend.” She played the video clip in fast-forward, slowing only when there was movement in the corridor.

“Why? What happened?” Trevor asked.

Ariana pointed to the sheet of paper lying on her desk without taking her eyes off her monitor. “That. Put on a pair of gloves before you touch it. Top right drawer,” she instructed.

She set the video to run at regular speed when the cleaner entered the frame, unlocked her office door and went in and out, to and from her cart, as she performed her duties. She backed out of the office vacuuming the carpet. Pushing her cart, she moved out of the camera’s range.

“Is this for real?” Trevor asked, his voice shrill, as he placed the letter back on her desk.

Ariana shrugged. “We have to assume it is. At least until we prove otherwise.”

“So there’s a—”

“Wait!” Ariana cut him off. “Look at this.”

She rewound and slowed the video clip. A random dot pixel pattern of static, commonly referred to as snow, was all that was visible on the screen.

"Electronic noise. How could that happen?" Trevor asked.

"That's what we have to find out. The elapsed time was one minute and forty-eight seconds," she confirmed from the timer on her watch that she'd started when the disturbance had begun. "Long enough for a person to come down the hall, access my office, leave the envelope and disappear."

"After he'd disabled the camera," Trevor stated.

"It's not a far stretch to think someone can hack into our video management system, if he or she wants to. This won't help us for now. Let's get going."

Ariana thought about the new system she had just authorized Max to acquire and the additional security features it had. That system would make hacking more difficult, but even then it wouldn't be impossible. At the sound of a knock, she swung around. Two of the SDPD officers assigned to the airport stood in the doorway. Carl Rossi she knew but she hadn't met the other cop. Rossi made the introduction to Officer Haughton. "Captain O'Connor and his explosives detection dog are on the way."

"Good. Let's move to the emergency operations center boardroom and meet them there."

Ariana put her laptop in sleep mode. She rose, grabbed it and her jacket, and led Travis and the two cops out of her office at a brisk jog.

"Captain O'Connor filled you in when you spoke to him?" she asked Rossi.

"Yeah. You've got the letter with you?"

Ariana nodded as she entered the meeting room. A few of the members of the multiagency security committee were already present. She briefed them as quickly and succinctly as she could.

"I don't think I need to say this," she said to everyone in the room. "But you've got the full cooperation and assistance of my team. Let me know what you need."

Even as she said it, she heard footsteps, accompanied by the clicking of canine nails on the hard tile surface of the corridor. A moment later, Logan O'Connor stood in the doorway with Boomer. Ariana had a peculiar sensation seeing Logan, so imposing and virile. She suppressed her reaction. There was no time for it.

Nor could she dwell on the moment of fear at seeing the dog by his side in the doorway. *No escape route*, flashed through her mind before she quashed that thought, too. She took a determined step forward to extend a hand to Logan.

"Didn't think I'd see you so soon," Logan

said to Ariana with a ghost of a smile, voicing her thoughts.

Quick introductions were made to those who'd not met before.

"The SWAT team is right behind me, as are two explosive ordnance disposal technicians. The EOD techs should be here any minute." He gave Ariana a quick appraising glance, the only hint of anything remotely personal between them. Then he was all cop. "Can I see the note?"

Logan pulled on gloves and accepted the sheet of paper from Trevor. Ariana didn't need to see the letter again to know what it said.

> You think you're smart? So secure? Can you find the bomb before it detonates? Look where you'd least expect it. Will lives be lost because of your failings?

"Is it credible?" Ariana asked, as others filed in.

"Specificity and intimate knowledge are indictors that raise the threshold to a real threat. 'Where you'd least expect it' could imply knowledge of the airport's operations. Impossible to say if it's credible based on what we have. We can't ignore it, though."

Ariana nodded. She felt the same.

Although Homeland Security's Office of Intelligence and Analysis hadn't picked up any online chatter or other advance warning, they couldn't discount the incident being the act of an organized terrorist cell.

"Where's Stewart?" Logan asked the TSA supervisory special agent present.

"On his way, I've been told."

Logan was well aware of the hierarchy, which gave the FBI overall responsibility, but they had no time to waste for all the key participants to arrive.

"We've got to get moving." Logan said, taking charge until someone else stepped up to do it. "What else do we know about the person or persons responsible and consequently where the bomb might be? The airport has an enormous floorplate for us to cover. If we can prioritize, it would help."

He turned to Ariana. "How did he get into your office? Did you check for tampering with the lock?"

"Yeah." Trevor responded, as he'd been the one to do it, while Ariana initiated the critical incident response plan. "There's no indication of the lock being forced. The guy had a key or knew how to pick a lock."

"So it's someone who has access to your corridor, has a key to your office or is skilled at picking locks. He knows where the security cameras are located and has the expertise or access to resources to tamper with them. What do you make of the comment about it being where you'd least expect it?"

Ariana glanced at Trevor and Max, who'd just joined them, to see if either of them had any ideas. When they shook their heads, she offered hers. "I'd interpret it in one of two ways. Either a noncritical area where the bomb wouldn't do much damage, or a secure area where the person would've had to get in through a TSA checkpoint or alternate means of security screening, for example a gate to the airfield. Since the note mentions lives being lost, I favor the latter. A public area with a concentration of passengers—for example when they're congregated at a gate just after arrival or before departure, or in security screening lines—would be my guess."

"Makes sense," Logan said.

"Do we have any reason to suspect it would be a domestic or international area?"

Ariana gave the question some thought. "Not that I can think of."

"Anyone else?" he asked.

When no one had other thoughts, they quickly reviewed the airport plans to establish a strategy.

"Should we begin to evacuate the airport? Even partially?" Max asked.

"That's not my call to make," Logan responded. "If you want my opinion, we don't have enough to go on at this point. The likelihood of a major event is low but the consequences, if it happens, are significant. We have no corroboration that the threat is credible. We have no location. Without a known or suspected location, with a full-scale evacuation, people might get injured because of the hysteria that could result. Our dogs are trained to search with members of the public present and with distractions. It won't compromise their effectiveness. We should reassess if we learn more."

Again, Logan's comments were in line with Ariana's own thinking.

"All right, let's get going. We have no idea how long we have if this isn't a hoax. We need to work fast, and our best chance is our explosives detection dogs."

Ariana's breath hitched at the mention of dogs—plural.

Logan gave her a quizzical look. "I have two more dogs and handlers coming in to cover the areas as quickly as possible. Rick Vazquez and his dog, Nitro, are on their way. You'll remember meeting Rick," Logan said with a small smile. "So is Shannon Clemens, and Darwin. She was here the other day. We'll work with

Boomer and Nitro off-leash, for maximum speed. Is that a problem?"

Ariana forced her head to turn side to side.

"Good. The airport is too large to cover in any reasonable time otherwise. To keep passengers calm about a couple of dogs running around, I suggest you make an announcement that we're conducting a drill. Let people know that they shouldn't be afraid of or interfere with the dogs."

"Of course," Ariana said, her voice tight, trying not to think of two big dogs *off leash* and a third one, leashed or not, likely in close proximity to her.

At the sound of people and dogs approaching, Logan turned to the doorway. "Great. Thanks for coming in," he greeted Rick and Shannon. "Sergeant Rick Vasquez works narcotics mainly but his dog, Nitro, was an explosives detection dog before he was retrained for drugs. Nitro's smart and fast. He's worked the airport previously. Officer Clemens is new to the K-9 Unit as is her dog, Darwin. They'll assist us," he said to everyone in the room.

Both dogs were sitting between Ariana and the door. Including Boomer, Ariana now had *three* dogs between her and her escape route from the boardroom. She gulped some air. She knew her best defense against panicking was to breathe deeply and distract herself enough to let the fear subside.

She had a bomb threat to deal with, and this one carried more weight than the ones they experienced periodically. She wouldn't let her phobia get in the way of doing her job.

Although Ariana managed to hold off the anxiety attack, she breathed easier when everyone present, the three dogs included, left the boardroom.

Logan slapped Rick on the back, before they headed in opposite directions at a run. Logan and Boomer took Terminal 1. Rick and Nitro, with Shannon and Darwin assisting, Terminal 2.

FSD Stewart showed up just as they were heading out. He was out of breath and disheveled. He grabbed Ariana's arm as she was rushing past. "What's the status?"

"Go with the captain," Ariana told Trevor. "I'll follow when I'm done here." She had no choice than to provide a brief overview to Angus. Ariana excused herself as quickly as possible so she could catch up to Logan, leaving Angus and his subordinate, who'd stayed back after the briefing, to notify other area airports as they deemed appropriate. There was no way of knowing if it was an isolated threat or others might be targeted, too.

Ariana's priority was her San Diego International.

Before long, the airport was swarming with law enforcement officers. The FBI rapidly assumed leadership of the investigation along with the Department of Homeland Security through FSD Stewart and TSA. Although detection dogs were the best, if not only, line of defense in this type of situation, the TSA didn't have any to deploy on short notice. As such, Logan and his team retained primary responsibly for sweeping the airport for explosive devices and associated components. They hadn't wasted any time starting the process.

Ariana found Logan near Gate 8 and fell in step beside him. He glanced at her without slowing. "What are you doing?"

"Sergeant Vasquez has Max to give him access to restricted areas. I'll do the same for you."

"Trevor's with me. We can manage."

She'd debated leaving Trevor to do it. Then she wouldn't have to be near the dog, possibly in confined spaces. But this was a serious matter and it was *her* responsibility. She couldn't—*wouldn't*—delegate it.

They both fell silent as they listened to the announcement over the public address system, advising passengers that a security exercise was under way. With no time to waste, they carried on. Boomer was already hard at work and, with little guidance from Logan, moving at a rapid pace. He was thorough, checking passengers, goods, luggage and storage spaces.

Ariana walked toward a children's play area and came to an abrupt halt. A young mother was holding her infant on the seat of a small seesaw, while a toddler grasped a monkey bar and bounced up and down with a happy gurgle. It terrified Ariana to think that someone could be so depraved as to set an explosive specifically targeting children. She did a careful visual inspection of all the components, forcing a smile for the young mother. For an instant, she second-guessed herself if she should have ordered an evacuation of the airport, as a precautionary measure.

No. Based on the intelligence they had, it wasn't warranted. Everyone present had agreed.

All seemed to be in order, but Ariana was still relieved when she saw Boomer approaching. She stepped back so the dog could clear the area. Boomer was oblivious to the children, who squealed excitedly at seeing the animal.

"He's a police dog," Ariana told the anxious mother. "He won't hurt your kids. We're running a drill." She repeated what had already been communicated. Even with the added assurance, the mother lifted the infant and, taking the other child by his hand, led them to a seating area.

Ariana rejoined Logan and Boomer. They were inside a retail shop when there was a loud rumble and an unmistakable vibration, strong enough to cause the glassware on the shelves to rattle.

Logan's arm shot out in front of Ariana to bring her to a stop.

It was eerily silent for a few heartbeats, before panic ensued.

People were yelling and running. There was general chaos.

In near unison, they yanked out their phones. Ariana called Trevor. "Do you know what just happened?"

"Yeah. A bomb detonated."

She'd presumed as much, but hearing it confirmed caused a cold dread to slither up her spine. "Is anyone injured?"

"I'm with one of the SWAT guys, not far from it." She could tell he was running based on his breathing. "I can see it now. It doesn't appear that anyone's hurt."

"Good. That's good."

"Where did it happen?" Logan cut in.

"What's your location?" Ariana asked Trevor, then listened. "Okay, we're not far from Gate 16. We're on our way."

"No, *we're* not," Logan retorted, having holstered his own phone.

"Trevor, get a hold of Max. Start evacuation of this terminal, and keep me posted." Disconnecting the line, Ariana stared at Logan. "What are you talking about?"

"It's simple. We're lucky no one was hurt. We're not far from the location and I'll get the EOD techs there. We'll investigate. In the meantime, we can't assume that there's only one explosive device. I no longer need you for security access as we're already in the departure area. Get passengers out of this section of the airport."

"I've got that started already."

"Look," he said, his voice softer. "I'll handle this with our team. Like it or not, I don't want to risk you getting hurt."

His last comment gave Ariana pause. He was trying to shield her. She was as qualified for her job as he was for his. "This is *my* airport and arguing will serve no purpose. It's a waste of time. We've activated the airport's critical incident response plan and, like it or not, I'm incident commander for the airport. There's no point arguing," she repeated.

She could see the resistance on his face, but he must have come to the same conclusion that they had no time to spare.

They arrived at Gate 16 in no time. It was obvious where the explosion had occurred. Gray smoke was billowing from the charred furnishings. As they'd already been told, no one had been in close proximity at the time of the detonation, and the explosion appeared to be relatively small. Ariana was immediately thankful that it had occurred in a quiet area of the departure lounge. Consulting the status board, she ascertained that a flight had just left and there wasn't another one scheduled to arrive at that gate for a couple of hours.

An EOD tech rushed over, while Logan instructed Boomer to check the rest of the area. Boomer's concentration didn't seem to be impacted by the noise and confusion around them.

While Logan and Boomer worked the area between Gates 16 and 18, Ariana wandered ahead to the next section of the concourse. She watched the members of her team and other airport personnel undertake an orderly evacuation. People had obviously been shaken by the explosion, but the staff were communicating that it was a minor incident to keep everyone calm. She followed in the wake of the evacuation, scanning the area for anything that might've been out of the ordinary, although she knew it was futile.

She was glad she hadn't dismissed the letter as a ruse. Ariana had been in her job long enough to know that the airport received a considerable number of false threats on a regular basis.

In this case, the threat just hadn't felt like a prank, and Ariana trusted her instincts. Whoever was behind it had access to her office, making it far more likely that he'd have means of entry to other secure areas, as well. Granted, security in most areas of the terminals was electronic and far more advanced than the rudimentary manual lock on her office door. And she *always* kept her door locked when she wasn't in it. Electronic security was harder to breach, but if someone wanted in badly enough, there were ways. No easy feat, but possible.

Ariana checked in with her team to get status updates about the search. For the time being, they believed they were dealing with an individual. Even so, they couldn't assume that only Terminal 1 was targeted. They had to check the entire airport.

She monitored the evacuation process for Terminal 1, and she kept Calvin and Molly informed.

From the cryptic updates Logan received, Ariana assumed that Sergeant Vasquez and his dog had left Terminal 2 and were heading to Terminal 1.

She caught up to where the passengers were exiting the concourse and paused. She watched Logan as he supervised Boomer. When he glanced at her, she could picture the bright blue gleam of his eyes, although he was too far for her to discern their color. It was only a moment in time, but Ariana felt a spark pass between them, across the nearly empty concourse.

Disconcerted, she broke eye contact and made her way toward the concession area, still seeking anything that might not appear right.

Suddenly, Boomer rushed by her in a blur and she heard her name called from a distance. Swinging around, she saw Logan sprinting toward her. She felt the floor shudder, and an ear-splitting sound reverberated around her. Before she could process what was happening, she was flying through the air.

CHAPTER SIX

"ARIANA. ARIANA!" Logan continued calling her name as he cradled her in his arms. They were in the exact position they'd landed when he'd tackled her. He didn't want to move her, in case she had injuries beyond the obvious. He'd been able to protect her from the worst of the explosion when he'd grabbed her. Fortunately, he'd been wearing his body armor, as his back would probably be a mess if he hadn't been. A quick scan of the area showed him that three other people had been hurt, but they'd been far enough away that their injuries were unlikely to be serious.

Logan gently tapped Ariana's face. When her eyes slowly opened, relief flooded through him.

What was she thinking, going off on her own like that, when they'd already established that the threat was real and were in the process of evacuating the public? And she was injured because of it. "Damn it all."

"Sorry, what...?" she murmured. "What happened?"

"There was another explosion. You were almost on top of it when it detonated. Boomer alerted me to it."

Ariana pushed up and looked around frantically. "Oh, my God! Where's your dog? Where's Boomer?"

"Relax." It surprised him that her first concern was for Boomer. "Over there." He pointed to Rossi, who was keeping pace with Boomer, as the dog worked the rest of the area. "He's okay." Thankfully. "Boomer was circling the area and was behind a column when the IED detonated. But you..." He bit off thc rest of what he was going to say. There was nothing to be gained by browbeating her, although she could've been killed or seriously injured, if not for the fact that it appeared to be another small explosion. If there'd been more explosive material... He didn't want to think about that, especially until they knew her condition.

"Was anyone else injured?"

Logan scanned the spot where the passengers were. "Three people. Nothing significant, from what I can see."

"Good. That's good."

"You should've stayed behind us, in the areas we'd cleared," he said more gently, and rubbed a smudge from her cheek just below where an angry bruise was forming.

He reached out to brush her hair back to examine the bruise and scrapes. She flinched.

"Sorry, did that hurt?" He'd barely touched her. On closer inspection, he saw a jagged scar from her hairline nearly to the top of her ear. "That's not new."

Shrinking away from his touch, she swatted at his hand and tugged her long bangs back down to cover the side of her face.

He wanted to ask how she'd gotten the scar but it was obvious she didn't want to discuss it, nor did he have time. A group of paramedics was running toward them. Giving them a quick overview of what happened, Logan directed them to the three injured passengers and made room for one of them to attend to Ariana.

As he was edging back, he heard Rick Vasquez call to him. Rick must have caught up to them while he was occupied with Ariana.

"We've got something here, Jagger."

Logan glanced over his shoulder to where Rick was with Nitro. Nitro was staring at a chair, a passive indication that he'd found something. When Boomer rushed over to join Nitro, his reaction was the same.

Leaving Ariana with the paramedic, Logan signaled to one of the EOD techs and ran over to join Rick.

"What have we got?" he asked the technician,

glancing around to ensure no one else was in the vicinity, in case it was another bomb.

The tech swept his electronic trace detector over and around the chair. "Not much. Some dust at most."

"Our subject of interest sat here?" Rick speculated.

"I don't think so. The dust is *under* the seat. As I said, not much of it."

That was a relief. "Rick, I'll deal with this. Keep checking the rest of the area with Nitro, would you?" He looked around. "Where's Shannon?"

"I left her in the other terminal to work with Darwin. It's cleared, but I thought it would be a good exercise for them."

Logan nodded then dropped down on his hands and knees and peered under the chair. There was an envelope taped to its underside.

"You want to check this again before I pull it off?" he asked and edged to the side to let the EOD tech squat down beside him. He ran the detector across its length. "It's nothing to worry about. Our subject of interest probably handled the envelope or what's in it just before or after he'd set the IED over there." He gestured to where the explosion had occurred.

Logan slid on thin latex gloves and tugged the white letter-size envelope off the bottom of the chair. It wasn't labeled or sealed. It was similar to the one left in Ariana's office. He pulled out the sheet of paper, unfolded it and read.

When he heard Ariana groan, he spun around. The paramedic was helping her to her feet, probably to transport her to the hospital.

It seemed Ariana had other ideas, though. She nearly toppled over as she shook off the paramedic's grasp. Despite his protest, she lurched toward Logan.

"I'm fine," she grumbled. The paramedic made a grab for her again. "I said I'm fine," she repeated with more heat.

Logan took in the bruise and scrapes on her right cheekbone, and the blood on the corner of her mouth, probably a result of her having bitten her tongue or the inside of her cheek as she'd landed. One of her sleeves was torn, and it appeared that she might have a broken finger on her left hand.

"You don't *look* fine," he observed with a glance at the paramedic, who responded with a frustrated shake of his head. "You should get your injuries checked out. We can handle it here."

Ariana gave him an annoyed expression. "I said I'm fine, and I decline medical care," she added for the benefit of the paramedic, no doubt. "Note it down. It's on me."

Logan was surprised to feel the corner of his mouth twitch, but it passed quickly. They weren't done yet and he didn't want anyone else getting hurt on his watch. He needed to get back to work.

"At least let the man take care of your finger," he said. "But read this first."

Logan held the note out to her and her eyes skimmed over it.

He was glad he'd been standing close, because she nearly collapsed. He and the paramedic steadied her and helped her to a chair.

"Oh, no," she whispered. "It's not over."

"Doesn't look like it," Logan responded.

While the paramedic splinted Ariana's finger, he scanned the words again.

There's more but not today. The clock—or in this case, the bomb—is ticking!

There was a blue smear on the bottom right corner. It was some kind of powder. Since neither Boomer nor Nitro showed any interest specifically in it, it must not have been explosives dust.

The note might have indicated that there would be no more explosions that day, but they couldn't trust the subject of interest. Were more

IEDs already set, or was the bomber planning to return?

The airport went into lockdown. They weren't taking any chances. The evacuation was expanded to include the entire airport. A facility the size of San Diego International, with an estimated fifty thousand passengers passing through the airport that day, required significant time to evacuate. They were working as fast as they could.

In the meantime, Logan and his team had to complete the search.

As soon as Ariana's finger was in a splint and bandages had been applied to the worst of her cuts and abrasions, she was back in action. There was nothing Logan could do to dissuade her. At least now she kept to the areas cleared by the dogs.

As they swept the remainder of the concourse, Logan was more and more convinced that they wouldn't find any more IEDs. At least not that day. He wasn't surprised when he was done with his section and he hadn't found anything of concern. Logan told those present that he'd wait for Rick to finish, and they'd meet them at the airport's emergency operations center.

He watched Ariana as she walked away with the others. She'd held up despite her injuries.

To see her beautiful face marred, her elegant but capable hand splinted—anger rose up in him. If for no other reason, he wanted to get the person responsible for what he'd done to Ariana.

He saw victims on a regular basis. It was the nature of his job. He'd never grown so callous that it didn't affect him each and every time. But his emotional reaction to what had happened to Ariana—and what *could* have happened—was unprecedented in his experience. He didn't have the time or inclination to analyze it just then.

He rolled his shoulder in an attempt to ease the ache that had settled there. It must have been where he'd hit the ground. He reached back to rub the spot. His hand came away damp.

There was a smear of blood on his palm. Clearly, he hadn't been unscathed. He wiped his hand against his pant leg and took out his phone to call Rick to see how he and Nitro were progressing. Before he had a chance to do so, he heard his name called from behind him.

He turned to see Rick approaching at a fast jog, Nitro easily keeping pace by his side.

"Find anything?" Logan asked Rick when he caught up to him.

"We searched the entire place. There was no further evidence of explosives, residue or dust. Nor did we detect any failings in security. Her senior manager, Max Golding, told me that Atkins has been using whatever funds she's been able to scrape together to progressively address weaknesses that had existed for a long time before her arrival. Golding said it hasn't been easy for her, as she's been getting a lot of pushback, even from members of her own team. If there haven't been issues, why spend the money? That sort of thing."

Logan glanced at Rick as they started walking toward the emergency operations center.

"Wasn't it a former FBI director who famously said 'security is enough until it is not enough'?"

Rick chuckled. "Yeah, and isn't it the truth. Bottom line, Atkins runs a tight ship."

Logan agreed.

"She's going to face some heat over the incident occurring in a secure passenger area and the letter being left inside her locked office," Rick added.

"She probably will, even though we don't know yet how the subject of interest got in. She'll come out of it okay. As you said, Ariana runs a tight ship. She's intelligent. She's professional..." His voice trailed off as he reflected on her other attributes.

"And she's a looker," Rick supplied, in an uncanny echo of Logan's thought.

"Yeah, she is that, too."

"She doesn't like dogs much, does she?" Rick asked as they exited the concourse.

"You've noticed that, huh? Actually, I don't know if it's not liking them rather than being afraid of them."

Rick glanced down at Nitro by his side, sleek and dark and fit. "Is it just police dogs, you think?"

Logan pursed his lips. "I can't answer that. I haven't seen her with other dogs. She just seems…uneasy." He paused. "You know when that second IED exploded and she was hurt? The first thing she did when she came to was ask if Boomer was okay."

"That says something, doesn't it? Especially if she's afraid of dogs." They turned down the corridor leading to the EOC. "I didn't get the chance to ask how your date with her at Buster's Beach House Bar was."

Logan shot a look at his friend and colleague. "It wasn't a date…exactly."

Rick smirked. "If you say so. So you're not interested in her?"

Logan contemplated the muddle of feelings he'd been experiencing since he'd met Ariana, not the least of which being the degree of concern he felt for her. More than that, there was that undeniably strong attraction. "I might be interested, but…"

"But what?"

No matter how close they were, Logan couldn't explain to Rick the reason he avoided relationships. Rick was waiting for an answer, though, so Logan grasped at the first excuse he could come up with. He let out a short laugh. "You just lucked out, pal, that your fiancée is a veterinarian who loves dogs. You know as well as I do that none of us could contemplate having a relationship with a woman who didn't like dogs."

"Yeah. That's a fact. The dogs are a part of our lives. Some of the guys say even more so than their spouses." Rick chuckled. "I wouldn't go as far as that. So are you going to ask her out?"

Logan shook his head. "Weren't you listening? A woman who doesn't love dogs is a no-go for me."

"I *was* listening! But we weren't discussing a relationship here. When was the last time you've dated a woman with the intention of anything serious developing? If ever? Why should Ariana be any different?"

Rick had a point. Logan had no plan to get involved with a woman other than on a casual basis. It wasn't in the cards for him. He'd resolved that a long time ago. When he'd taken the oath to serve and to protect.

Logan was well aware of the pressures the

job put on a relationship. The realities could be even harder for the partner or spouse of a cop, as he'd seen.

Sending their loved one off to work, not knowing if that would be the day he or she would be injured or killed. He'd seen firsthand how it had affected his mother—the constant worry and fear.

Logan thought about it as they strode along the corridor.

His parents had loved each other deeply and his mother had managed to hide her stress and fear reasonably well from his father, but she hadn't been able to conceal her worry from Logan. Innumerable times he'd watched her cast furtive glances at the phone when his father was late getting home. If the phone rang during those times, she'd literarily jump out of her chair. It if was the doorbell, she'd freeze with terror etched on her face.

Ultimately, the dreaded knock on the door had come. His mother's worst fear had materialized. His father had been killed in the line of duty. Only three years before he'd been planning to rctirc and two years after he'd made police chief, a position that came with greater responsibility but supposedly less personal risk.

Thank goodness Logan had been home at the time.

He'd never forget how his mother had broken down, keening inconsolably as a wounded animal might. Logan had felt the pain, too, for the father he'd loved and idolized his whole life.

In an instant, his mother had aged a decade. She'd never been able to fight her way out of her grief. She passed away eighteen months after his father, of natural causes, they said. Logan knew better. It had been from a broken heart.

He'd been the one to find her that morning. She'd seemed peaceful for the first time since his father's death. He'd stood watching her for long moments, appearing so much her old self. Recollections of his family, together and happy, had flooded in. She must have had a similar memory when her spirit had left her, if the gentle smile on her lips had been an indication.

It was the influence of his own parents' situation that had made Logan determined to avoided relationships.

Maybe when he had a desk job…

He'd accepted a long time ago that his relationships wouldn't be serious. So why *should* it be any different with Ariana? And why did that thought make him feel as if he'd be missing out on something precious?

As they walked through the doors leading to the emergency operations center, Logan felt an immediate constriction in his chest when he saw Ariana standing inside.

There was nothing wrong with spending some time with her, he rationalized, as long as he kept it casual. He might just have to push her for that dinner date.

Rick made a scoffing sound, interrupting Logan's thoughts. Rick, too, was watching Ariana. They both saw her look at the dogs with rounded eyes.

"I don't get how someone can't like dogs," Rick said under his breath.

CHAPTER SEVEN

ARIANA LOOKED AROUND the airport's emergency operations center and noted that almost all the members of the multiagency security committee had arrived for the debrief. They'd done everything they could to ensure the safety of the airport and its passengers. The first order of business was to decide whether the airport could resume normal operations. She expected the answer would be yes.

While they were waiting for everyone to arrive so they could start the meeting, Logan excused himself to return some calls. Ariana assumed he had to check in with the division and provide an update.

She was glad of the few minutes she had before the meeting. She could use the time to settle down. Her head felt as if it would explode from agony and frustration. Her left hand was throbbing with pain, too. In hindsight, she should've accepted the painkillers the paramedic had offered. She'd refused them because she didn't want to dull her brain. She should have taken them and saved them until now. She could have used them.

Despite her pain and fatigue, she had to get through the debrief. They needed to do it while the events of the day were still fresh in everyone's mind. Cyn had stuck around to help with coordination. Ariana wanted to hug her for having set up coffee. She didn't know how long the urn had been sitting there and didn't care, as long as the brew was hot and strong.

When Rick stepped away to make a call, as well, Ariana took a long, bracing drink of coffee.

Self-critical as she was, she believed she'd handled her role the best she could. Outwardly, she was certain she'd seemed efficient, calm and in control. The way she was trained to be.

Outwardly capable—yes. Inside was another matter. She was second-guessing everything she'd done and was plagued by a feeling of failure. She thought back to her time at Sector Security and Bryan Carpenter. It wasn't just because of Bryan that she'd been working so hard over the past year to improve security at the airport and close all the gaps she'd found. It had surprised her that George Dennison, her predecessor and occasional mentor, would have allowed some of the glaring weaknesses to exist. No matter, as they'd been easy enough to fix.

She believed she'd been addressing the highest-risk areas, but if that was the case then how did the person or persons responsible get the explosives into the secure area?

For now, they had no answer. If it turned out to be through a security checkpoint, that fell under the auspices of TSA, but she couldn't shirk her duty. She saw her role as integrator of all the various entities that contributed to the safety and security of the airport and its passengers. That included TSA. The general public and the media didn't care who did what directly. Placing blame—which wasn't her style to begin with—would only work against her. Whatever happened at the airport, people saw as the airport's responsibility. If it was security or safety related, it was *her* responsibility.

Should she have done more, once the weaknesses in TSA's procedures had been made public through the leaking of the covert testing results? One of the recommendations had been to increase the use of detection dogs. Bomb-sniffer dogs were far more accurate at detecting explosives than electronic detection devices, *and* they cost less. She'd put her personal phobia aside and had been pressuring FSD Stewart for dogs to be assigned to the airport since the recommendations had been made public. He'd been unresponsive. Would dogs have been able to prevent what they were dealing with?

She mulled over providing a quick update to Calvin before the meeting started. All she had at this point was that there were no more explosives on site. That had already been communicated through the emergency notification system. She decided to put off calling Calvin. She had no answers for her CEO yet.

Logan walked back into the meeting room and to where she stood. His close proximity made her feel edgy, unexpectedly so, since he and Rick had left their dogs in the office assigned to the SDPD to let them get some well-deserved rest.

With mug in hand, Ariana moved to the table and sat. Logan topped up his own mug and took the chair directly opposite her. As others joined them at the table, he continued to hold her gaze. It caused that churning in her belly again. She was unreasonably relieved when her phone rang.

Ariana checked the display and her relief was short-lived.

It was her boss. She berated herself for not calling him and headed to a quiet corner of the room to answer her phone.

"Yes, Calvin." She forced her voice to sound as normal as possible.

"What's happening, Ariana? It seems everything is going crazy around here. The media are knocking down my door. Under the circumstances, I can't keep redirecting them to Molly," he said. "Ralph has called a special meeting of the board. As chairman, he wants answers. And so do I. I need you there and ready to brief the board. I might also need you to handle some of the more technical aspects of the media queries." There was a pause. Calvin had clearly covered the mouthpiece of the phone. She heard a muffled conversation before he came back on the line a moment later.

"I've got to go," he announced. "We need to talk, but for now are we clear?"

She'd never heard Calvin so abrupt. Sounding so *outraged*. Calvin tended to be passive-aggressive at worst. He'd never been antagonistic. "Yes, we're clear." What choice did she have?

While she'd been on the phone, the rest of the people attending the meeting had arrived. They gathered around but not everyone sat. The adrenaline was still surging too strongly for many of them.

Ariana did take a chair because she wasn't certain her legs would support her. "Shall we get started?" she asked to get everyone's attention, before turning the meeting over to the FBI special agent leading the investigation.

"What's his or her motivation?" someone asked, once everyone was brought up to speed.

No one seemed eager to jump in, so Logan shrugged. "We'll get brighter minds than mine to theorize, but the note has the condescending tone of a terrorist group toward infidels. Comments like *Think you're smart. Secure. Failings*. Another hypothesis, if we factor in that the explosions were both relatively minor—" he glanced sympathetically at Ariana "—and considering that no terrorist group or individual has taken responsibility, at least not yet, it could be someone who wanted to send a message. *Watch me. I can do this*." He looked to Angus for confirmation.

Angus mumbled something noncommittal.

"Does anyone have any ideas about how he got in?" Ariana asked.

"Not through a TSA checkpoint," Angus replied.

"How can you be certain?" Ariana didn't want to seem openly challenging, but there was no way to categorically make that determination based on what they had to go on.

"We've checked our procedures—we don't allow any departure from standing orders, since…since last year."

Ariana glanced at Max. He shrugged and rolled his eyes.

They had a roundtable discussion about it but didn't come to any satisfactory conclusion or supposition. The TSA checkpoint remained the obvious path of least resistance, no matter how much FSD Stewart protested. One thing they all agreed on was that they couldn't discount that the person might be an insider—someone who worked at the airport. Insiders tended to pose the greatest threat for most organizations because of their knowledge and their familiarity, since most people wouldn't question them if they saw them around, perhaps even if they were acting strange. No, they couldn't eliminate the insider threat principle.

"I don't like the tone of the notes," Logan said, moving on to another point for discussion. "I believe the mention of 'more' isn't just an idle threat. Since we didn't find additional IEDs today, it means our subject of interest intends to get other explosives in." He looked at Ariana directly. "And security at the airport is solid. He'd know that we'll tighten it further."

Ariana appreciated the compliment, although she couldn't acknowledge it right then. "It's brazen of him to give us a heads-up and think he can outsmart security again. I don't understand why he wouldn't have done everything he plans to do today," she added.

Logan shook his head slowly. "I don't have an

answer to that. Combined with the fact that the two IEDs didn't have sufficient explosives in them to do a lot of damage, it's as if he's toying with us. We have no insight into his motivation or what he plans to do?" He scanned the faces around the table. "He'd have to know we'll be watching for him and it'll be harder if—*when*—he tries again. It's brazen, as Ariana said. Any ideas, Angus? I know it's not something you want to consider, but theoretically, how likely is it that our subject of interest got in through a TSA checkpoint?"

Nice lob, Ariana thought and waited to see how Angus would respond. He opened his mouth a few times and his face turned bright red before he spoke. He sputtered on at some length about the integrity of the TSA processes and the improvements that had been made in the past year. Partway through his discourse, Logan got up and joined Rick, who'd been leaning against the counter at the side of the room. They were speaking in undertones that Ariana was unable to hear.

"After all, security isn't entirely our responsibility," Angus concluded, giving Ariana a hostile glare. "Have you considered the weaknesses in *your* systems and procedures?"

Whatever Logan had been saying to Rick, he stopped abruptly and pushed off the counter to approach the table. "Now, hold on a minute. We don't know how the perpetrator got in or where the failure occurred. There's no need for accusations. We'll determine what happened through our investigation. Then we'll discuss who, if anyone, dropped the ball."

Angus must have been truly agitated, as he pointed an accusatory finger at Ariana. "Why don't you ask her and her people?" he said scathingly. "If she's that good at her job, why is *she* the one who got hurt?"

EVERYONE IN THE room fell silent. They all became preoccupied with their cell phones or the papers in front of them.

Logan was astonished by what he'd just heard.

Looking at Ariana, seeing the livid blue-green bruise against a face that had gone suddenly white, Logan felt his protective feelings for her rise up.

"There's no correlation between her injury and the state of security at the airport." He was tempted to add "you buffoon" but decided against it. He'd made his point. The others in the room could read between the lines.

"So how *did* she get injured?" Stewart persisted. "If your dog is supposed to be so good?"

Logan closed the distance between him and Stewart. He got satisfaction out of towering over Stewart, who had to crane his neck back to maintain eye contact. "Not that it's any of your business, but she got ahead of us."

"Ahead of you? What do you mean?"

"There was a lot going on and we were all doing our best in a tense situation. It wasn't her fault," Logan said and gave Stewart a long, hard stare he usually reserved for suspects. Stewart compressed his lips, the edges turning white from the pressure, and shifted in his seat. "We were sweeping the departure lounge for explosives," Logan began as he heard the door behind him open. "She was almost on top of the IED when it detonated. It could've been a lot worse…" Thinking about it caused the horror and the dread he'd experienced to surface again.

"She should've waited until you'd cleared the area. Isn't that standard procedure?"

"Yeah, but she got ahead of me and Boomer," he acknowledged and glanced at Ariana. She'd gone paler still, if that was possible. She was staring at the door behind him. Turning to see who'd entered, he saw Calvin Murdoch, the airport's CEO, standing in the doorway.

"You're injured." Calvin stated the obvious, his face flushed and jaw clenched. "Are you okay?" he asked Ariana.

ARIANA'S TENSION MOUNTED as she heard Calvin's voice directed at her. He must've come straight to the EOC after he'd dealt with whatever had interrupted their telephone conversation.

She could see the stiffness—and displeasure—on Calvin's face as he, much as the others had before, scrutinized her face, her rumpled clothing and splinted hand.

"I'm fine," she repeated for what seemed like the thousandth time since the explosion.

"Good. And what were you and FSD Stewart discussing?" he asked Logan. "About procedure?"

Logan's features were taut. He glanced at Ariana. "We were all doing our jobs."

Calvin slid his gaze back to meet Ariana's. "But you shouldn't have been ahead of the officers?"

She felt the blood—what was left of it—drain from her face as she replayed the final comments between Logan and Angus from the time Calvin had entered. She expected that sort of treatment from Angus. It was his nature and she knew Calvin didn't put much stock in it. But Logan? He'd never said a word about not getting ahead of the dog until *after* the explosion. It made sense, of course, in hindsight.

"Ariana, what were you doing not following police direction?" Calvin demanded.

She was at a loss for what to say. She couldn't believe this was happening in front of the other members of the multiagency security committee. There was a lot of paper-shuffling and topping up of coffees.

"You were supposed to provide *access* for the law enforcement professionals. Not try to do their job. Isn't that right?"

Is that what she'd been trying to do? Looking around? Searching? Had she been wrong… *again*? Ariana's heart was pounding so hard, she thought it would burst right out of her rib cage. Why was Calvin fixated on this, when they had much more serious issues to deal with?

"Calvin, we're in the middle of a debrief here," she said with a strained voice, forcing the words past the constriction in her throat. "I'm happy to discuss your concerns with you later. In the meantime, you're welcome to join us, if you wish."

Her comment hung in the air for long seconds, before her boss shook his head. "Be ready to brief the board," he said. "I want a full report on what happened and what we're doing about it before the end of the day. At present—and this is the reason I came down here—I need assurance that the airport is secure. That there are no more bombs. I have a media conference in thirty minutes. Can you give me that assurance?" To Ariana's consternation, he was posing the question to Logan again.

"There are no more explosives," Logan responded.

"Can I safely tell the media that? Categorically? It'll be my credibility and that of the airport on the line."

"Yeah. We've cleared the airport," Logan responded. "For now."

"What does that mean?" She could hear the displeasure in Calvin's tone.

Logan shrugged and looked at Ariana again. Was he giving her the opportunity to jump in? She didn't see how it could help her current situation.

"It means what I said. We have reason to presume the perpetrator isn't done. I don't believe this to be a random act, and it wasn't an isolated IED. He went to a lot of trouble to get into the concourse with the explosives. He could've planted much more powerful IEDs. There could have been significant casualties and injuries. Far more damage. We'll see what our Homeland Security colleagues have to say." He nodded toward Angus and some other members of the group congregated around thc table. "But my read is that this guy's intention was not to do physical harm. Rather he wanted to demonstrate that he could waltz in here and do what he did." Logan fleetingly considered whether it could be someone trying to reveal more weaknesses in TSA's procedures.

"He got the explosives through security. How did that happen?"

"Yes, he breached security," Ariana said, finally finding her voice. "If you'd let me explain—" But Calvin cut her off again.

"You'll have a chance to explain to the board." There was a pause as he checked his watch. "I've got to get ready for the media conference. Ariana, be in the boardroom in an hour and a half. Does that give you enough time to do what you need to do here?"

She nodded slowly.

"Don't be late," he said. "And make your explanation a good one."

She let out a strangled sound after Calvin walked out, then quickly glanced around to see if anyone had heard. If they had, they were pretending not to have. Only Logan was watching her, and he gave her an encouraging smile.

"All right," the FBI special agent chairing the meeting cut it.

Ariana could tell he'd run out of patience with the interruption, and she was thankful for it.

"Let's review where we were?" he said.

The rest of the debrief took nearly an hour. At this stage of their investigation, they couldn't discount terrorism, and decided to operate on the assumption that it was. That meant the FBI, with responsibility for counterterrorism, retained the lead.

They agreed to heightened surveillance and other defensive measures, as well as regular coordination meetings for the foreseeable future.

The blue residue on the bottom corner of the second note stumped them. They didn't know if it was relevant but couldn't ignore it. The letter was taken by Homeland Security for testing.

Ariana purposefully avoided Logan at the conclusion of the meeting. She left while he was having a conversation with Rick and Max. Cowardly perhaps, but she didn't have the energy to face him just then. She made it to the boardroom with only minutes to spare, without time for preparation.

The normal procedural matters associated with convening the meeting were dispensed with quickly.

"How could this have happened at our airport?" Ralph Sterling, the chairman of the board, demanded of Calvin. "That was a secure area. If someone can get into that area with two live explosives, what does that say about our security?"

"I understand and share your concern, Ralph," Calvin responded. "I can assure you no one is more troubled about it than me. I'd like to redirect that question to our chief of security." He turned cold, hard eyes on Ariana.

"We're continuing to work with the various law enforcement agencies—"

"Don't give us any of that BS," Ralph interrupted her. "Just answer the question."

There were a couple of coughs, some sounds of agreement, including from those directors who were participating in the meeting by teleconference. "Let me repeat. How could this happen?"

"Sir—" Ariana tried to keep her voice from shaking "—we haven't determined that yet."

"What?" he boomed. "What if there are more explosives?"

"We've eliminated that possibility. We're investigating, in collaboration with the appropriate law enforcement agencies, through the multiagency security committee. We will—"

"Let's try this, then," Ralph interjected. "*Why* did it happen?"

"Right now, the security committee is operating on the assumption that it's an act of terrorism."

"Terrorism?" Ralph repeated, an appalled expression on his face. "I ran into the TSA head on my way in. Angus, I think his name is. He said he agreed with the SDPD that it's most likely a disgruntled individual trying to prove something. Ariana, you think otherwise?"

Yes, Logan had said that in the meeting, but it was speculation. Angus had no right to say that to the chairman of the board. "We're still in the early stages of our investigation, but the committee is treating it as an act of terrorism for now."

"You should get your stories straight. You have no idea how they breached security?"

Ariana wanted to snap back. How *could* they know? Didn't Ralph understand how large the airport was? How complex its operations? And that security screening was a TSA responsibility and not under her direct supervision, regardless of how often she wished it was? But she knew there was nothing to be gained by pointing any of that out. She thought about mentioning the possibility of an insider being responsible, but that was based only on probabilities and they had no specific evidence to corroborate it. If she raised it, she expected it would only increase the level of agitation in the room. "No, sir. Not yet."

"Let's move in camera with our CEO," Ralph responded dismissively. "I need a motion."

With the vote unanimous, Ariana left the boardroom. As she was walking out, Calvin called to her, asking that she wait outside.

She checked in with Max. There were no new

developments. She tried Logan's cell phone. It rang numerous times and went to voice mail.

She paced restlessly for interminable minutes while the board deliberated behind the closed doors. Periodically, she heard a raised voice, but the soundproofing prevented her from making out what was being said.

Marlene, Calvin's executive assistant, suggested she take a seat. Several times she offered her coffee or water. Ariana declined all three.

When the door swung open, Ralph hurried past her, barely sparing her a glance, followed by the other two directors who'd been able to attend in person.

Calvin stood in the doorway, his face pinched. "Ariana, can you join me, please?"

She took a fortifying breath and followed Calvin into the boardroom, feeling very much like a lamb being led to slaughter.

"Shut the door," Calvin instructed as he moved over to the coffee station and poured them each a cup. She thanked him but was horrified to find that the cup rattled in its saucer as she carried it to the table. The slight noise was enough to draw Calvin's attention to her shaking hands.

What was wrong with her? She usually handled stress well and calmly. She worked best under pressure. It was one of the traits that made her good at her job. It wasn't the incident that had flustered her. Nor her injuries, she concluded.

It was the apparent lack of confidence in her abilities topped off by the lengthy in-camera deliberations by the board of directors. She had no answers for them, but they should have realized that it was virtually impossible to know so soon after an incident exactly how and why it happened. Clearly, the chairman of the board didn't understand or chose not to accept that.

"Ariana," Calvin began in a detached tone, "the board is understandably perturbed about such a significant breach of security and resultant passenger injuries."

"As they should be. I'm also very concerned about it and we're cooperating fully with the investigation being undertaken by the authorities."

Calvin sipped his coffee without taking his eyes off Ariana. She sat motionless and straight-backed under her boss's intense scrutiny. She wished he'd just get to the point. "The in-camera session was long," Ariana observed to fill the uncomfortable silence.

Calvin nodded. "Yes, they had quite a debate."

"About what?" She felt a tickle at the back of her throat and resisted coughing.

Calvin leaned back. "I'm not going to lie to

you. In camera or not, these matters have a way of getting back to people. The board is deeply troubled about what happened today. They are, of course, concerned about the passengers first and foremost, then about the airport operation. Frankly, they're anxious—and rightfully so—about their own reputations. They want to know how, exactly, the security breach occurred, and what we're doing to prevent a reoccurrence.

"Ariana, you came to us highly recommended by George. George had held your position for nearly two decades before he retired. He'd done a good job." Calvin sighed heavily. "The board trusted and respected George. You came in and wanted to make improvements. You said we needed them, and I supported you. Although we've had to cut spending overall because of our economic realities, I found the money for you for most of the security improvements you said were critical.

"Yet here we are, with an unprecedented breach. The most significant security incident the airport has experienced in my time as CEO. You can understand why the board would be concerned." Calvin rose and walked to the windows overlooking the airfield and stood with his back to her. "Ariana, I won't hold information back from you. There was talk of bringing

George back on a fee-for-services basis. To help you out. Get things back on track."

"What?" Ariana's voice was thin and barely above a whisper. If Calvin did that, he'd effectively be taking away her authority. Undermining her with her team, ruining her hard-earned reputation with the law enforcement organizations she had to work with. It didn't matter if it was George or someone else. The outcome would be the same.

"You should know that it was only by a narrow margin that they decided not to have me immediately ask George to help us out."

Ariana felt light-headed. This job meant the world to her and she loved what she did. She saw everything she'd worked so hard for slipping away.

"I recommended that they leave it up to me," Calvin said. "I convinced them it was an operational matter. For the *time being* I'll hold off."

Ariana heard her own voice as if from a distance. "I appreciate it."

After Calvin dismissed her, she went directly to the south stairwell and outside to the airfield. She stood with her back against the wall and took several deep, fortifying breaths. She had work to do, but first she needed some fresh air and quiet time alone.

Ariana didn't wallow in self-pity easily. As

she calmed, she rallied. She'd gotten this far on her knowledge, skill and strong work ethic.

It troubled her that the improvements she'd been making were being brought into question. She wondered if she'd be able to implement the remaining ones, including the improved video management system.

A few more deep breaths and she was feeling distinctly better. She'd get through this and come out stronger. She would show the board that she *could* manage a crisis of this magnitude.

This would be the second major test of her career. Recalling the first, when she'd been operations manager at Sector Security and had sent Bryan Carpenter, a young guard relatively new to his job, on an assignment that had ultimately cost him his life, caused her confidence to waver again. She couldn't dwell on that now.

Steadier and ready to go inside, she pulled out her restricted area identity card, turned the corner and smacked solidly into a hard chest. A little dazed, she felt strong hands clasp her upper arms and she stared up into bemused blue eyes.

She blinked to make sure her throbbing head wasn't causing her to hallucinate.

It was definitely Logan. After her confrontation with Calvin, she couldn't help wanting to melt into his arms. The reaction unsettled her to such a degree that she did the opposite, swiftly stepping back.

As she did, she noticed Boomer. Logan must've gone back to get the dog. She had no idea why he and his dog were there. She stuffed her card back into her pocket and prayed for calm.

She leaned forward and shouted over the roar of a jet readying for takeoff. "What are you doing?" Realizing how close she'd come to his dog, she took another step in retreat. "And how did you get out here?" she demanded.

Logan eyed her pensively. "Your second in command gave me access. I'm here because this might've been where our subject of interest entered."

"But this is a secure area, too. Anyone in here would have to have a restricted area identity card, and at a high clearance level. Are you positive?"

Logan gave her another appraising look. "Watch."

With a hand signal, he directed Boomer, and Ariana backed up against the wall as the dog scented the area. She might not have trusted dogs—and with good reason—but she knew enough about how service dogs worked to realize that this dog had found something.

"So I believe this is where he brought the explosive devices through, or at least some of its components." He glanced around. "Assuming he had an access card, how would he have gotten here?"

If it was true, it was more troubling because of the number of highly sensitive restricted areas the perpetrator had to have passed through, but she turned her mind to Logan's question. "There's no direct, easy access." She inhaled deeply. "He had to know what he was doing, where he was going and, as we just discussed, he had to have high-level security access."

Logan glanced up and around.

She knew he was searching for cameras. "We should be able to see him on camera…unless he somehow disabled, blocked or avoided them. We'll also check for security card access," she continued. "See who might've entered this area in the time frame in question."

"Good. Thanks," he said. The small, encouraging smile he gave her settled her further. She *knew* what she was doing, she told herself, regardless of what her CEO or the board thought.

They'd conduct the investigation and find out what happened. The first step was to see what the cameras had picked up.

CHAPTER EIGHT

ARIANA HAD BEEN right about the video footage. After Logan put Boomer in his SUV, they watched the video file on the monitor in her office. She tried very hard to concentrate on the images. With Logan so close, she could smell the woodsy scent of his soap and practically feel the warmth of his body. She tried not to let it distract her and focused on the screen.

This time it wasn't snow. She'd expected that would've been too much to manage with the number of cameras involved. They had no trouble picking out the suspect, although they didn't get much. There were no obvious distinguishing characteristics.

"I'd say he's between five-ten and six feet, average build, good posture, confident gait," Logan said.

That was her assessment, too. She would've added cocky, based on the bounce in his step. Facial features and skin color were indeterminate. He'd worn dark clothes—a maintenance uniform to blend in, with a hoodie underneath.

The cowl was pulled low, obscuring most of his face. What was visible was in shadow, but she was almost certain he was smirking. He wore work gloves, had a tool belt around his waist and carried a large-diameter pale green PVC pipe that he transferred from one arm to the other to block his face from the cameras.

Not once did he glance up to check for them. He'd obviously memorized the locations to know precisely where they were without seeking them out. A plan like that wasn't readily accessible. Someone who worked at the airport—an insider, as they had contemplated during the debrief—was now the highest probability.

It troubled Ariana to think that the person responsible might be a person she knew and trusted. Someone she might have hired.

"He knows where the cameras are," she said, stating the obvious, and glanced over her shoulder at Logan.

He nodded. "That's evident. Any seriously disgruntled employees lately? Anyone that you know who might've experienced a personal crisis or otherwise been susceptible to radicalization? Or might hold a grudge against the airport?"

"Radicalized, no. We watch for the behavioral signs. Change in disposition. A personal tragedy they're having difficulty handling." Then

Dave Langdon came to mind. “I recently had to terminate one of our security supervisors. He’s a former SDPD officer. He’d worked for us for ten years.”

“When did you fire him?”

“A couple of weeks ago.”

“Why?”

“He’d had a negative attitude for some time. What tipped the scales in the end was that he compromised airport security.”

“How?”

Ariana explained the situation about the propped-open security door.

“He’d know where all the cameras were, correct? Or at least have had access to plans?”

“Yes.”

“You got his access card back?”

“Of course. The permit control office canceled it. I took care of that personally.”

“Does Langdon have any specialization in electronics or cybersecurity?”

She shook her head. “Not that I’m aware of. Not beyond a basic level of knowledge he’d gained in his job. I don’t think he’d be able to override cameras, if that’s what you mean.”

“Okay. Do you have facial recognition capabilities here?”

“Rudimentary, but yes. It’s one of the things I’m planning to upgrade.”

"Run him. See if he pops."

"Okay."

Logan rose. "Thanks." He hesitated as if he was about to say more. Instead he shoved his hands in his pockets. "I'll be in touch tomorrow. If you find him, call me right away."

She nodded and watched him walk out her door.

As soon as he was gone, Ariana called Max. In under thirty minutes, they were back in the emergency operations center.

"Oh, my God," Ariana murmured as she watched the security camera footage. "There he is. Even with the jacket and ball cap, I recognize him. Max, come look at this. See if you agree."

Max watched with her. "Yeah, that's Langdon. No question."

Ariana swiveled her chair to face Max. "You've known Dave much longer than I have. Do you think it's possible that he'd do something like this out of spite?"

"Most of his time here I didn't work with him directly. Only since you promoted me to senior manager. I don't recall hearing George express any concerns about Dave. It's true he's had it in for you since the day you started here, though." He shook his head slowly. "For all his faults, I can't see him doing something like this."

"If he was already angry and unbalanced, maybe struggling with marital issues, couldn't firing him have pushed him over the edge?"

Max nodded. "I suppose so."

"I wonder where he was going. We know he was in Terminal 1." She replayed a section of the clip. "He's heading toward the administrative offices."

She glanced at Max for confirmation.

"That would be my guess."

"Try to find out if anyone saw him while he was here. Check with HR. He might have had a meeting with them."

As soon as they left the EOC and Max headed to Human Resources, Ariana called Logan's cell number. "We've found Dave Langdon on camera. He's been back at the airport. A couple of days before the explosions." She gave Logan the date and time. "I have Max checking to see if there was a legitimate reason for him to have been back here."

"Good. See if you can track him on other cameras. Determine where he was going. Also, check to see if he was back at any other time."

"We're already on it."

It didn't take Max long to get back to Ariana. Dave had come in for a meeting with HR to discuss his pension benefits. He'd gone straight to the Human Resources Department and had a twenty-minute meeting, but there was a time gap from when he'd finished his meeting and when he was picked up on the camera exiting the administration area. Fifteen minutes of the time he'd spent at the airport were unaccounted for.

Facial recognition didn't pick him up again. That didn't mean he hadn't been back. Ariana asked her team to keep searching to see if they could find him on a video camera again that day or any other up to the day of the explosions.

Midmorning the next day, she was advised that Langdon didn't appear in any more footage. But they had no explanation for the fifteen-minute gap after he'd left Human Resources and before he was walking out of the terminal building.

What had Langdon been doing in those fifteen minutes, and was it relevant to their investigation?

Ariana had an odd mixture of feelings. First and foremost, she wanted the airport safe and secure, and the perpetrator apprehended, but she had to think ahead. Once the dust settled, would she still have a job? Was there something she'd missed? Did she make a mistake in the prioritization of her improvement initiatives? In letting Langdon stay on as long as she had?

She lifted the phone to call Logan.

When she heard a knock, she turned in time to see the door open. Max entered, looking morose. He was followed by Logan, minus his dog, and Calvin Murdoch.

Ariana felt Max was trying to send her a message. Before she could determine what it might be, Calvin pushed past him. He was furious.

"Where's your restricted area identity card?" Calvin asked without preamble. She slid her eyes back to Max, trying to get an indication of what this was all about, while at the same time pulling out her security card. It was attached to an extendable cord, the other end of which was clipped to her belt. She showed it to Calvin and flicked a glance at Logan.

Logan stepped forward and tugged on the cord, testing how secure it was.

"What's going on?" she asked. Calvin was making her nervous.

"Did you misplace your card at any time?" Calvin demanded, ignoring her question.

"Of course not." She shoved the card back in her pocket forcefully. "Why?"

"Your card was used to access the secure areas by the bomber," Max informed her.

Ariana shot out of her chair. "That's impossible! I wouldn't let my card out of my control. I never leave my card anywhere it can be accessed by someone else, and I don't lend it. It's basic security protocol."

"Well, someone got a hold of it," Calvin interjected. "If you didn't leave it or lend it, how is that possible?"

Ariana's gaze collided with Logan's.

"Could the permitting office have issued a duplicate?" he asked.

"I don't see how. We have safeguards against that. Even if a card is lost or damaged, the card is canceled and a new card is issued. The technology in our permit control office prevents duplication of a card."

"Could it have been copied elsewhere?"

"For that, the person would need a card to copy *from*." Ariana fingered the security card in her pocket and tried to figure out how that could have been possible, if her card hadn't left her possession. "I'd imagine they'd have to have a very sophisticated system to do it."

"Get to the bottom of what's going on," Calvin interrupted. "Any developments, I want to know about it right away." He spun around and marched out of the office.

Ariana met Logan's eyes boldly. She wished she wasn't attracted to him. It would've been easier not to like him. She didn't *want* to like him, but her traitorous heart had its own ideas.

"Did you *really* have to confront me with that in front of my boss?"

His eyes clouded. Regret? Sympathy? She could accept the former but abhorred the later. Then his eyes turned cool and distant. "Just doing my job. People were injured. Could've been killed. The person responsible is out there and could try again anytime. *Will* try again, based on his note. My priority is to stop him."

Before Ariana could say that it was her priority, too, Logan said a curt goodbye and left.

"Terrific," Ariana exclaimed, as she dropped into her chair. "What does Logan have against me?" She knew she sounded petulant. She'd obviously taken Max by surprise, based on the look on his face.

She wasn't an emotional person. She was a *logical* person, but her question had been filled with heat.

Max sat down in the chair across from her and leaned forward. "Ariana," he said gently, "you can't blame O'Connor for this. As he said, he's just doing his job. Don't take it personally."

"Then why did he go to Calvin?"

"He didn't."

Her head shot up. "Then who did?"

Max shook his head. "I don't know if anyone did. Calvin didn't say. All I know is he barged into my office. Logan was with me at the time.

We were going over the logs. I didn't have a chance to warn you. Calvin didn't leave me alone for a moment."

"And you're certain it was my card?"

"I checked the logs myself, Ariana. There's no mistake. We finished tracing the bomber's entire path. Over the time frame in question, your card is the only one registered to have been used along the path—the entire and exact path, I might add—that the bomber took to get to the departure lounge."

Ariana pulled out her access card again, stared at it, wanting to satisfy herself that it really was in her possession.

She turned it over. Her ID photo stared back at her. She raised it toward Max. "I've had it all the time. It couldn't have been physically copied. Could someone have hacked into our system?" She understood cyberattacks were a reality. The possibility that someone hacked into their security system terrified her. If the person could accomplish that and was able to replicate her card as a consequence, what else could that person do?

Max tilted his head. "You know as well as I do that cybersecurity is a vulnerability for any organization. Our systems are sophisticated. You ensured that, but no system is immune to cyber hacking. Consider how many hacking attempts we block every single day and how many major corporations have been hacked. Remember that security guy who tweeted while on board a 787 en route to JFK, claiming he could hack into the engine monitoring system of the aircraft?"

She nodded.

"The airline blocked him from his connecting flight and the FBI detained him for questioning," Max continued. "He alleged that he'd once hacked an airplane's systems and caused it to fly sideways.

"That might've been farfetched, but it was never disproved. There are lots of potential hackers out there who can break into just about any application—airlines and airports alike. If we were hacked, it wouldn't be the first time that has happened in the aviation industry."

"I realize that. However, I continue to lean toward an insider. Or at least a person who's using someone inside."

"I agree there's a high probability of that, but then we're back to someone getting a hold of your card and copying it. Are you positive no one had access to—"

Ariana's dismay must have shown on her face, as Max stopped midsentence. He straightened and held up a hand. "I'm on your side here, but we'll have to convince Calvin of that...probably some others, too. We need to get to the bottom of this."

Ariana sighed. "Yeah, we do."

"Ariana…" Max hesitated. "There's something else. Something Calvin doesn't know yet. I wanted to tell you first."

A cold dread filled Ariana. "What is it?"

"When we traced the bomber's path, we discovered that he got through the TSA employee checkpoint no problem and then accessed the secure areas from the airfield using his access card."

Ariana understood the implications of that. It meant that the failure was not entirely TSA's. The airport's internal security measures did nothing to prevent him from accessing any number of secure areas once he passed the initial checkpoint. He might or might not have had the bomb or any of its components with him, and he might not have brought them in through a TSA checkpoint. Once inside, he simply went where he wanted to with his access card. Things were getting progressively worse for her. "Does Logan know?" she asked softly.

Max nodded. "He did the tracing."

She felt some relief knowing that Logan hadn't initiated the confrontation she'd just had with Calvin, and that he could have made matters even more dire for her by sharing this latest bit of information with her boss. But he hadn't.

Regardless, she had to tell Calvin. She could imagine how much more disturbed her CEO and the board would be over this latest information. "Okay. Let's figure out how my access card got copied. You still don't think Dave Langdon is involved in this?"

Max seemed to mull it over for a few moments. "No, I don't. I don't think he's smart enough, and he's too hotheaded. Our guy had to be cool to waltz in the way he did and not cause any suspicion. Remember his gait in the video when you watched it? My read is that this guy didn't appear nervous in the least. He seemed to be enjoying himself. What do you think?"

"I agree with you about Dave, but then who? We have thousands of people employed at the airport. And why was Dave's visit and the explosions only days apart? It seems too coincidental."

"Is it possible Dave's working with someone? He has the insider knowledge, and he's feeding it to whoever is behind it?"

"It's possible, but that doesn't explain the timing of his visit to HR. If your theory is correct, he wouldn't need to be here to do that."

"Good point."

"The police will be interviewing him. Let's

see if we can find anyone else who might have seen him or talked to him while he was here and determine what he did during the extra fifteen minutes."

"Okay."

Ariana rose. "I'm going to the permit control office to have my card canceled and a new one issued. Then I'm going to IT to see if they have any ideas about how it could have happened."

"Ask for Wayne Gallagher in IT," Max suggested. "He's the best tech they have, and we need the best for this."

LOGAN STALKED OUT of Ariana's office and toward the parking garage. That woman was going to drive him crazy. He wished he could deal with her like any other contact on an active investigation—detached and indifferent. What was it about her that tugged at the core of him? Heck, *tugged* wasn't the right word. It grabbed hold and nearly strangled him. As much as it would probably irritate her, he wanted to protect her. To stand up for her. He'd done just that with the CEO of the airport, Calvin Murdoch, when the guy had cornered him in Max's office, wanting to know what the latest was with the investigation. No matter how many times Logan tried to redirect him to Ariana, he wouldn't listen.

When Murdoch started questioning what they

were doing, Logan had no choice but to tell him what they'd just discovered about Ariana's security card. That had prompted the guy to storm off to Ariana's office.

Logan couldn't ignore it...he *cared* about Ariana.

How was that possible after such a short time? It was more than professional respect and a natural attraction to an obviously beautiful woman.

Logan scrubbed his hands over his face. Wow, he was tired, and he'd promised Becca dinner. He felt guilty that he hadn't been available all day. He'd called her when he could, and was reasonably satisfied that she was doing better. He longed for her to be back to her normal, happy, energetic self. He was getting over his anger at Winslow, too. Now it was a mild irritation that the guy had hurt his sister so badly, and a reminder that Logan was wise to have avoided personal entanglements.

But the way he was drawn to Ariana was unlike anything he'd experienced before. His feelings for her were too unique—too disturbing—for even casual dating.

It would be safer to avoid getting any closer to her, he decided as he unlocked his vehicle and let Boomer hop in the back.

ARIANA UNLOCKED HER apartment door. Once inside, she bent down to scratch Sabrina. The cat wound her way between Ariana's legs with a self-satisfied purr.

"You had a good day, then?" Ariana murmured. "Sometimes I wish I could live your life. Spend a lazy day at home, with nothing more to do than eat and sleep."

She gave the cat another leisurely rub. Straightening, she pressed the palm of her uninjured hand to the small of her back and stretched, trying to ease the kinks that had formed.

Placing her briefcase on the dining room table, she went into the kitchen to rummage through her refrigerator. Inspecting the sparse contents, she grabbed a Coke Zero and tried to remember when she'd last bought groceries. Shopping wasn't a favorite activity at the best of times, but she needed to make an effort or she'd have to start ordering in. Faced with the meager contents of her fridge, she decided she wasn't that hungry. She settled on canned soup and crackers.

Leaving Sabrina in the kitchen to feast on her own meal, Ariana took her soup, crackers and soda into the dining room.

She set up her laptop and ate while she worked. She had three burning questions. Assuming the person responsible was in possession of a restricted area identity card, how did he get the explosives into the secure area of the international departure lounge or the airfield, if Logan was correct about how he'd entered? Even with an access card, everyone was screened. Second, how was the person able to duplicate her security pass? And *why hers?*

She might be overthinking it. Perhaps it was as simple as knowing that she'd have the highest level of access possible because of her job. If the system was hacked, one card was no more difficult to duplicate than any other. She kept circling back to an insider. Could someone working for their permit control office be involved? She'd mention it to Logan, but she doubted that was the case. Cards could not be duplicated within their system. But outside of it? As Max had suggested, she'd asked the airport's chief information officer for his best tech, Wayne Gallagher, to be assigned. Wayne hadn't had any immediate answers for her, but he said he'd look into it right away.

And while she was on the topic of Logan, he'd left her office abruptly without any sign of the friendly flirting she'd become accustomed to from him. Despite what Max had said, she wasn't convinced where she stood with him. *Was* he beginning to question her competence, despite his supportive comments during the multiagency meeting? Was he trying to undermine her?

Of course not. Stress and lack of sleep were getting to her. There was no gain for Logan in doing so. It had been bad luck that he'd been with Max when Calvin had visited Max's office. It wasn't Logan's fault. Max should have given her a heads-up. There were ways he could have alerted her. He could've sent her a quick text or email even if Calvin was with him. Why hadn't he?

She groaned. Now she was being paranoid.

Sabrina sauntered over and meowed mournfully. Ariana picked up the cat and gave her the attention she craved. When she placed the cat back down on the carpet, she shot her hind leg up in the air and went about grooming herself.

After finishing her soup, Ariana fiddled with the soda can. She understood there would be questions about how her security pass had been obtained and used to breach the secure area. If she had questions and doubts about it, what must Logan be thinking? Or Calvin?

She finished off the last of the Coke.

She thought of Logan, his height and broad shoulders. His easy, athletic stride. Those bright blue eyes that seemed to see everything. And when he smiled? Clichéd as it sounded, something just melted inside her.

And why did she keep thinking of Logan? Being aware of his reputation and having seen him with his *friends* at The Runway, she would have thought she'd be over him. Evidently, she wasn't.

She was attracted to Logan, whether she wanted to be or not. As for seeing him at The Runway, she'd probably overacted. If he had a relationship with either of the women he was sitting with, he surely wouldn't have left them and come after her. There were many plausible explanations for what she'd witnessed, if she thought about it logically. And there was the problem. With Logan, her emotions overrode logic. She longed to pick up the phone and call him. Just to hear his voice.

Wow! She must be overtired, or overworked, she reasoned. She didn't fall for guys that easily, especially when they worked together and when they had a reputation like Logan's.

Overtired for sure. She shook her head and called up the plan of the airport on her computer. She had a lot of possibilities to consider, and hopefully she'd come up with some answers.

CHAPTER NINE

LOGAN SAT IN his office making his way through the paperwork that had piled up over the last few days.

"Got a minute?" Shannon Clemens asked him from the doorway of his office.

"Of course." He motioned for her to enter and slid the papers he'd been reading away from him. "What's up?"

"One of the explosive ordnance disposal guys came by while you were out. They have the results of the tests of the IEDs that went off at San Diego International."

He gestured for her to take a seat. "And?"

"Here's the report." She passed a stapled document to him. "The EOD tech explained that the gist of it is that the first IED was on a timer. Small amount of explosives. In his estimation, not intended to do much damage. He said that generally that sort of device is used to draw attention rather than injure."

"And the second one?"

"It was different."

"How so?" Logan thought of Ariana so close to that IED, and his blood ran cold. Try as he might, he couldn't shake his feelings for her.

"It had more explosive material and it wasn't on a timer."

"Was it triggered by a cell phone?" That was most likely. If that's what it was, it meant that the person responsible had controlled when it went off…and who was in its vicinity. It also meant he'd probably been close by, within sight. He'd *been there…*

"Yeah." Shannon nodded. "Why would he have done that?"

"Why do you think?" Shannon didn't know explosives well, but she was smart and a quick learner. She'd been at the scene with him and Rick, and Logan wanted to see if she would come to the same conclusion he had.

She didn't take long to respond. "Triggering explosives by remote—a cell phone in this case—would mean that whoever was doing it wanted to decide when it went off. I know that's stating the obvious," she was quick to add. "But to me that means that he was targeting someone specifically. Maybe a passenger. It makes it unlikely to be an act of terrorism, in my opinion, if it's directed at a specific person. If it's personal, an ex-partner or a business associate might make sense."

Shannon's eyes rounded.

"What's wrong?"

"Just thinking..."

"What?" He didn't have time for games, but she was obviously distressed.

"I was in the other terminal when the bomb went off. I know there were injuries. I heard that three passengers and the head of security for the airport were hurt."

"Go on," Logan prompted when she fell silent.

Her shoulders slumped "I was just thinking about Jeff...having been shot by the cartel," she said, referring to a former K-9 Unit officer who'd been killed in the line of duty less than a year ago. "I wondered if it was possible that one of the injured was targeted...or maybe a police officer who might have been close by."

"No. I don't believe so," he said slowly, thinking of Ariana. "The outcome doesn't corroborate it. As for targeting an officer, none of us were nearby. It's a good point, though, and we're looking into possible motives. As for the rest, yeah, you're right about the use of a cell trigger." What Logan didn't say was that although three passengers were hurt—and he was digging into their backgrounds—the person closest to the IED when it had gone off was Ariana.

Was it possible that she'd been targeted? And if so, why?

"Other noteworthy points are," Shannon continued, "that although the second device contained more explosive material, neither had enough to cause large-scale harm in a facility the size of the airport. Neither device was a crude pipe bomb. He knew what he was doing."

"Anything else?"

"No. That sums up the highlights."

"Well done. Thanks, Shannon."

Shannon rose to leave, but stopped at the door. "Uh, actually do you have another minute? I'd like to ask you something."

Logan glanced up. "Sure."

Shannon walked back in and sat again. "It's about Darwin…or maybe me…I'm not certain."

It wasn't like Shannon to get flustered. "Go on," he encouraged.

"The day we were at the airport, doing the search for explosive devices?"

"Yeah."

"Well, when Rick and Nitro were leaving, Rick asked me to continue to search—essentially redo an area as a training exercise for me and Darwin."

"I'm aware of that."

"I don't know if it was me or something else set Darwin off, but he wouldn't leave a room that Rick and Nitro had already cleared for explosives," she rushed on. "Rick and Nitro are… well, they don't make mistakes…or miss a thing. But I couldn't get Darwin away from what I was told was a lost baggage secure storage area. So, to be on the safe side, I called one of the EOD techs over to check for me to make sure there really wasn't an explosive device in there."

Logan didn't know where Shannon was going with this, but he was concerned and not happy that this was the first he was hearing about it.

"Anyway, the tech got a security guard to open the door for us. Actually, it wasn't security, because his key didn't work so, since it was a baggage storage area, one of the baggage handlers' supervisors let us in. It was what they said it was. The room was filled with boxes of a variety of sizes and a few suitcases. The EOD tech checked it all and there was no indication of any trace explosives."

"The dogs aren't perfect, Shannon. I'd rather have a false positive than the other way around. Besides, Darwin is still in training."

"Yes, but it got me thinking. We all know how much more accurate dogs are than the trace detectors. And Darwin was definitely alerting. So I didn't know if it was something I did wrong or maybe there's a problem with how we're training Darwin."

Shannon was good and all the reports he'd received so far stated that Darwin's training was coming along well. He was excelling. Although they hadn't settled on the dog's specialization yet, Logan was leaning toward explosives. What Shannon was saying surprised him, as Darwin had been showing high levels of detection accuracy. Still—as he'd said to her—Darwin was in training.

"I don't think it's you, Shannon," he reassured her. "You said there were mostly boxes in the storage area?"

"Yes."

"Did anything appear out of the ordinary to you?" Logan wondered if maybe the perpetrator had stored his explosives materials in that area, but then why didn't the trace detectors pick it up? Was it the accuracy issue associated with the equipment?

"No. If it had, I would have reported it to you right away. The tech said Darwin might have been overzealous, with the excitement of the day, everyone on edge and all." Shannon glanced down at her hands in her lap. "That bothered me, because Darwin is such a good dog. So, after the tech left us, I opened a couple of the boxes, just to be certain. There were some electronics equipment, canned goods and stuff like that."

The mention of electronics equipment sent up a flag for Logan. He wondered if the equipment could be related to the explosives mechanism. "How did Darwin react?"

"He didn't seem interested in what was in the boxes. More the room in general. Any idea why?"

Logan shook his head. "No. You did the right thing telling me about it, Shannon. I don't think you or Darwin missed anything, but I want to go out there with you and have a look." He checked his watch. "How about we leave in fifteen minutes?"

"Yeah. Sure."

"We'll take Boomer and Darwin with us, and see what they tell us."

She nodded and gave him a relieved smile, before rising again.

As soon as Shannon left his office, Logan started reading the report on the explosions. She'd covered all the salient points, and he didn't like the implication.

They'd have to acccle rate the background checks for the injured passengers.

Logan kicked around the idea of Ariana being the target, but it made no sense. What possible motive could there have been in that? He'd ask her if she was aware of anyone who might have it in for her. He didn't think that was likely.

She'd been in the wrong place at the wrong time. That was all.

As he was about to put the report aside, a concluding comment captured his interest. The blue residue on the bottom of the note paper was printer cartridge powder.

What did that mean?

He'd used a defective printer to generate his note?

The type on the note had been black. The residue was blue. He'd see if they could determine the type of printer and cartridge based on the residue. It was probably a waste of time, but he had to follow up on all possible leads.

DESPITE SPENDING MOST of the night going over all the possibilities, Ariana hadn't been able to come up with any plausible ideas as to how her access card had been compromised or how the explosives had gotten into the secure area of the airport. She'd been advised that morning that the FBI special agents had satisfied themselves that it wasn't coordinated terrorism or a matter of national security. The impact had been too small and no group had claimed responsibility. Other than the note they'd found taped to the underside of the chair, there'd been no indication of further incidents. The feds relinquished their leadership role to the SDPD. They could be called in anytime and would attend briefings, but it was now up to Logan and his team.

FSD Stewart wasn't pleased about the turn of events. It was obvious that he would have preferred to call the shots.

Both airport security and police presence would remain at heightened levels for the time being. TSA was adding extra personnel, too, but security clearance lines grew longer with the added scrutiny applied to all passengers.

Calvin was furious about that, because it impacted passenger flows. Ariana had just finished a tense meeting with him—not the way she liked to start her mornings. He'd questioned—grilled was more accurate—her at length about how long the extra precautions would be in place. He hated inconveniencing passengers any more than they had to be. Unhappy passengers spent less money shopping, resulting in lower revenues for the airport, causing further budget pressures.

Ariana tried to focus on the positive as she left Calvin's office. They'd been fortunate to avoid serious injuries and fatalities. All three impacted passengers had sustained minor injuries only. She glanced at the splint on her finger. As much as it made it awkward for her to do normal tasks, such as type, she'd been lucky, too. And bless Molly for her mastery with communication to have been able to manage the flurry of media attention effectively. Airport operations were back to normal, at least on the surface.

Ariana sighed. She hoped her relationships with Calvin and Ralph would regain their equilibrium, as well.

As for Logan? They had limited opportunity to be alone together, yet every time she saw him, her heart rate accelerated.

Ariana's head and heart were in two very different places where Logan was concerned, and she didn't know what to do about it. She hoped she wouldn't have to see much more of him unless she could figure out what it was that was between them…if anything.

But Logan was the least of Ariana's worries. Her feeling of guilt that the breaches in security were a personal failure persisted. Even her CEO and the board of directors seemed to think she'd failed. She didn't want to contemplate another incident for which she felt personally responsible, as she did with Bryan Carpenter.

With those concerns circling in her mind, Ariana was on her way to her office when her cell phone rang. Seeing Max's name on caller ID, she answered without slowing her pace. "Any news?"

"Not the kind you're hoping for."

She held back a sigh. "What now?"

"Where are you?"

"Terminal 1, passenger concourse." She glanced up. "Near Gate 15."

"Can you come to Terminal 2?"

"Of course." She didn't like how cryptic Max was being. "Why?"

"O'Connor and Clemens are on their way with their dogs."

"Why?" she repeated.

"He didn't say. All he said was that they wanted to have access to the Terminal 2 baggage claim area. He tried calling you, but your phone went direct to voice mail."

Now she did sigh heavily. "I was with Calvin." Instead of turning down the corridor leading to her office, she headed in the opposite direction. "I'll see you shortly."

LOGAN AND SHANNON arrived with their dogs at Terminal 2 shortly after ten o'clock. Logan had called Ariana on the way. When his call went directly to voice mail, he called her office number and pressed zero for her assistant. She told him Ariana was in a meeting and put him through to Max. It was probably for the best, Logan thought. With two dogs with them and Darwin still on the rambunctious side because of his youth, Ariana wouldn't have been comfortable.

Max met them in the terminal.

"Can you tell me what this is about?" he asked.

"I'm not sure. It's probably nothing. Darwin alerted to something in a storage area. He's young and still in training, but I didn't want to disregard it. Shannon can show us where it is."

They rode the escalator down to the baggage claim area and followed Shannon to the storage room in question. Logan watched Darwin carefully to see if he'd alert, but there was no visible reaction as they neared. "Did you direct him to search?"

"Well, we *were* searching but I didn't give him a specific command."

"Give him the command now."

She did and when they reached the room, Darwin sniffed under the door, but with only a mild level of interest. Soon he started off to continue his search.

"Okay. Call him back," Logan said to Shannon. "Max, can you unlock the door for us, please?"

"Of course." He tried his master key but it didn't work. He checked the key, seemed to satisfy himself that it was the correct one and tried again with the same result.

"Why isn't the room on card access?" Logan asked.

Max glanced at him, still trying to figure out

what was going on with the lock. "Hmm…it's just a storage space for lost or unclaimed baggage." He pulled out his cell phone and dialed a number. "Hey, Aaron. Can you unlock a baggage storage room door for me in Terminal 2 by domestic baggage claim or send someone to do it?" He paused. "Yeah. I'd appreciate it." He holstered his phone. "One of the supervisors from baggage handling is on his way to open it for us."

It took only a few minutes until they saw a lanky man in blue coveralls striding their way.

"Thanks for coming, Aaron," Max said to him.

Aaron unlocked the door and swung it open.

Logan stared into the nearly empty space. From what Shannon had told him, he expected the room to be packed with cartons and boxes. Less than a dozen suitcases were in there now, and that was it. He glanced at Shannon. Her surprise was evident and she shook her head at him. "This isn't the way the room was when I saw it. It was full."

"This room is used as secure storage for lost or unclaimed bags, until we can reconnect them with their owners," Aaron explained. "The number of items in here will vary day to day, even hour to hour."

"What about cartons or boxes?"

"Yeah, they can end up here, too, say as part of an unclaimed shipment of goods."

Logan nodded slowly. "Okay, Shannon, send Darwin in to search."

She instructed her dog and he ran into the room and headed directly to a couple of suitcases. Rather than focusing on the bags, he sniffed under them, repeatedly nudging one. It was an older bag without wheels and since it didn't move readily, Logan assumed it was heavy. Darwin persisted until he'd pushed it a few inches from where it had been, revealing small, dark-brown objects that had been beneath it.

Logan directed Darwin to cease and sit. When he didn't immediately obey, he stepped in and grabbed the dog's collar and handed him to Shannon to put him back on his leash.

In response to the uncertain expression on Shannon's face, Logan said, "Go ahead and praise him. He did well."

As Shannon happily obliged, Logan bent down to inspect the objects Darwin had revealed. He lifted the suitcase out of the way and pulled an evidence bag from his pocket.

Shannon approached with Darwin beside her. "What did he find?"

"Coffee beans." He crouched down and scooped a half dozen of them into an evidence bag.

Aaron stepped up behind him. "Huh. Ah... we must've had a shipment of coffee in here, and the packaging must have torn." He turned to Max. "I'll get the room cleaned up ASAP."

Logan wasn't so sure. Coffee beans were often used to mask other smells to confuse detection dogs. The strong, pleasant aroma could be effective at throwing dogs off the trail of the primary scent they were following. He sent Boomer in. If the perpetrator had hidden in the room or stored any explosive materials in there, Boomer was skilled enough to pick it up even with the passage of time. Similar to Darwin, Boomer did a thorough sweep but found nothing.

"Why is this door not keyed to your master?" Logan asked Max as he reattached Boomer's leash to his collar.

"It should be. When did you have the lock rekeyed?" Max asked Aaron.

Aaron rubbed the small goatee on his chin. "Oh, uh...about a week or two ago, I guess." He fidgeted with the key ring. "One of the airlines let a baggage handler go who said he'd lost his keys, so we rekeyed."

"Did he have keys to anything other than the baggage storage areas?" Max asked.

"Just that. His access card was lost, too, but it's been cancelled."

"Well, make sure this lock, and any others that might've been rekeyed, get rekeyed again to the master."

"Okay. I thought it had been. I'll take care of it right away. Do you need anything else from me?"

Max looked at Logan.

Logan shook his head. "No. That's it. Thanks."

"Sorry to waste your time," Logan said to Max, after Aaron had locked the door again and left.

"No problem."

"Just one question…" His words trailed off as he saw Ariana approaching at a quick pace. It didn't seem to matter how often he saw her, each time it felt as if he took a hard punch to the gut.

"Officer Clemens, Logan." Ariana greeted them with a smile and handshakes, while obviously trying to keep a maximum distance from their dogs. Logan held her hand a few moments longer than might have been expected. He liked the feel of it in his. Warm and solid.

"I'm sorry I took so long, but I just missed the shuttle. I didn't mean to interrupt."

"No problem. Thank you for coming." Logan wondered if his smile looked as silly as it felt, but he couldn't help it. He was glad to see Ariana. "I was just asking Max why a baggage handler would change a lock and not go through security."

Ariana raised questioning eyes to Max.

"The baggage handlers work for the airlines and the bags are the responsibility of the airlines, too. So technically, this storage area is their space, but we have to have access in case of fire or other emergency. They shouldn't rekey locks themselves, and they know they have to be keyed to the master, but sometimes these things happen," Max said.

"I'm not sure I understand. This lock isn't keyed to the master?" Before Max or Logan could respond, she pulled out her keys and slid her master into the lock. She turned the knob and the door swung open.

Max looked flustered. He pulled the door closed and tried his key again with no success. "I don't understand. Why does your key work," he asked Ariana, "and mine doesn't?"

"My key is a grand master," she explained, "but for this lock, it shouldn't matter. Yours should work, too. Please follow up with the airline when you get a chance." She turned back to Logan. "The more significant question is, is there a problem with this space that I should know about?"

"No. We were doing a follow-up on Darwin's training. He'd alerted to something in this room the other day. We wanted to check it out. I hope that's not a problem." God, he wanted to reach out and touch her! Just the arch of her cheekbone or the curve of her neck.

"No...not at all."

Logan could see that she wasn't buying it. At least not completely.

"Well, thanks again," Logan said and extended his hand to Max, then to Ariana. "I apologize for taking up your time."

"I'm sorry about that," Shannon said as she and Logan were walking out to their vehicles.

"It's better to be safe than sorry. You and Darwin both did well," he added as they stopped by her SUV. "And we might be on to something."

"The coffee beans you put in the evidence bag?" she asked.

He smiled. "Yeah."

"Okay, but why?"

"Darwin was very interested in something that was in the room when you were last there. Today, he found the beans, but he wasn't nearly as engaged, am I correct?"

She nodded, but her expression showed her confusion.

"Coffee beans have a strong and distinctive smell. They're often used to mask other scents dogs might pick up—explosives or narcotics, for example."

Shannon came to an abrupt halt and stared at Logan. "You mean Darwin might have been on to something and *I* missed it?"

"Don't beat yourself up. Rick and Nitro cleared the area, and Nitro's accuracy rate is nearly 100 percent. What the baggage handler supervisor said is plausible, but we'll check it out."

"You didn't mention it to Ariana and Max."

"No. As I said, it's a long shot, and they have enough to worry about right now. Who unlocked the door for you the day of the explosion?"

"It might have been the same guy. He was wearing similar overalls." She gave Logan an apologetic look. "I know I should remember, especially with that facial hair, but there were so many people around and...I was a little nervous."

"Don't worry about it, Shannon. It's all part of the learning process," he said and waited for her to put Darwin in the back of her vehicle and get in herself. "See you back at the division."

CHAPTER TEN

THE BACKGROUND CHECKS on the injured passengers didn't produce any major revelations. Logan interviewed each of them out of an abundance of caution. Of the three, two were possible targets: a man whose wife caught him cheating, leading to a recent and messy divorce, and a financial planner who'd lost sizable amounts of her clients' net worth in the economic downturn. The man's ex-wife was eliminated as a suspect. Not only did she have a solid alibi—she was hosting a charity luncheon—there didn't seem to be any lingering ill will. She was happy in a new relationship while her ex's love interest had left him shortly after the divorce papers had been filed. She didn't appear to have probable motive.

The most likely target was the financial planner. In her case, there was a clear motive and a number of possible suspects. It seemed that it wasn't only the economic downturn that resulted in her clients losing a lot of money. She was more interested in lining her own pockets through exorbitant fees than ensuring that her clients realized healthy returns on their investments. If they went by the amount of money lost, there were at least a dozen potential suspects. Logan wanted a thorough check of the woman's clients.

When Logan had broached the subject of someone targeting Ariana personally, she'd been genuinely dismayed. She obviously hadn't taken that possibility seriously. He understood it. It was sobering to think someone had it in for you that bad. He wanted to take her into his arms when he saw the horrified expression on her face, but they had been in her office, with the door open.

He encouraged her to think about it carefully. She said she had, and the only person she came up with was, again, her former employee Dave Langdon. As for the extra time Langdon had spent at the airport after his appointment with the Human Resources Department, it was still unaccounted for. He didn't appear on any other cameras and no one remembered seeing him or speaking to him. With the size of the airport, fifteen minutes wasn't a long time, she had rationalized, to do anything significant. Ariana had dismissed any possible correlation, but Logan wasn't prepared to leave any stone unturned and personally interviewed Langdon, too.

Langdon had shown surprise seeing Logan at his front door. He'd remembered him from the drunken-women-on-the-plane incident. He'd assumed that was why Logan was there. Logan's gut told him this wasn't their man. At least not directly or knowingly. His shock was too authentic. Despite being a former cop and fully aware how the process worked, Langdon didn't squawk about lawyering up. Another point in the guy's favor.

A lengthy discussion with Langdon corroborated what Logan had suspected at the outset. Langdon didn't seem to have motivation, other than his dislike for Ariana, and that wasn't a compelling enough reason, since he seemed to have an aversion to just about everybody they'd touched on. Nor did he have the skills, in Logan's estimation. He'd also told Logan the name of the person he'd spoken with during the fifteen minutes that had been unaccounted for. They could verify it easily. Yet Logan didn't strike him off their list of possible suspects.

The coffee beans also led to a dead end. There was no explosives dust or residue present. Nothing noteworthy. Plain, simple coffee beans.

He needed to talk to Ariana again. It wasn't just because of the investigation. She was constantly on his mind. The more he tried to block thoughts of her, the more entrenched she seemed to become in his mind. He *had* to see her.

No time like the present, Logan decided. As he gathered what he needed, he felt downright cheerful!

ARIANA WASN'T IN her office when Logan arrived. Her assistant, Cynthia, told him that she was doing a walkabout of the airport. He caught up to her in the terminal. There was no mistaking that mass of dark chestnut-colored hair, today loose and cascading down her back, even at a distance. She was near the foreign currency kiosk, crouched down in front of a blonde girl.

As Logan strode toward her, he noticed that the little girl was clutching a cat and the girl's cheeks were damp. Ariana was saying something to her. Whatever it was, it had the little girl giving Ariana a weak smile.

Ariana took the cat and lifted it up in front of her face, as if she was talking to it. Then she held the cat to her ear, obviously pretending that it was responding. Next she cradled the cat in her arms and petted it gently while she talked with the child. At the little girl's uncertain nod, she carefully slid the cat into a pet carrier on the floor.

Ariana rose, handed the carrier to the woman standing beside the little girl and had a short conversation with her. The woman nodded.

With a touch on the child's shoulder, she guided them toward a check-in counter.

When Ariana started to walk away, Logan called to her and jogged to catch up.

Based on how she'd spun around, he'd obviously startled her. It shouldn't have surprised him. Everyone involved in the current investigation was on edge, and likely no one more than she.

Yet she continued to hold it together. He would have respected her for that alone, but there was so much more.

He could see her relax when she saw him.

"What was that about?" he asked as he caught up to her, curiosity getting the better of him. She seemed so caring with the little girl…and the cat.

Ariana glanced at the retreating back of the child and her mother. "Oh, their family is moving to Washington. Kerry—that's the little girl—Kerry's father is already there, and they're flying to join him. Kerry said her cat was afraid to fly. She wouldn't get on the plane without her cat."

Ariana smiled, and Logan had trouble remembering what they'd been talking about.

"I think it was really about Kerry. She's never flown before." She gave him a mischievous smile. "So we made sure her cat was comfortable with flying."

Logan laughed. “So you have a soft spot for kids and cats… Why not dogs?”

“It’s a long story.”

“I have time. Tell me why you don’t like them.” He kept pace with her as she resumed walking.

“Oh… I don’t *dislike* them. They… I really wish it wouldn’t be the case, but I’m just not… not comfortable with them.”

“Hmm.” That got him thinking. “Do you have some time?”

“We didn’t have a meeting, did we?”

“No. No meeting.”

“Is there a problem?” she asked quietly as they turned a corner.

“No. If there had been, I would have told you already. I can update you about the interviews I’ve had with the injured passengers and your former employee, but that can wait.”

She glanced to his right and waved to someone behind him. “Oh…?”

There was that urge to touch her again. Her face. Her shoulder. Her hand. Just for a minute, to make a connection. To resist the temptation, he slid his hands into his jacket pockets. “So, can you take some time?”

She glanced around again, almost as if she was searching for a reason to say no. “All right,” she said with a doubtful expression.

"Good. When do you have to be back?"

"Not for a couple of hours. I was about to take a lunch break and I don't have any appointments scheduled immediately after."

"Are you hungry? Do you want to grab a bite?"

"No…"

He could see the bewilderment in her big blue eyes. He could understand why, because from her perspective, he'd been running hot and cold.

"I was going to take a walk outside. Get some fresh air," she added.

"Okay. Will you walk with me?" he asked and placed a hand lightly on her back. Seeing her with the cat and the child had given him an idea.

"Where are we going?"

"You'll see." He guided her out of the terminal building to the curb, and led her to his SUV. He opened the passenger door and held it for her.

She gave him a quizzical look.

"I want to try an experiment. Trust me?"

"I suppose."

He smiled at her reassuringly. "Hop in."

She did, but kept casting uncertain glances at him. When he pulled into a vacant greenfield near the airport, her curiosity must have gotten the better of her. "Why are we here?"

"You'll see. C'mon," he said as he climbed out.

He went to the back of the Explorer and

glanced at Ariana where she stood on the other side. "I'm going to let Boomer out. Trust me?"

After a brief hesitation, she nodded. Logan released Boomer and clipped on his leash. He went over to Ariana, holding Boomer on a tight leash. It was for her sake, as the dog didn't require it. "Here. Take my hand and walk with us."

Shooting an uncertain glance at Boomer, she put her hand into his.

He led her to a small park that had been constructed on one side of the greenfield. It was empty. "Have a seat," he said, pointing to a wooden bench. "Try to relax. I won't let anything happen to you."

She nodded, but he could tell she was apprehensive. He instructed Boomer to sit-stay and unclipped his leash. He walked back to Ariana.

"What are you doing?" she asked, casting wary glances at Boomer.

"Demonstrating that he won't move until I release him. His training and obedience are such that he does exactly what I say, when I say it. My life or his could depend on it."

She nodded slowly.

"Okay. Watch." He walked toward his dog. Pausing, he glanced back at her. "He won't hurt you. Without my okay, he won't go near you."

Logan took Boomer's Kong toy out of his pouch. He released the dog and put him through a number of drills, demonstrating how precisely the dog followed his commands. Although his attention was mostly on Boomer, he kept an eye on Ariana to ensure that she was okay.

After ten minutes or so, Logan gave Boomer a drink from a water bottle, instructed him to down-stay and let him have his toy.

He joined Ariana on the bench. "So, what do you think?"

She had a ghost of a smile on her face. "He's very obedient."

Logan nodded. "Yes, he is."

They watched him gnaw on his Kong for a few minutes.

"He seems happy...and friendly."

Logan smiled. "Yeah. He's both. Police service dogs enjoy their work. They're still just dogs. You're okay with cats," he commented, remembering her with the little girl.

"Yes. They're a lot smaller than most dogs." She smiled. "I have a cat. Mostly, I think Sabrina thinks she's a person."

"Cats are like that, aren't they?"

She nodded.

"Ready?" he asked her.

He'd been happy to see her relax while they'd been talking. But now, with his shoulder pressed against hers, he felt her tense up again.

"Ready for what?"

He took her hand and gave it a squeeze. "To say hi to Boomer." When she tried to pull her hand away, he held tight. "It'll be okay. I promise."

Standing, he drew her up and led her over to where Boomer was.

"Boomer, stay," he reinforced, more for Ariana's comfort than because Boomer needed any reminding.

Logan released her hand and squatted down in front of Boomer, petting him. Glancing up at Ariana, he was pleased to see the tentative smile on her face.

"He's a very handsome dog. He's not a purebred shepherd, is he?"

"He's not a shepherd. Boomer was bred in Holland and he's a Malinois. His coat isn't coarse like most of our canines. It's as smooth as satin. Do you want to feel it?"

She caught her lower lip between her teeth for a moment as she considered. Logan found it incredibly appealing.

"I'd like to," she said.

"Okay." He reached for her hand. When she was crouching beside him, he held their joined hands out to Boomer, his hand on top. He let the dog sniff his hand, then turned their hands to let him sniff the back of Ariana's. She chuckled. Boomer's cool nose on her hand must have tickled. He reversed his hold, placing his hand on top of hers, and laced his fingers through hers. He guided her hand across Boomer's head and along his back. "What do you think?"

She gave a short laugh again. "He *does* feel silky…what I'd imagine a mink would feel like."

"Will you be okay if I release your hand?"

There was another brief pause before she nodded.

He slowly drew his hand away, and she continued to stroke Boomer gently.

"Had enough?" he asked after a few minutes. He wanted it to be a positive experience for her. Baby steps. She rose, and he saw pleasure in the depths of her eyes. That simple thing and knowing he'd helped put it there made him feel inordinately happy. He clipped the leash to Boomer's collar and rose, too.

He took her hand in his again as they walked back to his SUV. Logan let Boomer jump into his compartment, and then he held the door for Ariana.

After parking at the curb in front of the terminal building, he got out and opened the door for her as she climbed out.

She shifted her eyes toward the back of his SUV and smiled. "Thank you for that. For letting me get to know Boomer a little."

"We enjoyed it. There's something else I would enjoy. Have dinner with me tonight," he said on impulse, not giving himself time to reconsider. "Come to my place for a barbecue."

"I appreciate the invitation," she said hesitantly.

She was going to say no. He knew it. He could read it in her eyes. Disappointment flared up, immediate and intense.

"Are you sure?" she asked.

He was glad he'd been wrong. He couldn't blame her for her hesitancy, though, after the mixed signals he'd been sending. "Yes, I am." He gave her his best smile.

"Okay. I'd like that."

Clearly inappropriate, but he wanted to do a fist pump, he was so happy. "Great! How's seven? Do you want me to pick you up?"

"I'll drive myself, thanks."

He wrote down his address and handed her the paper.

"I'll see you tonight." She glanced wistfully toward the back of his SUV. "Boomer's a beautiful dog. Thanks again for the...introduction."

"No problem." Logan leaned against his SUV and watched her walk away until she entered the terminal building and disappeared from his view. Damn, he had it bad for Ariana!

CHAPTER ELEVEN

ARIANA PULLED INTO Logan's driveway at five minutes to seven. His house was a sprawling bungalow situated on a large lot. The property appeared to back onto greenspace, with tall eucalyptus and sycamore trees visible over the rooftop.

She climbed out of her car and stood beside it, admiring his home. It was neat and welcoming. He must have had a way with plants—or he had a grounds service—as the lawn and gardens were healthy, attractive and well-tended. She saw the little stone statue of a dog adjacent to the garage and smiled. It was a miniature version of Boomer, so she figured it was a Malinois.

She walked around to the other side of her car, opened the door and hoisted the bag holding a bottle of wine, a smaller sack from a pet store and a baker's box containing a lemon meringue pie. She'd had Max call one of his contacts at the police department to find out what Logan's favorite dessert was. She'd made up a story about wanting to send him a token of appreciation, because she didn't want anyone to know she was having dinner with him. She smiled again. Her investigative skills weren't lacking!

When he'd invited her to dinner, it had taken her by surprise. As she mulled it over, she'd decided she must have misinterpreted his relationship with Becca based on the snippet of discussion she'd overheard. And she'd accepted.

Ariana felt remarkably happy and carefree… and excited about spending the evening with Logan. He had a way of lifting her spirits. It didn't mean that she wasn't concerned about what was going on at work, but she needed a night for herself, preferably with an attractive, fascinating man.

Boomer barked as she approached the house. She came to an abrupt halt and nearly dropped the baker's box. "Coward," she whispered, then squared her shoulders and walked up to the front door.

Boomer must have alerted Logan to her arrival, because he swung the door open before she had a chance to knock. Her breath caught not from surprise but the impact of seeing him. He wore jeans and a black lightweight sweater with a short row of buttons at the neck, the sleeves pushed halfway up. Unremarkable perhaps, but the clothes suited him. His smile alone was enough to get her heart racing. "Let me help you with that," he said, reaching for the bags and the box. "Come in."

With a light touch on her lower back, he guided her through a wide hallway. She glimpsed a cozy living room to the right and a well-equipped media room to the left. At the end of the hall, they turned right into a large, airy kitchen.

Logan placed the bag and the box on the counter. He pulled the wine out of the bag and looked at the label. "Nice. Do you want a glass of this or what I already have here?" He pointed toward the open bottle of red sitting next to two wineglasses. "I also have a bottle of chardonnay chilling in the fridge, if you prefer, but we're having steak. Your choice."

She smiled. "Since you already have that one open, I'm good with it."

"What's in the box?"

"See for yourself."

He lifted the lid and grinned broadly. "Lemon meringue. My favorite! Good guess."

She raised an eyebrow meaningfully.

"Hmm. Not a guess? I won't ask how you found out, but thank you for going to the trouble."

"Now open the other bag," Ariana prompted.

He reached in and pulled out a rawhide bone.

"I hope that's okay. I didn't know if Boomer could have things like that."

"It's very thoughtful of you. I know he'll love it. Thanks for thinking of him."

Logan filled the two glasses with rich burgundy wine and handed one to her. "To new... friendships," he said, clinking his glass lightly against hers.

His toast caused a warm sensation inside her. She took a sip of her wine.

"Let's not talk about the explosions tonight, if that's okay with you," he suggested. "We could both use some downtime."

She nodded and glanced around the kitchen. The steaks were marinating, the salad had already been tossed, and asparagus spears were in a clear bag, also in some sort of marinade. "This is very nice. You seem to have dinner preparations well under control, but can I help with anything?"

"Thanks for offering, but I have it in hand," he said, moving efficiently around his kitchen.

"What time did you get off work?" she asked. It had to have taken him some time to do everything he'd already done, considering it was a spur-of-the-moment invitation.

"Five o'clock," he responded as he turned the steaks in the marinade. "For once, I left on time. I had to pick up some groceries." He smiled. "I like to barbecue and steak is my specialty. Speaking of which, come out back so I can check on the potatoes and put the meat on."

Ariana followed him. She was barely through the door when Boomer bounded up to greet them. She immediately stiffened.

Logan must have sensed her reaction, because with a hand signal, he had Boomer dropping like a rock into a down position.

Ariana's relieved hiss was out before she knew it was coming. "That's some trick," she said with a nervous laugh.

Logan gave Boomer the stay signal and turned to her. "Boomer has a repertoire of tricks, mostly to entertain kids when we visit schools, but that was basic obedience like I showed you earlier today. An essential element of a police dog's training is to stop and stay if told to do so, regardless of what he's doing."

Ariana eyed Boomer uneasily. She'd enjoyed meeting him earlier in the day and was grateful to Logan for wanting to help her overcome her fear. As gentle as the dog had seemed, having him off-leash and wandering around still made her feel uncomfortable.

"Why don't I put Boomer in his kennel, if it'll make you feel better?" he offered.

"You don't have to..." Her words trailed off as Boomer shifted in his down position, startling her. "Yes, thank you," she amended quickly. "I know I shouldn't be afraid. I wish I wasn't, but he makes me nervous. Even after today."

Logan walked over to Boomer and crouched down. He ruffled the dog's fur, scratched him behind his ears and glanced up at Ariana. "Why don't you say hello to him first?" He held his hand out for hers. When she didn't immediately offer it, he smiled encouragingly and added, "You did it earlier today. Will you trust us again?"

Ariana placed her wineglass on the patio table and wiped her suddenly damp palm on her jeans before placing her hand in Logan's. Logan gently tugged her forward and down, and as he'd done at the park, he held their joined hands out for Boomer to sniff. The dog did so gently, with a soft touch of his cool, damp nose. Ariana knew Logan was watching her.

"Okay?"

She took a minute but nodded.

He then guided her hand down the dog's glossy back. This time, when he glanced up at her, she gave him a small smile.

He pulled their hands away and stood, helping her up, as well. "He won't hurt you. I promise."

Ariana rubbed her palms together. "I know that with my head. Emotionally? Well, that's another thing." She smiled and shifted her gaze back down at Boomer, who hadn't moved since

Logan had instructed him to stay. She took a cautious step toward him. Bending forward, she held the back of her hand out for him to sniff again. When he did so once more and licked her hand gently, she touched the top of his head.

"Thank you for that," she said to Logan as she stepped back, pleased with herself.

Logan opened his mouth as if he was about to say something, but was interrupted by the ding of a timer on his barbecue.

"That's my cue to get the steaks on. I'll put Boomer in his kennel first."

"I feel bad that he has to be confined because of me."

"It's not a problem. The dogs like being in their kennels. Think of it as their den. I'll show you." He first went to the patio table, where he'd left the bag with the bone in it, then gave Boomer a release command, tapped his thigh and had Boomer follow him toward the far side of the yard. Ariana trailed behind at a safe distance.

On the other side of the house was a large chain-link enclosure. Boomer ran into the kennel unprompted and sat watching Logan expectantly. Logan reached into a cupboard affixed to the side of the house. He offered Boomer a treat first, then handed him the rawhide bone.

Ariana drew in a sharp breath when Boomer

sprang at the bone in his enthusiasm. She relaxed again, amused by Boomer curling up with his toy. "He seems to like it! He looks happy in there."

"That bone's a treat for him, and he is happy. I told you it's no hardship for him to spend quiet time in his kennel."

"I've never thought of police dogs as being so...good-natured," she said as they walked back to the patio.

"The dogs have a job to do, but they're just dogs. They're pack animals and bond with each other and their handlers like any other dog. Just give me a minute, please, so I can put our steaks on the grill."

LOGAN PLACED THE steaks on the barbecue and checked the potatoes again. He swirled the asparagus spears in their marinade and set them aside. He had a few minutes before they needed to go on the grill. When he finished his preparations and turned around, his gaze was immediately drawn to Ariana.

He liked the way she was dressed. White jeans that weren't too tight, a royal blue short-sleeved blouse and espadrilles. Her hair was straight and loose, and cascaded down her back.

She was wandering along the perimeter of his yard, her back to him. She paused here and there to lower her nose to a blossom or trail a finger along a velvet-smooth petal. She stopped by a large sycamore tree where he'd hung a wind chime. With a fingertip, she set it tinkling.

As he watched her, she tucked a strand of it behind her ear. When she spun around and her gaze met his, there was a smile on her lips and in the depth of her deep blue eyes.

Logan had never seen a more beautiful sight: the woman he'd discovered to be capable and strong, now soft and wistful, the spears of sunshine filtering through the canopy of trees casting speckled light on her.

She made a sweeping motion with her hand. "This is such a lovely spot." Her laughter blended with the fading tinkle of the wind chime. "All the trees and flowering shrubs. The little koi pond. It's not what I would have expected of a tough cop."

Logan shook free of the trance that had come over him at the sight of her and joined her where she stood. He reached up and sent the chime twirling again.

Ariana watched it for a few moments. "Fairy sprites?"

He glanced at the shapes suspended from the thin nylon threads and nodded. "Something like that."

"So whimsical. I wouldn't have thought that of you."

He smiled. "I didn't buy it, if that's what you mean. It was a gift from my sister. It's made of Venetian glass. She bought the chime for me in Murano when she was on her grand tour after graduating from college. The sprites, as you called them, are supposed to have protective powers. Keep me safe at work." He remembered that Becca had given it to him shortly after their father had been killed. She'd had tears in her eyes. He knew she'd wanted to beg him to quit the force. Instead, she'd sternly told him she trusted him to stay safe.

"That's a lovely gesture," Ariana said.

Logan took a step closer to her. When she remained where she was, her eyes steady on his, a small smile on her lips, he raised a hand and touched his palm to her cheek. Her smile wavered as her mouth opened slightly on a throaty "ohhh."

"I shouldn't want you this much, barely knowing you, but I can't seem to help it." He trailed a finger along her throat and down her arm, and felt the goose bumps form on her otherwise smooth skin. Reaching her hand, he laced his fingers through hers. He was tempted—oh, so tempted—to lean in and kiss her. Not just a touch, but something deeper. With any other woman he would have. With Ariana, he wanted to take care.

To fight the temptation, he took a step back and tugged her hand so she would follow him.

"Have a seat," he said, indicating the chairs around the patio table. "I'll top up our glasses."

"Not much for me, please," she said. "I have to drive."

He poured her just a little more.

ARIANA SAT AT the table, sipping her wine, while Logan busied himself at the barbecue. His backyard was large and the mature trees around its perimeter gave it privacy. Here, too, the lawn and gardens were neat and well-groomed. She thought of her little apartment. It was close to the airport. She didn't need a lot of space, especially with how much time she spent at work. But Logan's backyard caused an unexpected longing for a place of her own. Not just a rental. A *home* with outdoor space, a nice yard…

She shifted her gaze to where Logan stood and realized that the yard she was thinking of had a play set for a child. She was shocked to realize that, in her musings, she wasn't thinking in terms of being alone in the home, but with a husband and a child. Is that what people referred to as the ticking of the biological clock? She'd never felt it before. Was that what was going on?

She watched Logan turn the steaks on the grill. It wasn't some obscure, faceless man she'd pictured in that fantasy yard. It was Logan. That thrilled and scared her at the same time.

She forced herself to look away and took another drink. It was just the circumstances, she told herself. It wasn't that she was thinking along those lines about Logan specifically.

She took another sip, rose and walked over to where Logan stood. "Can I help?"

He hung the tongs on a hook on the side of the grill, gave her a wide smile and ran a hand down her arm. "I've got it covered. If you could take my glass to the table, I'll go in and get the salad and bread."

She did as he asked and sat down again. Through the patio door she could see him moving around inside, until he came back out with the rest of the fixings for their dinner. He went inside one more time for the bottle of wine.

"It's nearly done," he said as he placed the asparagus spears on some sort of flat sheet on the grill.

Within minutes, he was serving their dinner. It all looked and smelled delicious. Taking her first bite, Ariana had to admit it tasted even better.

"I remember you saying you've always loved aviation, but how did you end up at the airport?"

"Before San Diego International, I worked for a private company, Sector Security. We provided guard services to the airport. I started out as a coordinator, advanced to operations manager. It's a large company and the scope of my responsibilities was bigger than what the title implies. I reported to their national head of operations. We had a big contract with the airport, and I developed a really good relationship with my predecessor, George Dennison." She glanced up at Logan. "Do you know him?"

Logan shook his head. "No. Tom Brody was the one to deal with any calls we got for the airport."

Ariana took another bite of her steak. It was done to perfection. "Well, George had been at the airport for almost twenty years. When he decided to retire, he approached me and encouraged me to apply." She chuckled. "More like coerced actually. Not that I needed much convincing. It was my dream job. I just wasn't certain if I was ready for something so huge. George persuaded me that I *was* ready. He offered to be there for me, if I needed it. A mentor I could always reach out to." She spread her hands. "And the rest is history."

"Any regrets?"

Her gaze shot up. She thought about how perfect the timing had been for her, and the reason she had already been contemplating leaving Sector Security at the time. "Why would you ask that?"

He shrugged. "Your eyes."

Ariana cast those eyes that obviously showed too much down at her plate. She concentrated on cutting a piece of asparagus. "No. I don't have any regrets," she replied.

He reached out and with a fingertip, he raised her face to his. "Then what?"

She didn't want to talk about what had happened at Sector Security, Bryan Carpenter's death and the guilt she still carried over it. She shrugged. "I found a number of areas of potential weaknesses at the airport after I started. The TSA covert testing failures had been leaked shortly before I started. I saw it as cautionary and did a thorough review of our systems and protocols, to ensure our operations were solid. I've been addressing them steadily, when I've been able to secure the funding."

"There's nothing wrong with that. That's your job, isn't it?"

She nodded. "I started the improvements shortly after I started. George has been true to his word. He's been there for me every time I've had a question, and he checks in with me on a regular basis." She placed her utensils on the edge of her plate and took a drink. "When

I've discussed some of the improvements with George, he's made me feel…foolish about some of them. He had me second-guessing myself a few times, but I thought they were the right things to do, and did them anyway."

"What sort of improvements have you been making?"

"I've introduced an RFID—uh, a radio frequency identification—guard-tour system for guards to check in when they're doing their rounds, changed some of the standing orders and procedures, enhanced some of the equipment. Right now, we're working on upgrading the video management system."

"Those all seems logical and necessary. Have you considered—and no offense meant—that maybe George had been in his job for too long and had become complacent? I'm not aware of any major incidents at the airport in the time I've been at SDPD." He shrugged. "Maybe he didn't see it necessary to keep up with current technology and practices?"

Ariana was surprised by the gratitude that flooded her at Logan's validation. It had troubled her that George, a man she liked and respected, didn't always see the things she wanted to do as necessary. So much so that she'd pulled back from him. Now it was mostly him checking in with her. It was nice to have another man whom she also liked and respected, and who was in the business, back her up. "Thank you for the vote of confidence," she said.

"It's impressive to have implemented so many positive changes in a year. Maybe George is intimidated by your competence," he added with a warm smile.

Ariana felt the heat rise to her cheeks and concentrated on finishing the last of her meal. When they were done, she helped him clear the plates, and she brought out the pie.

"Did you ever want to be a cop?" Logan asked as they were starting on their desserts. "This is fantastic, by the way!" he added after sampling the pie.

Ariana glanced away and shrugged. "For a time."

"And?"

She was silent for a moment. "It just wasn't meant to be."

He gave her a contemplative look and she was grateful when he let it go. They moved on to other topics while they finished their coffees. Despite his objections, she helped him clean up.

The evening had passed quickly, and she was sorry to have it end. When he walked her out to her car, there was an intense pink wash smeared across the sky. Some trick of perspective made the rising moon, partially cloaked by diaphanous clouds, appear enormous. A call of a loon, the scrambling of some small creature in the brittle underbrush and a distant dog's mournful howl were the only sounds until Logan spoke.

"I'm glad you came tonight. I'm enjoying getting to know you."

"Thank you for dinner," Ariana responded.

He was standing so close, she could see the fine lines at the corners of his eyes and mouth in the muted light. Focusing on his smile lines, she wondered if he'd kiss her and hoped that he would.

When he leaned toward her and his lips parted, her eyes closed and she savored the gentle touch of his mouth on hers.

As they drew apart, there was a smile on his lips and it caused a tightness in her belly.

She turned to her car and he opened the door for her, offering a hand to help her get in. "I want to see you again…outside of work," he said before he shut her door and waved as she backed out of the driveway.

Ariana found herself grinning the entire way home. She fell asleep in a cheerful, cozy cocoon of bliss.

The feeling didn't last.

Bryan Carpenter, a guard with Sector Security, might have been murdered nearly two years ago, but in her nightmare it was as fresh and vivid as if it was happening in the moment. And the burden of responsibility hadn't subsided.

She jerked upright up in bed, her face and sleep shirt damp with perspiration. Her breathing was ragged and harsh. She thought back to that sweltering summer, as she'd done innumerable times, and whether she could have or should have done anything differently. Ariana had just been promoted to operations manager at Sector Security, and she'd sent Bryan to his death. It didn't matter to her that it hadn't been her decision.

Should she have refused? Resigned?

There was no room for error in her field of work. People's lives could be at stake.

BY THE TIME Ariana arrived at work the next morning, she'd shaken off the vestiges of the nightmare. She'd covered the dark circles under her eyes—the telltale signs of a sleepless night—with light foundation she seldom used. To force the debilitating memories of Bryan and his murder out of her mind, she tried to focus on her time with Logan the evening before.

She was still thinking of Logan when he arrived at her office, Boomer with him.

The grin on his face looked as silly as she was certain hers did. "Thanks again for dinner last night," she said in hushed tones, surprised that she hadn't immediately been bothered by Boomer's presence. "I had a nice time."

"So did I." He walked in and gave her a quick kiss before she could object. She glanced around swiftly. She felt like a schoolkid sneaking a kiss behind a portable so the teacher wouldn't catch them.

Logan dropped into the chair across from her desk, keeping Boomer close. "Don't worry. There was no one out there to see that," he mollified her. "But it's a nice start to my day," he added with another grin. "How about we grab a couple of coffees and…talk?" Logan suggested.

Ariana smiled. "I'd love to, but I have a pile of work to get through." Her smile turned grim. "And more worrisome, I'm waiting for a call from Calvin."

Logan's grimace nearly made her laugh. "Problem?" he asked.

"No. Just the usual. He wants a daily update."

Logan nodded. "Then how about I go get the coffees and we drink them here?"

"Sounds good. I should be finished with the call by then."

Logan eased out of his chair. "I'll be right back. Can I leave Boomer with you for a few minutes? I'll secure his leash to the chair."

"Um…" She glanced at the large dog, lying

quietly beside Logan, his snout resting between his extended paws. "I'd rather you didn't."

"Okay. We'll keep working on that," he said with a gentle smile. "We'll be right back." He gave Boomer a heel signal and they left her office.

Ariana sighed. She was glad he hadn't pushed the matter of leaving Boomer. She ran the tips of her fingers along the hard, jagged scar near her hairline. She hated the fear, all because of one bad experience, which she had to admit wasn't the dog's fault. Intellectually, she truly believed there were no bad dogs, just bad owners. It didn't ease her apprehensions, though.

She exhaled heavily. Between that and Bryan's murder, she was lugging a lot of baggage around with her.

By the time Logan returned, she'd finished her call with Calvin and most of her team had arrived. With the corridor bustling, she and Logan avoided personal topics and talked about the SDPD's new procedures at the airport and the investigation. The whole time Ariana kept a wary eye on Boomer.

"Do you feel more comfortable with him at all?" Logan asked softly.

"I'm comfortable," she said through tight lips.

Logan signaled for Boomer to sit up beside him. Ariana immediately drew back in her seat.

"That's comfortable?" he questioned. "You only have to worry about Boomer if you're a bad guy…or you attack his handler," he said with a grin, obviously trying to put her at ease.

Oh, how she wished it was that simple. "I know. We have dogs at the airport, too, through US Customs and Border Protection, mostly to check for narcotics, but also for meat and plants being brought in from foreign countries. TSA has occasionally used dogs, as well. Not often enough in my opinion."

He nodded slowly, then got up to close the door. He sat back down, leaned across her desk and linked his fingers with hers. "Will you tell me why you're afraid of dogs?"

Ariana took comfort in the contact for a moment before withdrawing her hand self-consciously. She hadn't told many people about her phobia and the reason for it. She considered herself sensible…except in this case. She liked Logan and understood that Boomer was important to him. If they were to have any sort of relationship—which after last night she didn't think was out of the question—he should know about some of her baggage.

She took a bracing sip of coffee. "I'd just turned fourteen." She didn't have to think about how old she'd been, whether the sun had been shining or the exact spot where it had happened.

Everything about that day was indelibly etched in her memory. "We'd just moved to a house in Carlsbad, because my father was starting a new job there. My parents were renting the house until they found one to purchase. It was a nice neighborhood. My parents wouldn't have moved anywhere they didn't consider safe for me."

Ariana had liked the little bungalow at first. So close to the ocean, walking distance to her school. She took a deep breath and continued. "Not long after we moved in, my parents were out and I was playing in the backyard. I hadn't made any friends yet. I was new to the neighborhood and school hadn't started.

"My dad had set up a contraption for me so I could practice hitting a baseball." She smiled. "I loved sports as a kid and wanted to try out for the school team. I hit the ball but instead of landing in the netting, it struck the metal frame and ricocheted up and over the hedge our neighbor on that side had along the property line. From the sound of it, the ball hit metal. I was thankful that I hadn't broken a window.

"I'd met our neighbor once when we'd first moved in. He was middle-aged and as far as I knew lived on his own. I went over to his house to apologize and retrieve my ball, but he wasn't home. I decided to quickly run into his backyard and get my ball." She held up a hand and smiled without humor. “I know. You don’t have to tell me I was trespassing. At the time, I didn’t think there’d be any harm in it. No one would know, and I wouldn’t get in trouble.

“As it turned out, the ball had bounced into an aluminum window well. It was pretty deep. I wouldn’t fit into it, but I thought if I stretched out on my stomach and reached down, I’d be able to grab my ball.

“I was like that, reaching in, my head and shoulders in the well, when my neighbor showed up. He must have gotten home, saw that I’d left the gate open and decided to investigate. Anyway, he had a dog. The dog was some sort of mixed breed, maybe seventy-five or eighty pounds. I didn’t know he had a dog. The man was furious and shouted at me. I pulled myself out of the window well as quickly as I could, but my shoulders were wedged in tight. Before I could get up, he set his dog on me.”

Logan straightened abruptly. Ariana saw the outrage in his eyes, a bright flash that burned like fire. “A grown man let a dog loose on a child?”

Ariana held his gaze. “Yes.”

“That’s unconscionable. Unbelievable! Just because you were in his backyard?”

“It wasn’t that simple. Luckily another neighbor heard me screaming. He called the police and an ambulance. The police contacted my parents and I was rushed to the hospital. I was bleeding but I wasn't badly hurt. Just this." She pulled back her hair and showed Logan the scar he'd noticed the day of the explosions.

He leaned forward and examined the jagged white mark he'd remembered seeing the day of the explosion. "The dog *bit* you?"

"No. He didn't. When he ran at me, I fell sideways. The window well had an exposed corrugated metal edge—I'm not sure why it was left like that. Maybe because the owner was doing his own repairs, and didn't want anyone on his property. Anyway, I fell against it and it sliced me. I needed a few stiches, but it could've been a lot worse."

He took her hand into his. "What happened to the guy?"

"The police determined he had a grow-op in his basement. He'd thought that was what I'd been after."

"But you were a child! How could he possibly think that you were there—what—*spying* on him?"

She lifted a shoulder, let it drop. "You'd think he would've known better. But the police also discovered that he had an addiction problem. He was high as a kite when he found me. Crystal meth. He wasn't in his right mind. At least that was his defense when he tried unsuccessfully to fight the charges."

"And the dog?" Logan asked quietly. She understood that he'd hate to think of an animal being put down.

"It wasn't the dog's fault. Intellectually, I know that in spite of how I feel. It was lucky he didn't actually bite me. My injuries were a result of my fall. The dog was taken to a hard-to-place shelter." Ariana gave him a half smile. "Believe it or not, I've always loved animals. I pleaded with my parents to make sure he wouldn't be euthanized. When my parents realized I'd developed a phobia about dogs, they took me to see him—on the advice of a doctor. He seemed happy and healthy. There was nothing threatening or mean about him." She shrugged again. "I could *see* that, but it still didn't change how I felt about dogs. As I said, I wish I didn't feel that way, but it's just there."

Logan pushed out of his chair, tugged her out of hers and wrapped her in his arms. He tucked her head against his chest, under his chin. "I'm so sorry..." he whispered.

She ignored that they were in her office with the door open, and anyone could walk by. Craving the comfort he offered, she held tight until her heart rate settled. "I'm okay now. Thank you," she said when she finally stepped back.

Logan skimmed a gentle finger along her hairline, tracing the contour of hardened skin. "This is a constant reminder, isn't it?"

She nodded, knowing that her emotional scars were deeper than the physical ones. Something good had come out of the incident. It had fueled her passion to become a police officer, to stop people like that man from harming others. She might not have made it into the police force, but she loved what she did.

When Logan pressed his lips to her forehead, she wanted to melt into his arms again.

CHAPTER TWELVE

"GOT A MINUTE, JAGGER?" Rick asked from Logan's doorway.

"Yeah. What's up?"

Rick walked in and sat in the chair facing Logan's desk. "I got a call from one of my Drug Enforcement Administration contacts. They got a tip about drug smuggling at San Diego International Airport."

"That's nothing new." Logan was aware that any major airport experienced a degree of smuggling. His team had been involved in a couple of major busts in the past.

"Except they believe it's been going on for some time, that it's organized and that it's not just drugs that they're smuggling. They mentioned stolen goods and possibly firearms."

Logan leaned back in his chair. "That is new. I wonder why Ariana hasn't said anything to me about it."

Rick gave him a considering look. "You're seeing her, aren't you?"

"I wouldn't call it 'seeing.' At least not yet.

We had dinner a couple of nights ago. I barbecued."

Rick let out a soft whistle.

"What?"

"To my way of thinking, if you barbecue for a woman, it's as serious as it gets for you. And so soon?"

"Never mind. How did we get on this topic, anyway? We were talking about smuggling."

"Right. And you asked if Ariana was aware of it. I know for a fact that the DEA wouldn't have mentioned it to her. They believe the ring has someone on the inside. Baggage handlers perhaps. For them to be able to do what they allegedly have been doing..." Rick paused. "Maybe someone from security, too."

Logan didn't like what he was hearing. "You said they've been operating for a while. Ariana has only been there for a year. She wouldn't be involved, if that's what they're thinking."

"I didn't say she was. Nor did they. I'm not sure how long they think it's been operating, but I do know they have an investigation under way and would like cooperation from us. Until we know more, sharing of the information is on a need-to-know basis, and Ariana doesn't need to know right now... Sorry, Logan," Rick said, as he rose to leave.

Logan felt as if he'd been hit by a truck. The

coffee beans he'd found in the storage room at the airport took on a whole new meaning. If they had been used to throw dogs off the scent of narcotics, not explosives, that would explain why Nitro didn't alert but Darwin did. They'd been retraining Nitro and it must have taken.

He'd have to inform the DEA of what he'd found. He thought about the storage room having been filled with boxes and cartons when Shannon had first seen it.

The baggage handler's and Ariana's keys worked on the door, but not Max's. Was that relevant? The DEA thought insiders were involved—baggage and security. There was no way Ariana would be embroiled in something like that, but he wasn't at liberty to discuss it with her. Holding something as important as that back from her was *not* a great way to start a relationship.

Had he just thought that?

A relationship?

"Man," he murmured and rubbed the top of his head, thinking of Ariana and worrying about how she'd take it when she found out.

ARIANA WAS HAVING difficulty concentrating the next morning. Her mind kept straying to Logan and the time they'd spent together over the last couple of days. There was no question. She was falling for him, and hard. The thought made her feel nervous and giddy at the same time.

"I think this'll be of interest to you," Max said from Ariana's office doorway.

She put her coffee mug down and glanced up expectantly. "What?"

"We might know how the explosives were transported into the departure area."

"How?" she asked, the adrenaline rush kicking in instantaneously.

"Let me show you." He moved over to her laptop and inserted a USB drive. Opening a video file, he clicked Play.

Ariana watched as an office supply delivery truck pulled up to the loading dock the retail tenants used for their deliveries. A skid was unloaded. A young woman, presumably a representative of one of the retailers, appeared to do a quick inventory check, signed what must have been the bill of lading and cleared the skid through security. On the other side of the screening point someone out of camera range called to her and she walked out of the frame. The skid remained on camera but there was no further activity.

"I don't understand."

"Just wait... Ah, here we go," Max said when a man in dark clothes, his face obscured by a baseball cap, walked into the frame. He turned his head side to side—but not enough to be seen on camera—as if checking that no one was watching him. He moved around some boxes until he found the one he must have been searching for and grabbed it. He rearranged a few more boxes, pulled out a brown paper bag and disappeared.

The clip ended.

Ariana shook her head. "What am I missing?"

Max rewound the clip and paused it where the man had the box tucked under his arm and the bag in his other hand. He zoomed in.

"He's got a printer cartridge box, by the looks of it, and his…lunch? Wait, did a cartridge go missing from the woman's inventory?"

Max nodded. "That's what alerted us. We checked the video files for the date and time of delivery, and this is what we found. The plain brown paper bag? There was nothing on the bill of lading that might have been in that bag. But see here…" He fiddled with her mouse and paused the video clip once more. "It was buried in the middle of all those boxes. We also caught our guy on another camera dumping the bag in a waste receptacle. I don't think he took anything out of it."

"Maybe it's theft. Nothing more sinister."

Max gave her a wounded expression. "C'mon, Ariana. You really think so? What about the paper bag? And why search the whole skid for a single cartridge box?"

"Okay, so the bag was planted there, along with the cartridge box, when the shipment was packed. There's nothing in it that would have alerted security during the screen and he obviously didn't need what was in it."

Max nodded.

"Assuming the explosives were in the printer cartridge box, the bag must have contained something with a strong enough smell to mask the explosives, if a canine was to check the skid."

"That's what I think."

"Go back to the frame where he's got the box under his arm, please. Yes. Stop right there. Zoom in. It's a blue printer cartridge. That could explain the smear on the letter he left us. It must have contained the explosives!"

"You got it."

"This *is* significant. Can you get that bill of lading?"

"Already have it." He reached into his jacket and handed her a folded sheet of paper.

"Thanks for this, Max," she said as she ejected the USB drive and checked her watch. It was nearing seven thirty. "I'll be back in a couple of hours at the latest. Let Cyn know when she gets in, would you?"

"Okay. We'll get him," Max said emphatically as Ariana put on her jacket.

"Lock up, will you?" she asked.

"No problem."

Ariana grabbed her phone and called Logan's cell on her way to her car. It went straight to voice mail. He'd told her his shift was scheduled to end at midnight the night before, and he wasn't due at the division until noon. She left a short message that she had important news and she'd try to catch him at home. If he got the message before she saw him, she asked that he call her on her cell. She thought about calling him at home but didn't want to wake him this early, if he was still sleeping.

Once Ariana was in her car and driving to Logan's, she briefly questioned the wisdom of simply rushing over without an invitation. But she was too energized to wait until she saw him at the airport to show him what she had. She'd left him a message, so she wouldn't be completely unannounced.

She pulled up in front of his house and was surprised to find a sporty red Mustang in his driveway. Unbidden, her conversation with Max at The Runway about how Logan had gotten his nickname sprang into her mind, as did the image of the two women, one on either side of him. Did the car belong to one of them? To Becca?

She tried his cell number again. It still went directly to voice mail. He might be charging it and not had it with him, she rationalized…or he was still sleeping.

What Max had discovered was too important. It might be the breakthrough they were hoping for. Besides, there had to be a rational reason for the car being there.

Even so, she didn't want to block the car so she parked in the first available spot along the curb. Hopping out of her car, she walked back and climbed the steps to his front porch.

The sound of a playful bark made her glance to her right.

And it felt as if her heart was lodged in her throat.

Logan was walking along the sidewalk with a lovely young woman. Boomer scampered alongside the couple. Even at a distance, Ariana could see that she was beautiful, with flawless features and thick, near-black hair secured in a high ponytail. She was dressed in loose-fitting yoga pants and an oversize T-shirt. She held a coffee cup in one hand. Dressed casually, she still had an innate elegance.

Judging by the hour and their attire, there was no question in Ariana's mind. The red Mustang belonged to the woman, and she'd spent the night.

Ariana sucked in a huge gulp of air while she tried to rationalize that Logan didn't owe her anything—they really didn't have what could be called a relationship. Yet…

In her mind, she'd been well on the way.

The woman laughed at something Logan said.

This must be Becca, Ariana decided, and her vision blurred. She needed to get away from Logan's house before they saw her. As a large cube van temporarily blocked Ariana's view of them, she took the opportunity to dash back to her car. She was fumbling to unlock her door when they reappeared on the other side of the van. She saw Logan look directly at her as she wrenched open her door. Desperate to get away to save at least some of her pride and dignity, she jumped in, backed up quickly and would have torn away from the curb if Logan hadn't sprinted forward and blocked her path.

"Whoa!" he yelled loud enough that she could hear him inside her car and over the sound of the radio. "What's wrong and where are you going?" His arms were spread, and she inched the vehicle forward in an effort to get him to move before she fell apart right in front of him and his girlfriend.

He didn't budge. He simply slapped his hands on her hood.

There was a car parked behind her and Logan in front. She couldn't move her vehicle without running him over. Looking around, searching for a means of escape, her eyes locked on the woman standing some distance away, Boomer sitting quietly at her side. She was sipping her coffee and watching the interplay with apparent curiosity.

Ariana knew she had to get away before what remained of her composure disintegrated. She opened her window and leaned out. "Logan, please," she pleaded. "Move so I can leave."

He cautiously edged his way around the side of her vehicle. He must have realized that if he gave her an inch, she'd take off. Reaching the driver's side, he leaned his arms on the window frame.

She was staring straight ahead, trying hard to ignore him.

"Ariana, what's up?" he asked softly.

He extended a hand to touch her face but she jerked her head out of the way.

"What's gotten into you?"

She swallowed hard. She looked briefly at the woman who stood drinking from her cup, unperturbed and giving every indication that she was amused by the little drama unfolding in front of her.

Logan followed Ariana's gaze. "Oh, for Pete's sake!" he exclaimed, throwing his hands up in the air.

Ariana's head snapped toward him. She didn't understand his exasperation. Seeing an opportunity, she moved her car forward, but Logan forestalled her with a hand on her shoulder.

"Just hold on a minute!" He signaled to the woman with his other hand for her to join them.

Ariana was horrified. Did he actually intend to make a friendly introduction? Glancing at the woman again as she reached Logan's side and seeing her smile, Ariana could only marvel why *she* didn't seem at all troubled by the occurrence.

"Ariana, I'd like you to meet Rebecca." Logan paused until Ariana's eyes met his again.

She'd been correct. This *was* Becca.

"My *sister*," he added.

Ariana felt the flush across her face.

"Becca, this is Ariana. The woman I was telling you about."

To Ariana's chagrin, Becca grinned disarmingly and extended a hand. "It's a pleasure to meet you, Ariana." She spared a glance for her brother. "Logan has told me a lot about you."

No longer panicked, Ariana immediately saw

the family resemblance. The hair, the eyes, the build and the easy smile. Embarrassment replaced Ariana's anger. "Oh. Well," she stammered. "It's nice to meet you, too."

Appearing relieved that the crisis had passed, Logan stepped back from her car. "Ariana, why don't you park? I'll put Boomer in his kennel. Come join us for a cup of coffee."

With her mind cleared, she remembered the reason she'd come over unannounced to begin with. "Logan, I… I'm sorry to intrude, but we might have a break in the case."

Over mugs of coffee, Ariana showed Logan the video clip and the copy of the bill of lading, and summarized what she and Max had concluded. Logan agreed with her. He made a couple of phone calls and got the ball rolling to see if they could figure out how the cartridge box got into the shipment and if it had been tampered with. "We should have some answers before the end of the morning. I have to go to the division early in case we need to move on it right away. I need to get ready."

"Well, I'll go, then, and get back to work, too."

Logan rose and rested a hand on her back. "Stay and finish your coffee. There's nothing more you can do at present. Leave it with me. Becca will be here awhile longer and she can lock up when she goes." He glanced at Becca for confirmation.

She nodded.

Once Ariana got over her embarrassment for how she'd behaved—which wasn't easy—she found she liked Logan's sister a great deal. Becca was intelligent, had a great sense of humor and was obviously very fond of her brother. Becca explained to Ariana why she'd spent the night at her brother's place. Although she was over her heartache, her ex, Winslow, had apparently decided that he wanted her back and had become a nuisance.

"My loving, overprotective big brother wanted to intercede. I assured him that it wasn't serious enough for a restraining order. It wasn't an easy sell, but I can be quite stubborn, if need be," she said with an impish grin. "He grudgingly dropped the idea. To avoid uncomfortable confrontations, I've been hanging out here on and off, knowing Winslow isn't foolish enough—or brave enough—to cause a stir at a cop's house," she said with another smirk.

They both glanced up as Logan came back into the kitchen. "You two okay?" he asked as he poured more coffee into his mug and refreshed theirs.

"Oh, yeah," Becca supplied. "It's nice to have

a woman to chat to about my…uh, recent problems."

Ariana noticed the searching look Logan gave Becca.

"Not to worry, big brother. No change in how I feel about Winslow. I'm happy he's in my past, and he'll stay there." She motioned with her coffee mug toward Ariana. "I'm so glad I got a chance to meet you!"

Checking his watch, Logan gave Becca's ponytail a gentle tug. Next, he brushed his lips over Ariana's. "I better get going." Placing his mug in the dishwasher, he walked toward the hallway.

"So tell me, Ariana, what exactly is it that a beautiful, intelligent woman like you sees in my brother?" Becca asked just as Logan was about to turn the corner, her voice laced with as much humor as affection.

He paused and glanced over his shoulder. "I might come to question the wisdom of leaving you two alone," he said with a smile and a wink at Ariana, before heading out of the kitchen.

ARIANA FELT AS if she was floating on a cloud as she walked through the terminal building.

She was crazy about Logan!

Who would have thought that something so exceptional could have resulted from a disaster?

Her euphoria stayed with her as she breezed by Cyn's desk on her way to her office. She started up her computer, and began reviewing and responding to emails. The splint on her broken finger slowed her progress, but by midday, she was almost done.

"What are you doing sitting here?"

Ariana jumped at the unexpected interruption as much as the harsh tone of Logan's voice coming from her doorway.

"And you're having your lunch?" The question sounded accusatory.

She glanced at the plate beside her computer with her half-eaten sandwich on it. "Is that a problem?" she asked. "Even a dedicated police officer, such as you, must eat now and then."

She could see Logan was perplexed. Well, so was she. She had no idea what had brought on his mood. "Did you learn anything about the printer cartridges?"

He gave a slight shake of his head. "Nothing substantive."

"Then what's wrong?" She didn't understand why he was behaving the way he was.

"I want to know why you're sitting in your office having lunch when you've got an active shooter incident in Terminal 2."

Ariana could feel the blood drain from her face and she shot out of her chair. "An active shooter incident…?" Her voice trailed off. "What's happening? Why wasn't I informed?"

The confusion on Logan's face intensified. "What are you talking about? You sent the notification as incident commander—"

"What?" The word exploded from her. "I didn't send a notification, and I'm not aware of any incident at the airport."

Logan stepped into her office. "Do you have an emergency operations training exercise underway?"

She shook her head. "No. We don't have them during the day and certainly not at peak traffic times. When we do hold them, we provide advance notice to all law enforcement organizations and most participate. You would've known if we were."

He pulled his cell phone out of its holster and held it out to her. "Then how do you explain this?"

Ariana quickly read the notification. Her shoulders sagged and her exhalation was an audible gush of air. It *was* a notification of an active shooter incident. It called for immediate evacuation of Terminal 2 and a request for police response. The notice had her electronic signature as incident commander on the bottom. Whoever sent it had to have had her passcode for access to use the notification system.

She felt nauseous and unsteady as she handed Logan's phone back to him and grabbed her own. She dialed Max's number and could hear in his voice what she'd feared. "Max, what are you doing?"

"I'm overseeing the evacuation of Terminal 2, as you directed."

"What's the status of the active shooter incident?"

"We haven't seen or heard anything, Ariana. I was about to contact you to find out the exact location."

Ariana sucked in three deep breaths. "Abort the evacuation. Do a sweep of Terminal 2, just to be sure. I don't think you'll find anything, but check anyway."

"Then why did you send the notification? What's going on, Ariana?"

Ariana's eyes met Logan's. "I didn't send out a notification."

"Your signature…your authorization passcode. How's that possible?" Max asked.

"I don't know." Her voice dropped to a near whisper. "We need to find out and fast."

She sat down and turned to her computer to check her sent messages. There was no record of the email there or in her trash folder. That didn't mean much. Whoever sent it could have deleted it immediately. She'd have her computer checked. The airport's IT people would be able to determine if the message originated from her laptop.

She called the airport's chief information officer, outlined the situation, gave him the time stamp from Logan's copy of the email and asked that he get a search done for the IP address and location it was sent from. He was understandably concerned and said he'd have Wayne Gallagher look into it immediately. When he mentioned Wayne's name, Ariana thought to ask if there had been any progress on determining how her identity card had been duplicated. He assured her that if there had been any developments, he would have informed her immediately. In view of the significance, he'd assigned another tech, Tyler Adams, one of their cybersecurity specialists, to work with Wayne, but they hadn't come up with anything, and at this stage he doubted they would.

Ariana made a quick call to Calvin's office. He was out, but of course he would have received the notification on his cell phone. Ariana gave the information to Marlene and asked that she communicate it to her boss the first chance she got. Ariana didn't want Calvin hearing about this latest fiasco from someone else.

When she finished, she turned her attention

back to Logan. "I don't understand what's going on."

Logan closed her door behind him and pulled a chair in front of her. He sat down and took her hands into his. "Ariana, one explanation is that someone has it in for the airport and is using you and your credentials to mount these attacks—physical and cyber."

"But—?"

"Let me finish. The more probable explanation is that it relates to you. Unfortunately, that's what I'm leaning toward right now."

She shook her head. "Why?" Her voice came out as a squeak.

"If we knew that, we'd be in a much better position to apprehend the perpetrator."

"Dave Langdon…?"

Logan nodded. "We've questioned him. We have him under surveillance, but it doesn't feel right to me. Can you think of anyone else who might have cause to harm you or your reputation? Have you collaborated with the DEA in a major drug bust at the airport, for example?"

"No, but that doesn't make sense, though. I wouldn't have been lead, and the cartels wouldn't simply play with me like this, would they?"

"You're not wrong. I'm trying to cover all possibilities."

When Ariana's phone rang, she grabbed it. It was the vice president of IT. She listened and thanked him before hanging up.

"The IP address isn't going to help us," she told Logan. "Whoever sent the email knew what they were doing. The IP address is untraceable. The signal bounced around five cities in four states."

"That's serious masking."

"Yeah."

"We're not dealing with an amateur."

Ariana had to agree. But Logan couldn't be correct about the rest, she tried to assure herself. It wasn't possible that all this was happening because of her.

And if it was, why?

CHAPTER THIRTEEN

LOGAN OFFERED TO take Ariana home. She refused. He wanted to be there for her, but he also understood her need to sort things out herself.

He expected she wouldn't have an easy night. The airport's CEO had been justifiably furious about this latest incident and the associated media attention—all critical of the airport—and had demanded answers.

They had none.

The investigation seemed to be consuming all of Ariana's time—and if not her time, her thoughts—day and night. When Logan wanted to take her out to dinner or just see her after work, she declined. She explained that she had to work. Yes, she was preoccupied, but he thought it was mostly an excuse.

She needed to figure out what was going on and if it involved her. He wasn't certain if she'd fully accepted that she was the common denominator of the incidents. If she did, she kept coming up empty as to why.

Logan could tell Ariana was jittery. He couldn't

blame her under the circumstances. When they'd finished for the day, he made sure he had a quiet moment with her in a sheltered corner. He ran his hands along her upper arms. "I miss seeing you," he said softly.

She laughed. "We just spent most of the day together—again. How can you say you miss seeing me?"

He held her gaze. "You know what I mean. I miss being with you outside of work. Just us." He was surprised by how true that statement was. He could tell she hadn't expected it either. Her lips parted slightly, and the desire to cover her mouth with his was nearly overpowering. "This Saturday is the police service canine tactical competition," he said instead. "It's held every year at Qualcomm Stadium. Boomer and I will be trying to hold on to our championship title. It would mean a lot to me if you'd come watch us compete. Afterward have dinner with me and the other members of the K-9 Unit. Hopefully to celebrate another victory for Boomer and me. What do you say?"

He saw the uncertainty in her eyes. He understood that her acceptance would mean that they were going public with their…relationship.

"Don't worry about the dogs. They'll be on the field. You'll be in the stands with our group."

Ariana smiled. She waited to let a couple of people pass by them. "Okay. I'd like that."

"I have to be at the stadium with Boomer early. Since I doubt you'd want to be with us on the field for check-in and trials, are you okay with getting there on your own?"

"No problem." She cast a surreptitious glance around them, rose up on her toes and gave him a quick kiss. "I have to get back to my office now."

With a smile on her face, she waved and set off at a brisk pace. Logan was glad she'd accepted. It would be a good distraction and it seemed to put a spring back in her step. He hated to see her so stressed.

With a bounce in his own stride, he headed back to his vehicle, and the division.

RICK WAS WAITING for Logan when he arrived. He followed him into his office and sat on the corner of Logan's desk.

"I heard about the latest incident at the airport," Rick said.

"Yeah. It makes no sense."

"Well, we have another problem."

Logan had been rounding his desk but stopped. "What?"

"We got a call from my DEA contact again today. He gave me a heads-up that an agent from the Bureau of Alcohol, Tobacco, Firearms and Explosives would be calling you. He did while you were at the airport today. Dispatch directed the call to me in your absence."

"And?"

"ATF is now involved with the DEA in investigating the smuggling ring operating out of the airport. They still don't know how long it's been in place, but early this morning they confiscated a major shipment that included not just stolen electronics and drugs, but guns and ammunition. The drugs were hidden in sealed cans of tomato sauce." Rick shook his head. "It never ceases to amaze me how innovative criminals get."

The mention of canned goods used for smuggling triggered a memory for Logan. Shannon had said that the baggage storage room Darwin had alerted to at the airport had contained cartons of canned goods and electronics. Darwin could have detected the narcotics, if there were any in the cans, while Nitro would have purposefully ignored it, because of his retraining to focus specifically on explosives.

"Most concerning is the gun trafficking," Rick continued. "Logan, ATF confiscated the shipment of guns and ammunition as it was leaving San Diego International. The feds believe the guns and ammunition were purchased at gun shows in Texas—no background checks required—and smuggled here as cargo on a commercial flight. That means there have to be operatives at both airports. ATF suspects the trafficker was transporting them from here to Mexico to sell to the cartels. Not a good situation."

No, it wasn't, and it was particularly concerning for Rick, because of his interaction with the cartels. "What do they need from us? The feds handle that sort of thing routinely on their own without local police involvement."

"I'm not sure it's anything they want from us. I took it to be more of a heads-up and to just keep our eyes and ears open. They're obviously aware of the explosions and associated investigation at the airport. They're not saying that there's any connection, but they wanted us to be aware of what's going on and that they're investigating."

Logan dropped heavily into his chair and dragged both hands through his hair. The only thing he could think of was how Ariana would react to this latest news. He could already see the effects of the pressure she was under, and he worried about her. She was strong, but everyone had their limits. "Did they share any details?"

Rick shook his head. "Not really. The ATF agent did confirm what my DEA contact had already suggested. That they suspect there are insiders at the airport involved."

"That's not earth-shattering, as it's usually the case." Logan again thought of Ariana and another hit she'd have to take. "Any indication how they're doing it and who might be involved?"

"No, other than what I already told you about a commercial flight, and that the insiders are likely from baggage handling and security. If they're not directly involved, they're accepting payment for allowing it to happen. On the plus side, the feds think they have a lead on the insiders at the airport in Texas. If they get them, identifying those involved in San Diego will be much easier."

"Yeah. Okay." Logan closed his eyes for a moment, trying to piece it together in his mind.

"Have you considered Ariana Atkins?"

Logan's eyes flew open, his gaze drilling into Rick's. "What about Ariana?"

"Look, I know you like her, and we've talked about how solid she is and all the improvements she's been making at the airport, but why are we faced with two major investigations there in the short time she's held her job? Prior to her arrival, the airport hadn't experienced any major threats or incidents in years, other than routine drug smuggling. If security is tight or at least tighter than it was before, and this stuff is going on, wouldn't it make sense that one of the insiders would have to be an influential member of the security team?"

Logan immediately thought of Langdon and wondered if he'd read him wrong. But he'd been gone for weeks now, and the shipment was intercepted this morning. It had to be someone else working inside.

"Logan...?" Rick asked quietly.

"No, it doesn't make sense for the two incidents to be connected. Why draw attention to the airport and cause heightened levels of security if you're operating a smuggling ring?"

"That's a fair point. Unless, of course, you know how to work around the tighter security. Any further thoughts about Ariana?"

"No. She can't think of anyone who might have a reason to target her." Other than Langdon, Logan thought. He might have to take another look at him.

"That's not what I meant."

"Then what?"

"Have you considered that Ariana might have something to gain from what's going on?"

Before Logan could jump to her defense, Rick rushed on.

"I'm not saying the bombs and the smuggling are connected. Let's put the smuggling aside for a minute. Remember that security guard at the residential development who was starting fires in the homes that were under construction and then showing up in time to call 911 and have them put out? He did it to prove that they needed him, because he was worried that he might be laid off."

"C'mon, you can't seriously think that—"

"Just hear me out, Jagger. I find it hard to believe, too, but what else have we got? Overriding a sophisticated video management system, knowing where the cameras are, unrestricted access to the areas impacted, her security card being used, the active shooter notification originating from her email address and with her passcode..."

Logan was trying to control his temper and not take exception to Rick's train of thought. If he put his personal feelings for Ariana aside, he had to admit Rick was asking the right questions. He leaned back in his chair and folded his arms across his chest. "I'll take the huge leap to say what if. Let's say there's some validity behind what you're saying. Why would she do it to make herself the target? Why not someone else, and she's the hero for resolving the problem?"

"Maybe she wants to be seen as a sympathetic victim."

Logan thought about the self-doubt he'd seen developing in Ariana. No! She wouldn't do what

Rick was suggesting. She had a strong moral compass and truly cared about her work. "No, she wouldn't do something like that," he stated categorically.

"Okay, but sometimes people do things they don't want to or that are out of character because they're forced to," Rick continued. "Ariana's smart and knows her job. We've already agreed on that. Her team respects her. We can agree that she's not incompetent nor would she unintentionally let problems arise."

Logan nodded.

"Is it possible she's being blackmailed to provide access or plans? Or at least allow it to happen?"

Logan raised his eyebrows and straightened in his chair. "No way. Whatever else might be going on, Ariana has integrity. She'd sooner suffer the consequences than compromise herself, or be part of an illegal act."

"Maybe she has debts she can't repay and—"

"No," was Logan's curt rejoinder.

Silence stretched between them for long moments.

"You sure about that?" Rick finally asked.

"As sure as I am about myself."

"Okay. Have you checked her background?"

Logan gave Rick a withering look. "There's

been no justification for me to do it. I can't invade her privacy without cause."

Rick shrugged and smiled grimly. "People have been known to do things that have surprised even those closest to them."

"No. Ariana wouldn't," Logan said firmly.

Rick pushed off the desk. "Just saying..."

"If we're done with that topic, I have some good news. I hired a new K-9 officer to work explosives. To replace Brody. He's an experienced handler. He's coming from the Port of San Diego's Harbor Police Department K-9 Unit. You've met him. He's the guy who's given me the toughest challenge at the service dog competitions for the last two years. He'll need a dog. Are you up for training another one?"

"Always," Rick responded. "But what about Shannon? I thought you were considering her for Brody's slot."

"I talked to her about it. What happened at the airport rattled her. She'd rather go into search and rescue, and I think she'll do well. Cal has more work than he can handle, and he'd welcome her assistance."

"Good to hear you won't have to keep doing double duty," Rick said and rose.

Logan watched Rick through the glass wall of his office as he made his way back to his desk, stopping to chat with Shannon and Cal for a few minutes. He shook hands with Shannon and she grinned at whatever he said to her.

Logan's thoughts turned back to the discussion he'd just had with Rick. No, he hadn't looked into Ariana's background. For the job she held at the airport, she would have had to go through a rigorous background check. Was it possible that there was more there? Could he have been wrong about her?

He thought about the smuggling and the empty storage room that Shannon had said Darwin had alerted to the day of the explosions. And that it had contained mostly boxes and cartons. When he'd gone back with Shannon, they'd found only a few bags and the coffee beans. Was there a connection? If there was smuggled ammunition in the room, Darwin could have picked up on that, even though they hadn't been specifically training him for that. But Nitro would have, too, since his training included firearms. That made Logan think of drugs again, possibly in the sealed cans. It'd been known to happen. Sealed cans were also a way of transporting illicit money. Boomer was a single-purpose explosives detection dog, so if firearms, ammunition or drugs had been stored in the room, he wouldn't have hit on any of them.

Ariana's key had worked in the lock, as had the baggage supervisor's. Max's hadn't. If she was involved, why would she have revealed that? He wanted to ask her but knew he couldn't. If the ATF and the DEA started thinking along the lines Rick had, she could become a possible suspect. If that was the case, he'd be walking a very fine line if he maintained a personal relationship with her.

No way Ariana was involved. It irritated him that Rick had caused if not doubt at least questions in his mind about her. He was…falling for her. The realization shocked the heck out of him, but it wasn't unpleasant.

Whatever issues Ariana might have, whatever was or wasn't between them, he remained steadfast in his belief in her honesty and integrity.

Logan swiveled his chair to face his laptop, logged in and did a couple of quick searches.

Nothing popped on Ariana. Everything she'd told him about her background, her family, her education all seemed to be aboveboard. He made a few additional entries. At his level, he could dig a little deeper, access certain files that might not be available to others. He didn't expect to find much, but since he'd already started, he figured he might as well make his background check as thorough as he could.

As he did, he got a flag.

"Well, what do you know?" he murmured. There was an SDPD file on her. He tried to access it, entering his password. It opened the file one layer but blocked him from the rest.

Accessing what he could, he was surprised to discover that she'd applied to become an officer with the department. She hadn't told him that when he'd asked her if she'd considered becoming a cop. That gave him a moment of unease.

From what he could see, she'd passed the written test. She'd graduated from police college. What had derailed her goal to work for the SDPD? The file showed that she'd applied to the department but had been rejected.

The rest was sealed to him. It required high-level human resources access.

He turned away from the screen and reclined in his chair. He considered the possibilities for her to have gotten as far as she had in the application process, gone through the intensive training, received positive scores and yet ultimately have been rejected. If it was a matter of passing the physical fitness testing or written examination, he knew that most applicants would try again. It wasn't unusual for some to try several times before they made it on the force. In Ariana's case, she'd applied once and only once. No second attempt.

Was it possible that there *was* a blemish in her background that had made her ineligible?

He didn't like what he was thinking. He'd

been so sure of her. He'd done the background check, the deep dive, certain he'd find her entirely clean. Was there something there that might be influencing her now? Something that would result in her being involved in smuggling or even hurting people?

Impossible!

He could read people well, and Ariana was a straight arrow. She was dedicated, lawful and ethical. He was certain he wasn't wrong about her.

Then Tom Brody came to mind. Brody had been with the SDPD, part of his unit and under his command the entire time Logan had been captain. He hadn't liked Brody on a personal level. That wasn't a requisite for an effective working relationship. But he'd never suspected him of collusion and double-crossing.

He'd been wrong about Brody, and the guilt he felt over the resultant consequences cut deep. Was it possible he was wrong about Ariana, too? Was it possible that his professional judgment was being clouded by his personal feelings?

CHAPTER FOURTEEN

WITH THE LATEST INCIDENT, the multiagency security meetings were now taking place every day, generally first thing in the morning. TSA, SDPD and Ariana's own team each had more than the usual number of representatives attending. The meetings had grown to a size that required Ariana to start using the airport's main boardroom, generally reserved for director meetings, instead of the smaller ones in her own department. The FBI had not been present since the initial investigation, but Ariana knew that they were monitoring any new developments and risks.

She recognized that the meetings were necessary and beneficial, but they took their toll on her. She had to be on her game. Even her CEO attended every once in a while. That unnerved her, as she suspected he did it to check up on her rather than to stay current, since she briefed him thoroughly after each meeting.

They tried to keep the meetings short to get the participants back to their responsibilities as quickly as possible. Today's meeting was scheduled for the afternoon because of preexisting conflicts and ran longer than usual. It surprised her when a federal agent she hadn't met before showed up. He introduced himself as Hansen and declined to take a lead role. He stated he was simply there to observe.

Although they were certain that the explosives had been smuggled into the airport in the printer cartridge, the office supply shipment came up as a dead end. The supplier had no idea how a box could have been switched or a bag buried in the shipment. The company didn't have a video camera system in its warehouse.

The injured passengers had also been eliminated as potential targets. Time was passing and they had no viable leads. All they knew was that they were dealing with someone who had strong IT skills or easy access to an expert, and that wasn't much to go on.

Special Agent Hansen sat at the opposite end of the table from her. He hadn't contributed much, nor did he show any particular interest in the discussions. During most of the meeting, she felt her skin prickle as if his eyes were on her. Whenever she glanced over, his gaze had been averted.

Ariana shook hands in parting with all the attendees. Her team members left along with everyone else, and it was only her, the federal agent and Logan. The two men had a brief conversation, and they both stepped out of the room.

She was organizing the papers in her file folder when Logan reentered. He sat in a chair and watched her finish.

"You got the splint off your finger," he observed as she closed the file folder.

"Yes, this morning." Ariana glanced down and cautiously flexed the finger that had been fractured.

"That was a tough one," he said.

She gave him a tired smile. She felt a warmth spread through her watching him. The muscular arms, broad shoulders, inky-black hair slightly longer than a brush cut. Her heart lurched then did one steady, slow roll as it fell.

"Yeah, it was," she murmured in response to his comment.

"Are you done for the day?"

"I am."

"Then I'll go with you to get your things from your office and walk with you to the parking garage."

"I appreciate the offer, but you don't have to do that. I probably have some calls to return before I can leave."

He held the boardroom door open for her. "No

problem. I'll wait. There's something I'd like to get your take on. Let's swing by and get Boomer from the SDPD site office and then we'll go to yours to get whatever you need to take home."

It was late enough in the afternoon that the office staff had left. Although Ariana kept a respectful distance from the dog, she was amused at the excited, enthusiastic greeting Boomer gave Logan despite the fact that they'd been apart for only a couple of hours. Logan snapped the dog's leash to his collar. Ariana appreciated that, although she was a little less nervous around Boomer as she got more used to him, Logan positioned the dog on the opposite side from her and kept him on a short leash.

"I hadn't met FBI Special Agent Hansen before. What did you talk about when you stepped outside?"

Logan's expression became guarded. "He's not FBI, and nothing specific. He wanted an update and to bounce some ideas off me."

Ariana wanted to ask him to elaborate, but she could see that it was unlikely he would.

"Okay. What was it you wanted to talk to *me* about, then?" she asked when they were in the main terminal building, heading toward the administration area.

"It just isn't making sense for me. TSA continues to operate on the assumption it's someone external to the organization. If that's the case, how do they know so much about your protocols? We still don't know how they got access to your security card?"

"No. Wayne—that's the IT specialist who's been investigating it—said he has no idea."

Logan stopped and so did Ariana. "He has no idea?"

"Correct."

"Is he still working on it?"

"I don't think so."

"That's not helpful for us, but I've said this before—in my opinion, it's not because of any potential weaknesses in your operations."

It had hurt to hear that point kicked around again during the meeting. She was encouraged by the fact that Logan had expressed his confidence in her. "I keep coming back to that, too."

"I want to—" They had just entered the security and asset protection department when Logan stopped abruptly and blocked Ariana's forward progress with his arm.

"What's wrong?" she asked.

"Stay here," Logan instructed, his tone all business. "Boomer picked up a scent."

Ariana glanced down at the dog and noted that his stance was no longer relaxed. His ears were pricked, his posture taut.

"Wait here," Logan repeated as he moved forward with Boomer, letting the dog lead. They skirted the reception desk. Boomer alternatively sniffed the air or the ground as he went. He stopped by the entrance to Ariana's office. He sniffed the gap beneath the door, its edge and the handle and sat, intently staring at it. Logan pulled a small flashlight from his pouch. Lowering to one knee, he shined it under the door and into the keyhole.

He rose abruptly and pulled out his phone as he and Boomer ran back to where Ariana stood. "Dispatch, this is O'Connor. I need an EOD team at San Diego International. What's their ETA? Okay. Thanks. I'll meet them at the entrance to the administrative offices in Terminal 1."

Ariana didn't need him to tell her that he'd found an explosive device. He turned to her as he holstered his radio. "Your door's been rigged. I need you to get clear of this area and make sure there's no one else in the vicinity.

"I'm betting it's set to blow when the door is opened, but I don't want to take any chances that it's on a timer. I don't want anyone near here until EOD clears it."

Ariana felt a cold chill snake up her spine. She'd been rejecting the suggestion that she was being targeted, primarily because she had no idea why that would be the case. Now it seemed improbable that it was anything else. She knew Max was on duty this evening and called his cell phone. He promised he'd secure the area right away, initiate their incident response plan and expedite the EOD techs through when they arrived. They agreed to meet in the emergency operations center as soon as they were all able to get there.

Ariana called Calvin, too. He needed to know what was going on, although she didn't relish the discussion they were going to have. It turned out to be a quicker call than she'd anticipated, as he was late for a business dinner.

"Keep me apprised," Calvin stated curtly. There was a moment of silence. "Ariana, I'm going to have to rethink bringing someone in to review things. George or someone else." There was another pause as Ariana could hear her heartbeat thunder in her ears. "I'm also freezing the budget allocation for your security improvements for the time being, and that includes the so-called upgrade to the video management system. I don't want any further changes to security systems or protocols until I satisfy myself we're doing the right things. I'm sorry, Ariana, but this is too much for me not to take action."

After Calvin had hung up, she found herself almost gasping for air. Calvin had just pulled the rug out from under her, and she didn't know what to do about it. Or if she should even try.

What if she *had* been messing up that badly somehow?

From where she stood at the far end of the corridor, she watched Logan greet the technicians Max brought over. She felt disconnected from what was happening, as if it was a movie flickering across a screen.

She thought of the last call she'd had with George. George had told her, maybe not in so many words, that she was wrong about upgrading the video management system. New-to-the-market systems could have glitches and could fail. If they were software-driven, they could be hacked. Sometimes the tried-and-true were the best way to go, he'd said.

In her eagerness to improve things, had she inadvertently weakened them instead? Was she too driven by not wanting to risk having another failure on her watch, as she had with Bryan Carpenter?

As much as Ariana wanted to stay, there was no point arguing with Logan. There was nothing she could do to help. It was in the hands of the EOD techs now. Besides, if she *was* the target, her being present might create another level of risk if the person responsible was somewhere in the vicinity and watching. And right now—after her conversation with Calvin—she didn't think she could face Logan, Max or anyone.

She thought she heard a noise behind her and spun around quickly, but she didn't see anyone.

She had to keep it together. She couldn't fall apart now. She'd go to the emergency operations center and wait for the others to arrive, once they were done.

Alone in the EOC, she paced like a caged animal, periodically pausing to look at the computer screen where she'd called up the camera aimed at the corridor outside her office.

Max was the first to join her after he'd cleared the EOD team through and ensured that the area was unoccupied.

Ariana kept an eye on the computer screen while she moved around restlessly. When she saw the men removing an object, she stopped, and she and Max watched the screen intently. The techs placed the object in a large metal container with thick walls. They continued to watch as those present had a short discussion, then everyone, except one officer who remained outside her door, walked out of camera range.

Ariana knew they'd be heading to the EOC.

Max went to the small coffee station and poured two cups, adding milk to one before handing it to her. "Ariana, what's going on here?" he asked as they sat down. "This isn't a general threat. Can you think of who'd be doing this?"

"Someone who's already injured people and

wants to do me harm?" She glanced down at her finger where she'd had the splint up until that morning. "I can't think of anyone. No," she said flatly.

"You might want to think harder. I expect the cops will have that question, too."

"Oh, Logan has already gone there," Ariana told Max. The questions would be asked all over again. Since Bryan Carpenter had been on her mind lately, she considered once more whether it could be someone connected to him. Wanting revenge against her. No. It wasn't likely. His friends and family had been distraught, understandably, but she'd always felt that she blamed herself for Bryan's death more than any of them did. As hard as she tried, she couldn't come up with anyone who could be doing this. She'd have to mention Bryan to Logan, to err on the side of caution. Under the circumstances, he'd want to know.

While they waited, they took the time to review the footage from the camera outside Ariana's office—and found the man responsible. Not surprisingly, he appeared to be the same one who'd been caught on camera when the explosives had been set in the Terminal 1 concourse.

He'd walked into the frame with a backpack slung over his shoulder, dropped down in front of her office door, almost appearing to tie a shoelace. There was a brief period of snow. When it cleared, he was gone. No one had been in the office area at the time. Similar to the previous incident, there were no distinguishing characteristics. Average height and weight. Dark clothing, a hoodie over his head. The one element that was new was that he was white. His hands and a partial glimpse of his face attested to it.

Logan took longer to get to the emergency operations center than she'd expected. When he entered, his face was grim, his eyes angry.

"Where's Boomer?" Ariana asked as she glanced down and around.

"I left him with one of the techs, let him do a complete sweep. Max, could you give us a minute, please?"

Max glanced at Ariana. At her nod, he rose and walked out of the room.

As Logan turned to close the door behind Max, Ariana noticed that the sleeve of his shirt was torn and bloodied. "Oh, my God! What happened?"

She rushed over to him to see for herself. He grabbed her by her upper arms. "Don't worry about that. It's just a scrape I got on the sharp edge of the device housing when I was helping the EOD tech."

"But, but…" She struggled to break loose from him so she could at least get a first aid kit, and clean and bandage his cut. All of it was getting to be too much for her. *She* was the target. If Logan hadn't been with her… But he and Boomer had been. He'd probably saved her life, but he was injured because of that. All these thoughts tumbled over each other. "Oh, God," she whispered and stepped into Logan's comforting arms. When they enfolded her, she broke down sobbing. Of all her concerns, she voiced the one that made sense to her troubled mind. "You're hurt. You got hurt because of me," she said with a quavering voice.

LOGAN HELD ARIANA as she cried. He never would have imagined this strong, determined woman capable of tears, let alone falling apart as she just had. Knowing that others would be joining them soon, he encouraged her to pull herself together. He recognized how fragile she was—and that caused a whole maelstrom of emotions to break loose inside him, not the least of which was a reminder of why he'd avoided relationships his entire life.

He'd sustained a minor injury and she'd broken down.

It had been a hell of a day. Even before they'd found the bomb, his chat with the ATF agent who'd attended the multiagency meeting had put him in a bad mood. The agent had attended the meeting not because he cared about their investigation but to unobtrusively observe Ariana and Max. Based on what they had so far, he believed someone in a leadership position in security was involved in the smuggling ring. And he'd fixated on Ariana and Max.

Apart from having to reconcile himself with what, if anything, he planned to do about his personal feelings for Ariana, Logan needed to find out what had kept her from joining the police force, and if that might be a sign of whether she could be involved. He had to tread very cautiously, because she was very close to being a suspect of an investigation. If that happened, he'd have to distance himself for the duration. And after? When the dust settled, it was doubtful that she'd want him back.

He still believed that she wasn't involved, but here was another incident targeting her directly, and they had no viable leads.

Logan had to get to the bottom of what was going on.

In deference to Ariana's fragile state, he took over as much of the discussion as he could.

"The IED was live. The EOD techs were able to disarm it without incident. It was connected to Ariana's office door, set to detonate two minutes after the door was opened. I don't know why there'd be a delay, other than to give the person entering—in all likelihood Ariana—the opportunity to leave the area once she saw the bomb inside the door.

"It also didn't have a lot of power. It would have caused some damage and possible injury to anyone in close proximity to it. However, it wouldn't have had much impact beyond a radius of a few feet," Logan explained.

He glanced at Ariana. If she'd been on her own and opened her office door, she would have seen the IED. Would she have gotten out of range quick enough? He had to believe she would have been smart enough to do that. But if she hadn't...

She was pale as a ghost. He was certain she'd been grappling with the same thoughts.

He moved over to the mini-fridge and drew out two bottles of water. "Here." He unobtrusively pushed one of them into Ariana's hands. He hoped the water would help. By getting a bottle for himself, too, he figured he wouldn't be drawing too much attention to her state.

He wrapped up the meeting as quickly as possible and sent the participants on their way.

"I need to make a phone call. I'll be right back," he said when he and Ariana were on their own.

He stepped out of the room. In less than five minutes he walked back in.

"You're getting protective detail. Whenever you're at the airport, one of the SDPD officers on duty will be with you..." He raised a hand to silence her when she was about to object.

"Like it or not, it's happening. It's been authorized by the chief. The threat is specific and *you* are the target. Since explosives are the weapon of choice, I'm primarily responsible, but I can't be with you all the time."

Ariana sprang up from her chair. "This is crazy. Why would anyone want to hurt me? And this isn't even about physical harm, because none of the bombs have been big enough to cause significant injury."

Logan was glad that she'd at least gotten her spirit back. He watched her pace restlessly. She eventually stopped in front of him.

"And what I just said is wrong...and stupid."

He trailed a hand down the length of her hair. He couldn't resist, despite his earlier misgivings. "It's not stupid. It's a natural reaction. But as you concluded yourself, it's wrong. You *are* the target," he added gently but with certainty.

"But why?"

"That's what I can't figure out. At least now we can focus our investigation. I know we've been through this, but try again, please. Try to think of anyone who might hold a grudge against you."

"Enough for everything that's been happening, including injuring innocent people? If that were the case, I'd know it." She shook her head. "I can't argue with what you're saying, but it has to be some nut targeting me because of my role here."

"Could be." But there was skepticism in his voice. "Give it some more thought, will you? Remember, there wasn't enough explosive material to seriously hurt you," he reminded her, hoping to ease her anxiety.

She nodded. "Okay. Good to know, but I don't need a security detail. I'll be careful."

"It's not an offer. It's done. Be thankful it's only while you're at the airport. I couldn't get authorization for around the clock, since the incidents have all been restricted to this location."

She shook her head but didn't object. Now that she seemed steadier again, Logan thought he might as well clear up the question of why she'd been rejected by the police force. He suspected she wouldn't react well. He believed in and trusted her, but he had to get it out of the way. "There's something else I'd like to discuss," he said and gestured for her to take a seat again.

The apprehension in her eyes was immediate and pronounced.

He sat down next to her.

"You never told me you applied to the SDPD."

Her eyes widened and her lips parted to form a small O. "How do you know that?" she asked, her voice barely audible.

He reached for her hand but she slid it back before he could touch it.

"I found it on file." He tried to make it sound more routine and happenstance than it had been. He suspected he wasn't fooling her, and she'd know he'd done a background check on her.

"Right. The information simply appeared on your computer screen."

He was about to explain, but she held up a hand. "I suppose I should have expected it." She broke eye contact. "I told you about when I was attacked by the dog. That's when I decided I wanted to be a police officer. I watched the officers who came to help me. They were kind and gentle with me, but they were fierce in their resolve to hold the man responsible accountable. To bring him to justice."

Logan could tell this was costing her. He wanted to take her in his arms but knew she wouldn't welcome it at that moment. She wouldn't even look at him, but she seemed determined to tell him the rest.

"So, when I was older, I went to police college, wrote all the tests, put in my application and thought I was on my way.

"I was wrong." She paused for long moments. "I didn't pass the physical. I have a heart murmur that hadn't been diagnosed at the time. They rejected me on the basis of health reasons." Her gaze swung back to meet his. "Does that answer your question? I can have it verified for you, if you want."

He hadn't noticed any sign of physical weakness in her and his concern was immediate. "Are you okay? The heart murmur, I mean?"

She shrugged. "It's no big deal."

Brave words, but Logan could see the pain of rejection on her face. He didn't know what to say, so he nodded.

"Fine." She rose. "I don't suppose I can go back to my office right now?"

Logan shook his head.

"Then I'm going home."

As she walked out of the meeting room, his heart ached for her and he wondered where everything that was happening left them on a personal level.

CHAPTER FIFTEEN

AFTER ARIANA WALKED out of the EOC, Logan had a silent debate with himself. Should he follow her or let her go? It was obvious that she wanted to collect her belongings and go home. He was probably the last person she wanted to be with. He wasn't going to give her the choice.

He'd seen the hurt and confusion in her eyes. He cared about her too much to let her go like that. He also wasn't prepared to allow her to drive home in the state she was in.

Catching up to Ariana, he dropped a hand on her shoulder. She must not have heard his footsteps, a sure sign of the degree of her agitation, because she gasped and spun around as if ready to do battle. He saw recognition register before he took her into his arms.

He could sense her desire to resist. To push back.

Her heart was racing, but as he continued to hold her, he sensed the tension easing. It felt just so darn good holding her in his arms. It didn't matter how strong she was. At that moment she needed comfort and Logan was pleased that she was letting him provide it, especially since they were in a public corridor.

She rested her head on his shoulder and wrapped her arms around him.

She appeared a little steadier when she stepped back and tilted her face up, questions swirling in her eyes.

He could see the cracks in her brave outer shell. He couldn't blame her. The attacks were getting more personal, and that worried him no end.

"Let's get you settled in the SDPD's site office, while I finish up."

He was mildly surprised when she didn't object or insist on going with him to see firsthand what was happening.

Once they got to the police office, Logan grabbed a blanket from their first aid supplies and wrapped it around Ariana. "Don't protest," he said when he saw that she was about to. "Let me take care of you for a minute."

He gave her another bottle of water and was relieved to hear that her voice, although subdued, was calm when she thanked him. He watched her closely as she took a long drink. There was a slight tremor in her hand, but he had to give her credit for keeping it together as well as she was.

She ran the cool bottle over her brow and hung her head. "What am I missing? What is it that I should be seeing that I'm not?"

"I wish I had the answers." Logan's frustration mingled with a sense of failure.

She raised her head. He could read the uncertainty, the exhaustion and the residual fear as clearly as if it was written in ink.

"I don't know what to do. This *is* about me. There's no denying it now. It's personal. But *why*?"

The expression on her face tore at his heart. He crouched in front of her, resting his forearms on his knees and taking her hands into his. He wanted to dismiss what she was saying and comfort her, but she was speaking the truth.

"I… I don't know what to do. Knowing I'm the target, and responsible for what's happening—"

He cut her off abruptly. "You're not far off the mark with most of what you've said, but you are *not* responsible for it. Stop thinking that."

Ariana nodded rapidly. "It is my fault. Like Bryan Carpenter's death was my fault."

"Ariana, it's *not* your fault, but who's Bryan Carpenter?"

Ariana was appalled that had slipped out, but the memory had hit her full force.

"Ariana…*who's Bryan Carpenter?*"

She knew what Logan had to be thinking. He had to be wondering if Bryan had something to do with what they were dealing with now. She had no choice but to explain.

"It happened nearly two years ago. Remember I told you about the job I had with Sector Security?"

"Yeah."

"We provided guard services to retailers and financial institutions. We had operating policies that said money transfers always required two guards. It was the middle of the summer, so we had more than a few guards on vacation, but we always kept the necessary number on duty. Then there was an unexpected job action by the union. We dropped down to a lower level of staff for a couple of weeks, but we were able to maintain our normal services, until one of our clients called late one afternoon. They'd run a special promotion and had a large amount of cash at their store. They wanted an unscheduled pickup."

She inhaled deeply. "I was overseeing scheduling and dispatch. I only had one guard available. Procedure required two for that type of transfer, but the client insisted he needed the pickup. My boss told me to go ahead with it, using a single guard. I offered to go with the guard, but I was told to stay in the office, since

I was the only manager on duty. I gave in and did what they told me."

She paused again, recalling vividly what Bryan had looked like—young, attractive, full of life. "Bryan took the assignment happily. He was at the end of his shift. He was a new father and welcomed the overtime pay. He was ambushed, the money stolen. When he tried to stop the robbers… He shouldn't have. He should have let them go." The anguish was as intense as it had been on that hot summer afternoon. "Bryan took a bullet. He died in the hospital later that day.

"So no, it's not related to this, but that was my fault and somehow so is this. I should have seen it. I should have known…"

"First, you're not responsible," Logan repeated again. "Not for Bryan Carpenter's tragic death and not for what's been going on here. *You're not*," he said with vehemence when she was about to object.

LOGAN FILED THE name in his mind. Ariana might not have thought there was a connection, but he'd do some digging before he was prepared to eliminate the possibility. An unbalanced, grieving and angry family member might be just the type of person they were looking for.

Ariana seemed to reflect on his outburst for a few seconds then nodded slowly. "Okay, but there are others who *do* think I'm responsible, and that was before what happened today." She took a drink. "For the first time in my job, I don't know what to do. How to stop this."

"That's why we're here. That's my job. You're not in this alone."

She nodded again. "Thanks. I can't help but doubt myself when it's obvious that my CEO and the board don't have confidence in me." Her voice cracked. "Calvin has frozen the budget for my improvements."

That astonished Logan. He would have thought that they'd want to accelerate the improvements, not curtail them, in view of what was going on.

"My team..." Her voice drifted off, but he knew what she was thinking. She was worried about her team losing trust in her. He hadn't seen any hint of that from anyone in her department, but she'd have to work through that on her own. As a leader, he knew how important it was for her.

"I don't know if I'm cut out for this," she said in a voice that was barely audible. "If these things are happening because of me...or I'm unable to stop them from happening... I... I have to think about whether I'm the right person for this job… If I don't quit, how long before they fire me? Or someone else gets hurt?"

"You can't do that! You're doing as well as anyone could be expected to, and they need you here." Listening to Ariana unburden herself, Logan felt an overpowering anger at whoever was doing this. He understood how important this job was to her. His determination to catch the person responsible intensified. He struggled to control his fury before he spoke again.

"Ariana," he said gently, "don't think that way. You're doing everything you possibly can and should. You're smart. You're very good at your job. Don't worry about things that haven't happened." He held her gaze until she broke eye contact.

"So where does that leave us?"

"We need to determine motive. If we get that, we stand a good chance of finding him. In addition to the added security for you at the airport, I'm officially going to become part of your protective detail until we figure this out." He could see the rebellion building in her eyes.

"What, exactly, does that mean?"

Logan understood that for the normally independent and in-control Ariana, the concept of someone having to look out for her would be troubling. He sensed that the objection was coming before she opened her mouth to speak.

"Let's not argue about this, okay?" he cut in. "It's a waste of time and energy. I know that with your background in security and threat assessment you would usually be perfectly capable of taking care of yourself." He squeezed her hand. "But we're dealing with explosives here." He stopped short of mentioning the close call in her office.

Logan didn't want to think about what could have happened if not for Boomer. He took some comfort in the fact that the perpetrator had had a number of chances now to seriously hurt Ariana but hadn't. That baffled Logan from a motive perspective, but he was glad for it. Regardless, he would be with her as much as he could manage. And she'd also have to get used to Boomer's ongoing presence, whether it unnerved her or not. In the situation they were dealing with, Logan had to admit that Boomer offered better protection for Ariana then he did.

When his cell phone rang, he answered with a curt, "O'Connor."

"It's Ramirez," the person on the other end of the line said. He was the officer Logan had left Boomer with. "Your dog found something else. You might want to come back here."

Logan shot Ariana a quick glance. As he'd anticipated, she was watching him. "Yeah. Sure," he said and disconnected.

"Is there anything you need from your office before you go home?"

"Just my laptop and briefcase," she said. "Is there something wrong?"

"No. No… I just need to go get Boomer. I'll check in with the team, get your things and meet you back here."

Logan hurried back to Ariana's office. He hadn't liked the tone of Ramirez's voice. If the bomb on the door was on a timer and not intended to harm Ariana, was it possible that there was a more powerful explosive inside?

"What did you find?" he asked as soon as he reached her office.

Ramirez handed him a sealed evidence bag with some papers inside.

"What's this?"

"They appear to be bills of lading, but there's explosives dust on it. You know, like the note that had been taped under the chair in the departure lounge the day those IEDs detonated."

Logan inspected the papers through the clear bag. There were two of them, back-to-back. One was a bill of lading for a shipment of children's toys. The other was for packaged foods, including canned goods, originating from Texas.

"Where did you find these?" Logan asked.

Ramirez pointed to her desk drawer. "In there. Just stuck in at the back. No file folder or anything. The rest of the drawer is very well organized, with printed labels on all the folders and alphabetically filed. These—" he gestured to the pages Logan was holding "—were stuck in the back, as if she was trying to hide them."

As if *someone* was trying to hide them, but who? Logan wondered. If they carried the scent of explosives, it had to be a setup, he told himself.

ARIANA WAS FAR more conscious of her driving than normal, with Logan following behind her. He'd insisted he would escort her home. She'd put up a bit of an argument, but it was more on principle. She was relieved, if she was honest with herself. Every time she glanced in her rearview mirror and saw Logan's headlights a few car lengths back, she checked her speed. She never drove in a reckless manner, but she had a tendency to go a little over the speed limit.

It had been a long, difficult day, but she found she could smile as she again glanced in her mirror and saw the headlights bounce as his SUV bumped over the uneven road.

Ariana had always prided herself on her fierce independence. She might have been overtired but somehow it didn't bother her, having someone looking out for her for a while. It was his *job*, she reminded herself, before she got all soft and dreamy over it. It felt surprisingly nice that he was following her home. And maybe she could fantasize a little about what it would be like to have her very own knight in shining armor. She thought about the dog competition on Saturday, the one Logan had invited her to, and the fact that they'd be going public with their relationship.

She pulled into her parking spot and glanced up at the windows of her apartment, comforted to find them dark. She waited for Logan to pull into a visitor's spot and then walked over to his driver's side window. Before she could tap on the glass to say good-night, he was stepping out of his SUV.

"I just wanted to say thanks for…for what you did today for me, and for…" she said. "You know. The police escort home."

"I'm glad we were there with you. But I'm not done yet. We're going up to your apartment."

She looked up at him with wide eyes.

"Ariana, I know you appreciate the seriousness of what might have happened today. When I said I was your protective detail, I wasn't joking. It's nonnegotiable." He rested a hand on her shoulder. "Consider it a sign of my confidence in you to take care of yourself that I'm not planning on spending the night."

Her shock must have shown because he amended his statement. "On the sofa." The lines around his eyes and mouth softened, and he gently cupped her face with his palms. "Don't misunderstand me. I care about you and hope to be able to spend time with you on a personal level. But right now? This is the job. I'm going to keep you safe until we catch this nut."

Ariana felt the comforting warmth seep through her again. She'd be stupid and ungrateful to push back. "All right," she acquiesced softly.

She heard Logan's release of breath as he moved to the back of his vehicle and let Boomer out. Ariana glanced at the dog. "I understand why you want to bring him, but I have a cat." How Boomer would get along with Sabrina was a legitimate concern, but she also didn't want to contemplate the dog running loose in her apartment.

"We're a team," Logan stated, obviously trying to ease her discomfort. "On a more serious note, I want to make sure your apartment door isn't rigged. I don't think it is," he was quick to assure her. "I don't believe his goal is to hurt you, and he's confined all his activities to the airport, but I want Boomer to do a fast sweep of your place regardless."

Ariana understood the wisdom of that, too.

She'd like to think she'd be safe in her own apartment, but there was no harm in making sure.

"As for cats—" Logan reached down to rub Boomer behind his ears "—he's gentle with other animals. If your cat's okay with dogs, Boomer won't be a problem."

She let Logan and Boomer lead the way. They checked her door before she opened it. Boomer did a quick sweep of her apartment, then Logan let him relax. Thankfully, there was nothing amiss.

No longer focused on his job, Boomer greeted Sabrina with enthusiasm. The cat wasn't quite ready to call the Malinois a newfound friend. She gave him a haughty stare and, with an imperious flick of her tail, sauntered away. Unmindful of the visitors, she sprang up on the sofa and curled into a tight little ball.

"Well, now that you're here, why don't you stay for dinner?" Ariana asked, thankful that she'd finally found the time to stock up on groceries.

"Are you worried about being alone?" Logan asked.

Ariana shook her head. "No. Honestly, I'm okay to be alone. I don't need someone babysitting me." She placed her hand on his chest before he could argue, and raised up on her toes to brush her lips across his and smiled up at him. "But I would appreciate the company."

LOGAN FELT A tightness in his chest. After everything that had happened that day, Ariana wanted to cook him dinner. She might become a suspect in an active investigation, and all he wanted to do was spend time with her.

He straightened, wrapped an arm around her and lowered his forehead to hers. The combination of his affection and need for her, and the realization that he could've lost her in any one of the recent incidents, terrified him. They'd have to talk about what had happened—including those bills of lading they'd found in her desk—but not now. He didn't want to revisit the horrors of what she'd been through just yet.

He drew back, released her and brushed a fingertip along her cheek.

"Let me get dinner started," she said, her voice not quite steady, saving him from saying something he might regret.

"You've been through a lot today. I don't want to put you to any trouble. We can order in."

"*I've* been through a lot? It's not as if you've had your feet up watching a ball game."

Sabrina hopped off the sofa and strolled over, giving Boomer a disinterested look. She wound her way around Ariana's legs, then wandered off again. Boomer's eyes followed her, but his only action was to thump his tail on the floor.

Ariana smiled at her cat, before continuing. "Neither one of us has had anything to eat since lunch," she said. "We both need to eat. It won't be fancy, but it's the least I can do."

Logan really didn't want to impose. Although he felt weary enough to sleep for a week, the thought of not being with Ariana caused a strange churning in his gut.

"Okay. As long as it's not much bother." He looked down at his torn and bloodstained shirt. "Do you mind if I take a shower and change first? I've got clothes in my duffel in the truck."

"Of course. It'll give me a chance to get organized."

While Ariana rummaged around in the kitchen, Logan secured Boomer's leash to a coffee table leg, tightening it to give the dog enough room to move without being able to get sufficient momentum to pull the table with him, should he think of attempting it.

"What are you doing?" Ariana asked when she reentered the room.

Logan tugged on the leash. "I thought you'd feel more comfortable with him secured."

"Thanks. I appreciate it. Will he be okay like that?"

"Yeah. He's had a long day, too. See?" Logan

motioned to Boomer, lying on his side and sleeping again. "He's already settled. I expect he'll stay that way while I get my duffel and clean up."

"Okay. I'll leave towels, antiseptic and bandages in the bathroom for you," Ariana offered.

Logan went down to his truck and by the time he returned, Ariana was humming some catchy tune she had playing as she prepared pasta... quick and easy, she explained, as it was canned sauce. She had garlic bread in the oven, heating up from frozen, and a bottle of cabernet sauvignon breathing on the counter. She offered to help bandage his arm, but he assured her he could take care of it.

Placing a gentle kiss on her lips, he headed for the shower. Stepping under the steaming-hot water, he let it run over his head and down his face, enjoying the feel of the massage setting on his skin. With eyes closed, he stood in the stream of water, thinking about Ariana.

He'd never enjoyed being with a woman as he did with her. She was smart and independent, and she was beautiful—inside and out. The more he thought about her, the more one thought crystalized in his mind.

He was in love with her.

When had that happened? They'd been on a roller-coaster ride since the day they'd met, but to think he *loved* her…that meant a long-term commitment to him. It had snuck up on him. He was in love.

When the memory of the life his mother had had to endure as the wife of a cop pushed its way into his consciousness, for the first time ever, he disregarded it. A lot of cops had happy family lives and their spouses accepted the risks they faced most days. Take his closest friends and colleagues, Cal Palmer and Rick Vasquez. Cal had already tied the knot and was happier for it, and Rick was ecstatic about his upcoming wedding. Thinking about having agreed to be Rick's best man, Logan grinned as he got out of the shower, dried himself, bandaged his arm and pulled on his clean clothes.

Yeah, it worked for his pals, and Ariana was as strong as Jessica and Madison. He hadn't been able to move beyond witnessing his mother's pain…until now. In addition to loving Ariana, he had a lot of respect and admiration for her. She was tough enough to handle it.

He'd never said the words "I love you" to anyone other than his immediate family.

He needed to lighten up; otherwise he might just blurt out to her the feeling that was consuming him. And that wouldn't be wise under the circumstances.

He ran a brush through his wet hair. After

stuffing his dirty clothes into his duffel, he hoisted it over his shoulder and exited the bathroom.

They had an enjoyable dinner, and after he helped her clear the dishes, they settled in the dining room with coffees.

Logan felt the urge again to tell Ariana that he loved her, but once he said the words, there was no taking them back. He wanted to be very sure before he said them.

Looking around the room, he tried to distract himself. "Where's your cat?"

Ariana chuckled. "I don't think she's terribly fond of Boomer. I saw her go into my bedroom. She's probably curled up on my pillow."

"Smart cat."

Ariana glanced at Boomer, lying on her living room carpet. "How can you do it?"

"Do what?"

"You seem so close to him. How can you face the possibility that he…?" She waved her hand. "You know…he might get injured or…worse in the line of duty?"

Logan drew his lips into a straight, hard line and shook his head. "It's not easy. We're told when we sign up for the K-9 Unit that our dogs are tools. That we shouldn't get too close to them. They're not family pets. We're not supposed to let them stay inside our homes." He laughed without humor. “I don’t know a handler who can do any of that.”

Logan thought of Cal Palmer having gone into a collapsed building after an earthquake, against a direct order, to rescue his dog, Scout. Cal had been injured, and Logan had to write him up for insubordination. There was no skirting it. He’d hated doing it, as he knew perfectly well that he would’ve done the same if it was Boomer trapped in that building. Their dogs were much more to them than simply tools of the job.

“Our dogs are like family to us.” He ran his palm along her arm, took her hand in his. They both watched Boomer, stretched out and snoring softly.

As if Boomer sensed their attention, he stirred and looked up at them with warm chocolate-brown eyes.

With a hesitant smile at Logan, Ariana let go of his hand and approached Boomer cautiously. She held a palm out to the dog. Logan could see it took a lot out of her to do it, by the tensing of her muscles, a slight tremble of her fingers. He saw her faint smile when Boomer touched a cold wet nose to her palm, followed by a wetter tongue.

“That’s major progress,” he said encouragingly and was glad for it, but he didn’t want

Boomer to accidentally startle Ariana and cause a setback. He joined them and took her hand into his and drew her into a hug.

LOGAN INSISTED ON a firm assurance from Ariana that she'd wait for him in her apartment until he came to pick her up the next morning. He was adamant that she shouldn't open the door for anyone…not even if she thought it was him, unless he'd texted her first that he was standing outside the door, and she confirmed through her peephole.

There was no point arguing with him. After she agreed to all his terms, he said good-night. Instructing Boomer to sit-stay by her front door, Logan circled an arm around Ariana's waist and slid his other up her back to her neck.

"I need you to stay safe," he murmured, before brushing his lips across hers.

When Ariana locked the door behind him, she found her normally steady hands were shaking—from fear or emotion, she wasn't sure.

CHAPTER SIXTEEN

LOGAN MET ARIANA at her apartment the next morning as he'd said he would. He followed her to the airport, waited for her to park and walked her to her office. He was still onsite when he got the request to attend a meeting with the CEO. He spent the time before the meeting with the SDPD officers on duty, and entered the executive boardroom a few minutes before the appointed time. Ariana not being there surprised him, as he knew her to be extremely punctual. He checked his watch and expected she'd be right along.

"Close the door, would you please?" Calvin Murdoch, the airport's CEO, called to him as he entered. "We'll get the meeting going."

Logan raised his brows but did as he was asked.

Calvin introduced Logan to Ralph Sterling, chairman of the board of directors, who was obviously presiding over the meeting. Logan already knew one of the other two attendees, TSA's federal security director, Angus Stewart.

He was shocked to learn the identity of the final person in the room, George Dennison, Ariana's predecessor.

"Help yourself to coffee, water, whatever." Ralph waved toward a sideboard holding a variety of hot and cold beverages.

"I'm fine, thanks," Logan replied, taking a seat at the middle of the table. He noted that FSD Stewart didn't hesitate to rise to help himself to a coffee and several cookies.

"Thank you both for coming on such short notice," Ralph began once Stewart was seated. "The board and our leadership are taking the recent incidents very seriously. Passenger safety is our top priority, and we will not compromise in that regard."

"Shouldn't we wait for Ariana Atkins?" Logan asked as soon as Ralph paused.

Calvin and Ralph exchanged glances.

"Where is she?" Logan persisted.

"In her office or somewhere in the terminal building, I assume." Ralph glanced to Calvin for confirmation. At his nod, Ralph gazed down at the notes in front of him. "So, as I was saying—"

"Hold on," Logan interrupted him again. "Why isn't she here?" He also wanted to know why Dennison was, but held back from asking.

"I don't see why that's your concern," Ralph retorted.

"Because we're discussing safety and security of the airport, and she's the head of your operation. I assumed you'd want her here as she's your expert, and our key contact," he said. He didn't like that they'd excluded Ariana. Had someone leaked the information about the bills of lading they'd found in Ariana's office? He might have his own questions about it, but she had a right to be presumed innocent until proven guilty as much as anyone. Then a thought occurred to him. *They wouldn't have let her go?* No, because Sterling had said she was still in the building. Were they planning to? Was that why Dennison was present? Yeah, Ariana had talked about quitting. As much as he'd tried to talk her out of it, at least that would've been on her own terms. For her to get fired? Not only was it unwarranted, he didn't want to think of what it would do to her.

Logan shifted his gaze to Dennison. His curiosity about why he was there must have been obvious, because Murdoch addressed it without Logan's having to ask. "In keeping with our fiduciary obligations to the airport, the chairman and I considered it prudent to retain independent expert advice." He smiled briefly at Dennison. "No one knows the airport and its operations better from a security perspective than George, with his twenty years of unblemished service to us before his retirement."

George stared at Logan, almost as if challenging him to argue the point.

"Does Ariana know?" Logan asked.

"Not yet." Calvin waved the question away. "But as Ralph stated, passenger safety is our utmost concern. Frankly, the recent events are unprecedented in my experience. We've always had a stellar reputation, and now it's being tarnished."

"We can't have that," Ralph added. "We plan to take every possible measure available to us to restore safety and security at this airport, and thereby our reputation. It's come to our attention that it might be Ariana who's attracting the occurrences."

Unblinking, Logan held Ralph's gaze. Thankfully, it didn't sound as if they were aware of the latest development or the possible smuggling ring operating from their facility.

"Isn't that right?" Ralph persisted.

"We're investigating," Logan replied noncommittally. He didn't like where this was going. Were they trying to lay the blame on Ariana? He had a moment of guilt, remembering that he'd questioned her involvement, too, but for a very short time. For him, it was all part of due process. Eliminate possibilities to concentrate on the probabilities. He adjusted his gaze slightly to take in Stewart on the opposite side of the table. He was curious about how he'd weigh in about Ariana. He'd witnessed Stewart's adversarial stance toward Ariana before, but didn't the TSA have some responsibility?

Stewart shifted in his seat, flapped his hand in a nervous gesture. "We all know it was her office door that was rigged with the IED. Doesn't that answer Mr. Sterling's question in the affirmative?"

Logan narrowed his eyes. So they did know about the incident…but not the bills of lading. Would Stewart throw Ariana under the bus to protect himself and his organization? And where did Dennison weigh in on all this? Ariana had called him a mentor. Said that he'd encouraged her to apply for the job. Surely, he would support her now.

Dennison's face was stoic, but he was fidgeting with his pen. *What was he worried about?* Logan wondered.

"Before you cast blame, how do you think the person responsible is able to keep getting into the secure areas to leave explosives and notes? We know how he did it the first time, but what about most recently?"

Angus made a sputtering noise. Logan expected he was about to protest again but Ralph cut in.

"The TSA's competence is *not* what we're here to discuss."

In Logan's opinion, it should have been an ongoing topic of discussion, but he held his tongue. He was so angry, he was tempted to storm out of the boardroom, but he couldn't do so without getting himself in trouble with the chief of police. More importantly, he wanted to know where they were planning to go with this meeting. If they were intent on setting Ariana up as the scapegoat, he'd rather know about it.

"We're thinking it might be appropriate for Ariana to…take a leave of absence," Calvin said. "George is willing to come back for an indefinite period of time."

Logan wanted to lunge out of his chair and grab the guy by the throat. The fury of it surprised him, but that wouldn't have helped his cause. Or Ariana's. He leaned back and folded his arms across his chest. "Why would you do that?"

"For her personal safety, of course." Calvin had a self-righteous expression on his face. "And if she's the target and she's not here, the airport can resume normal operations."

Logan leaned forward and rested his elbows on the table. "Let's take your assumptions one at a time, shall we? If she *is* the target it doesn't matter where she is. She might, in fact, be safer here, in a secure facility, than she would be somewhere else, on her own." He ticked the point off on his finger.

"Secondly, Ariana is knowledgeable, professional and dedicated. The short time she's been at the airport, she's made numerous improvements to safety and security, and—"

"We've put a stop to her *improvements* for now and are reassessing the ones she's already made," Calvin interrupted. "With George's assistance, we want to determine that they haven't, in fact, undermined the security of the airport. It seems too much for coincidence for us to all of a sudden experience the problems we have been since she came to us. There has to be an explanation."

"And there is." Logan clasped his hands, trying to contain his anger. He thought that it was a good thing that ATF and DEA hadn't shared information about their investigation of the smuggling ring with anyone at the airport, as that would surely have added fuel to the fire.

"You have someone wanting to cause harm and injuries at your facility. We intend to stop him from continuing to do so. You're fortunate to have Ariana in the role that you do." He wanted to say that her predecessor should have been making the improvements Ariana had been well before he retired, but again exercised discretion and held his tongue.

"If she were to take a leave of absence, or otherwise not be here..." Logan said the latter part as a way to test the waters for a reaction to determine what they might have been thinking about her longer-term prospects. He glanced around the table. He thought about the alleged smuggling and someone from the managerial level being involved. If Ariana was moved out of her role, he wondered how that would impact the feds' investigation. He wanted to make sure she was cleared of any involvement. For that it was best to leave her in place. He wasn't at liberty to mention any of that, but he could make reference to it in a circumspect way. "There are aspects of the investigation that would be negatively impacted by her absence. For the foreseeable future, your best course of action is to keep Ariana in place."

"C'mon," Stewart objected. "She's good—however, the current situation is getting to her. I'm not the only one who's seeing chinks in her demeanor and leadership."

Logan glared at him. Being confrontational was not his style, but this guy was really getting on his nerves, and he wouldn't let him slight Ariana. "What about the scrutiny you've been facing since the Inspector General's covert testing results were leaked? If I recall correctly, your region was at the bottom of the list, wasn't it?"

Logan took some satisfaction watching Stewart's face flush a bright red. Logan had reached his boiling point and he couldn't resist poking at Stewart some more. "Now, let me see if I remember this correctly..." There was no problem with his memory. Federal undercover investigators were able to penetrate security checkpoints at US airports while carrying illegal weapons or simulated bombs almost every time they attempted it. He knew the stats; he'd checked them. "Wasn't it sixty-seven out of seventy tests that failed? That's a 95 percent *failure* rate. Oh, and one instance in which your staff failed to find a fake bomb, even after the magnetometer went off and a pat-down was conducted? The Homeland Security agent was passed through with the fake bomb taped to his back, wasn't he?"

Logan noted the deepening of the color staining Stewart's face. "By comparison?" He smiled humorlessly. "My dog, Boomer? He has a 99.7 percent *success* rate."

"Well...there were extenuating circumstances involv—" Angus stammered.

"Extenuating circumstances be damned,"

Ralph interjected. "We are aware of the stats and welcome the government's actions to resolve the shocking issues with TSA. The test failure rate is a huge concern, especially with what we're facing here. What are we going to do about it, is what I want to know?" Ralph shifted his gaze from Stewart to Logan and back again. Stewart's phone vibrated and he suddenly seemed preoccupied with the device. Logan felt a small sense of accomplishment at being able to effectively redirect the conversation away from Ariana.

"Hard to say without your chief of security and asset protection here." Logan filled the silence. "As a starter, more explosives detection dogs should be deployed at all security checkpoints and patrolling passenger areas, *as was recommended by the Inspector General*. But our response needs to be comprehensive and coordinated, and for that we need to work with the airport's security personnel. So why isn't Ariana here?"

Ralph and Calvin both turned to Angus.

Confrontational or not, Logan felt good about having scored a point in Ariana's defense, but he knew neither he nor Ariana had a friend in Stewart. He'd heard that Stewart's job was on the line. With the results of the covert testing, if he lost this job, his chances of getting another one in his field and at his level were questionable.

Logan glanced at Stewart. Was it possible that the FSD was conducting his own sting and wanted to place the blame on someone other than himself and the TSA?

That might explain the direct attacks on Ariana. But why show more weaknesses in TSA's procedures? Then again, Stewart didn't strike him as the smartest of people.

And how did Dennison fit into the picture? He hadn't said anything during the entire meeting, but his presence would be a huge hit to Ariana when she found out.

Logan had some things to ponder and hoped he'd have answers soon.

"HOW DID THE meeting go?" Max asked Ariana as she walked by where he was standing at the desk of one of their security analysts.

Ariana stopped and turned. "What meeting?" She'd only been in the multiagency meeting that day, and Max had been there, too. In fact, she'd just finished an inspection of the new baggage handling system, including state-of-the-art screening technology, another important security improvement at the airport that she'd spearheaded with the TSA.

"The one with Calvin, Ralph, O'Connor and FSD Stewart."

She stepped to the side and Max followed. "I

didn't know there was a meeting. If there was, I wasn't part of it."

"Oh." Max cleared his throat. "Maybe I was wrong. I thought I'd seen George there, too. I thought I saw them leaving the boardroom, but I could've been mistaken. I don't know. I'm probably wrong."

Ariana could feel her heart pounding. Max was observant and didn't make mistakes often. Why would George be at the airport without her knowledge?

"I bet it was just a matter of crossed wires. Or they were unable to reach you."

She hurriedly pulled out her iPhone and checked to see if any meeting invitations had come in while she'd been on the inspection. No, none.

Trying to stay calm, she said, "Yeah. I'm sure it was."

Ariana walked to her office, forcing a leisurely pace. Once inside, she closed the door and reached for the phone. She punched in Calvin's number. She'd get to the bottom of this. It wasn't right or respectful of her position for the CEO and chairman to have a meeting with the police and TSA without including her. And if they'd included George, what did that mean?

Before the phone had a chance to ring, she slammed down the receiver. She needed to do this in person. She wanted to understand what was going on, and it would be too easy for Calvin to sidestep it over the telephone. She had to *see* his reaction.

She took the stairs to the executive suite. "Hi, Marlene," she greeted Calvin's executive assistant. As always, Marlene was elegantly dressed, her hair and makeup model-perfect. "Is he in?"

"Good to see you, Ariana. Yes, he just got back from a meeting. Go on in."

So there definitely *had* been a meeting, she acknowledged as she walked toward her boss's office.

"Calvin, do you have a minute?" Ariana asked from his doorway.

Irritation flashed across his face. It was so quick she wondered if she'd imagined it. He gestured for her to come in and be seated. She perched stiffly on the edge of a chair, her back straight, hands folded in her lap.

"What is it?" he asked without raising his eyes from the papers in front of him.

"Did you and Ralph have a meeting about airport security without me?"

"Yes, we did."

She'd expected him to deny, evade or seek to rationalize it, but he'd done none of those things. She realized that she'd hoped there was a mistake or at least a rational explanation for her not being invited. Calvin's admission threw her off. "Can…can you tell me why you chose to have a meeting with respect to my area of responsibility and not include me?"

Calvin compressed his lips, making his annoyance clear. "The last time I checked, I was the CEO around here, and that gives me the right to make decisions about who I want in a meeting," he said sarcastically. "However, if you must know, Ralph called the meeting. It seems some of our law enforcement partners have concerns about our operations here, and we wanted to give them the opportunity to speak freely."

Ariana felt queasy. She clasped her hands tightly together. "And what are the concerns?"

Calvin tossed down the pen he'd been holding. "Leave it with me for now. If I wanted to talk to you about it, I would have called you in. I'll get back to you."

"If there are any vulnerabilities that've been discovered and that I should be dealing with, I need to know."

"I said let it be. The authorities are not the only ones with concerns. George Dennison has also raised some with me. When and if you need to know, I'll tell you. Are we clear?"

Ariana felt again as if the rug had been yanked out from under her feet. She was inclined to argue, but she could read the expression on Calvin's face. She wanted to ask about George but was afraid to. She rose slowly, gave Calvin a slow nod and left.

"Have a nice day," Marlene called to Ariana when she walked by the EA's desk.

"Thanks. You, too," she mumbled. She took the back corridors, hoping to avoid anyone she knew. She stopped to grab a can of Coke from the fridge in her department's break room, since she stocked only water in hers and wanted the kick of caffeine. Once in her office, she closed the door behind her and dropped heavily in her chair. Opening the can, she gulped down the drink.

When her iPhone pinged, she checked the text message that had come in.

She emitted a harsh snorting sound and deleted the message without responding.

"*Now* Logan wants to talk to me?" she grumbled under her breath. "He couldn't do it *before* he attended a meeting with my CEO and chair?"

It hurt more than she would have expected. Just when she'd begun to believe that there might be a future for them.

She booted up her computer and started scrolling through the daily security reports. She did it to occupy her mind as much as to see if there was anything glaring that might've prompted the meeting that had excluded her.

Generally, she'd flip through them quickly, focusing on incidents that hadn't already been closed by her team. Now she took more time. She was searching for anything that might signify a weakness. Anything she might have missed.

Her iPhone pinged several more times and rang once while she worked. She ignored it all. She didn't want to break her concentration. She read report after report, until she finished. Closing the document folder, she leaned back in her chair.

There was nothing out of the ordinary, or indicative of a vulnerability in policies or protocols. The standing orders had just been reviewed and updated not more than six months ago. Everything was—or at least, had been—working well.

But there was something…something she had to be missing…

Using her mouse, she flipped through a number of screens until she got to the video footage of the suspect in the hoodie carrying the concealing pipe. She watched it through until he tossed what was obviously an empty pipe in a waste receptacle by the door to the international departure lounge and entered. He knew exactly where he was going. So confident…

Hearing a knock on her door, Ariana glanced

at her watch. She'd been reviewing the reports and then the video files for forty-five minutes.

She smoothed back her hair and rose to open the door.

"Why haven't you answered my texts or my call?" Logan demanded.

She glanced down to see if Boomer was with him. Not seeing the dog, she rested a hand on the door frame and blocked his entry. She wasn't in the frame of mind to face him. Logan was the last person she wanted to see. Well, maybe Calvin was.

"I do have a job," she replied coolly.

"It's your job I want to talk to you about." He grabbed the arm that was blocking his way and lowered it.

What the heck did that mean? She stood her ground. "I've got a lot to do. Say what you came to say, but I have to get back to work."

Two of her guards passed by and she greeted them.

Logan gave her a steely-eyed stare. "You want to have this conversation right here? In a corridor, with people walking by?"

She threw up her hands and stepped to the side. "Come in, then, but understand I'm not in the best of moods."

Logan took two steps in and closed the door

behind him. "Then we're well matched. Neither am I."

When Ariana remained standing where she was, Logan walked over to her desk and leaned against it.

"So what is it about my job that you wanted to discuss?" Ariana was tempted to ask about the meeting he'd had with Calvin and Ralph…and George, but doubted she'd get a straight answer. That would just have annoyed her even more.

"Can you sit down, please?" Logan asked.

She was feeling belligerent, and she had every right to be. "I don't want to sit."

"Ariana…" Logan rose and went to her. He grasped her shoulders gently. "Whatever's bothering you, can you put it aside for a minute?"

His touch on her arms nearly caused her to capitulate. The urge to step closer to him and into his embrace was almost irresistible. To counteract the temptation, she shrugged his hands off and took a bad-tempered step back.

What kind of a fool was she? Today he'd almost certainly criticized her to her bosses—possibly put her job at risk. Now he came and pretended like it didn't happen? His look of exasperation, maybe with some disappointment tossed in, didn't appease her. If he could go behind her back the way he just had, he obviously didn't care about her. More than likely, *Jagger* had just been angling to make her one of his conquests. Maybe that last thought wasn't fair, but she was feeling far from magnanimous at that moment.

Ariana crossed her arms. She had to, to keep herself from shaking, as the realization struck her that she'd been falling in love with Logan. Her mouth dropped open before she clamped it shut again. "Just say whatever you came to say and get out," she hissed. Her eyes stung. She needed him to go and go fast, before she shamed herself with tears.

Logan's irises turned a frosty blue. He was about to say something then his phone rang and he checked the display. Holstering it again without answering, he looked at Ariana once more. "I can't figure you out," he said.

"Then don't waste your time trying," she retorted, and was relieved that her voice remained steady, although she felt impossibly cold and each breath was a strain. "Get to the point, please."

He gave his head one slow shake. "Never mind," he said softly and moved to the door. Opening it, he glanced back at her over his shoulder. "Watch your back," he said before walking out and closing the door none too gently behind him.

Ariana exhaled, sank down into her chair

and rubbed a finger between her brows where a headache was brewing.

Had he just threatened her? To what end?

How could he be so sweet and funny and apparently caring a few short hours ago when he'd escorted her to the airport, and be so ruthless and cutthroat now?

Turning back to her computer, she had trouble seeing the screen through the sheen of tears.

HOW WAS IT possible for the woman to run so hot and cold in less than twenty-four hours? Logan marveled. Damn it all, he cared about her. He…he *loved* her. And that wasn't the only reason he continued to believe in her innocence, despite the evidence against her. He was putting his own reputation and job on the line by not backing away from her the moment she'd become a possible suspect associated with the smuggling ring.

He knew the discussion he'd heard at the meeting he'd been in was intended to be confidential, but he hadn't felt any remorse when he'd decided to tell Ariana about it. It had been obvious to him that the guy from the TSA was trying to deflect blame from his organization and onto Ariana. They weren't acting in good faith, so what was the point of him keeping it from Ariana? They should have had her in the meeting, to at least give her a chance to defend herself.

He now had to consider if the TSA federal security director had anything to do with planting the bills of lading in Ariana's office. But how would he have gotten in there? He certainly didn't strike Logan as someone smart enough and skilled enough to override the access control and video management systems.

Ariana was probably the most capable and competent woman Logan had ever met, but she brought something out in him that made him want to protect her. To stand for her.

He wouldn't believe that she had anything to do with the smuggling ring. The person responsible had been able to get into her office twice now. In the first instance, to leave the initial note, and most recently to rig the bomb on her door, probably to draw them in there so they'd find the planted bills of lading. That explained the timer on the bomb, too. Again, he doubted that the intention was to harm Ariana. He was fairly certain that it was to lead them to the bills of lading. And someone going to all that trouble had to be doing it for a good reason. He believed Ariana had no idea why it was happening, and he was at a loss for ideas, too.

But then a thought occurred to him. He and everyone else had been operating under the assumption that the threats to Ariana and the smuggling ring weren't connected. But this most recent incident raised two possibilities. First that it was a coincidence Ariana's door had been rigged, and searching her office had led them to the bills of lading. They were unrelated to the bombs but happened to have explosives dust on them from smuggled explosive material in one of the shipments. The conclusion would be that Ariana was involved in the smuggling ring. A stretch on all counts.

The more probable explanation was that whoever was targeting Ariana was part of the smuggling ring and was trying to set her up. The explosives dust would've been purposely planted on the bills of lading to ensure they were found. But if that was the case, why draw attention to the smuggling?

No, none of it made sense to him. It was time he had a chat with the ATF and DEA agents.

Logan had wanted to give Ariana a heads-up about what was going on. Both Calvin Murdoch and Ralph Sterling seemed to trust that sniveling spineless bureaucrat Stewart more than their own chief of security. He didn't know much about Dennison, but he didn't like him. Based on what Ariana had told him and their relationship, he'd expected her predecessor to stand up for her. After all, he had a vested interest, as he'd had a role in her getting her job.

Logan believed in loyalty, in integrity. Whatever they thought themselves, they should have stood up for her in the meeting. He'd anticipated one of them, if not all three, to speak up for her, defend her competence in the face of Stewart's allegations. When none of them had, and Calvin went on the attack against her, too, Logan did so himself. It shouldn't have been left to him.

He knew he hadn't endeared himself to anyone in that room, but he had to do what was right. He lived by a few simple principles, including doing the right thing, regardless of where the chips might fall.

He was prepared to breach confidence for Ariana, for her best interests. But whatever had gotten her so riled, she didn't give him the chance. He was pretty good at understanding women. He'd thought Ariana was as logical and rational as they came. She hadn't behaved that way just now.

He pushed through the exit doors to the parking garage.

Maybe it was fortunate they hadn't moved faster on their relationship, he considered as he climbed into his vehicle. If he didn't come up with a plausible answer to what those bills of lading were doing in Ariana's office, she'd be deemed a suspect in the investigation. If he didn't want to risk his job, he'd have to stay away from her until the investigation was concluded and she was cleared.

Tomorrow was the annual canine tactical challenge competition he'd talked Ariana into attending to see him compete. He wondered if, after what had just transpired, she'd show. Should he call her and remind her? See if they were still on for the competition and for dinner afterward? Maybe he should call and make some excuse to avoid having her show.

He let Boomer in the back of his SUV, climbed in and started his engine. He rubbed his hands over his face.

Sometimes it was smarter to let things take their own course.

He pulled out of the parking garage and called dispatch to get him connected with the two federal agents leading the smuggling ring investigation.

In view of the circumstances, even though it was Saturday, they agreed to meet early the next morning before he had to be at Qualcomm Stadium for the competition.

CHAPTER SEVENTEEN

ARIANA DROVE HER vehicle into the parking lot at Qualcomm Stadium. She found it hard to believe that she was actually here. With her fear of dogs, how on earth had Logan talked her into coming to watch the annual law enforcement canine tactical challenge? Add to that what had happened yesterday at work, and she'd considered calling him and making some excuse for not attending.

But then she'd thought about what *had* really happened. Logan had come to see her. Would he have been so brazen to try to undermine her with her bosses, then see her immediately after? Or was there another side to the story?

She hadn't given him a chance to say what he'd come to say. That was rude and unfair of her. On that basis alone, she decided she'd come and, given the opportunity over dinner perhaps, ask him what he'd wanted to talk about, and then draw her conclusions.

Qualcomm Stadium was the home of the San Diego Chargers and had ample parking, yet the surface lot was packed. The dog competition must be a popular event.

Most police departments from Southern California, the Port of San Diego's Harbor Police K-9 Unit and other law enforcement organizations with service dogs were competing for the annual honors. Still, the place was much busier than she'd anticipated.

Logan had told her that he and Boomer held the championship position in explosives detection two years in a row. He'd said he expected stiff competition from an up-and-coming contender from the Harbor Police but that he felt comfortable that they could win again. She admired his confidence and wished for his sake that it was true.

Finding a spot, she shut off her engine and shook her head, still surprised that she was actually here. There would be hundreds of dogs present…

Logan wanted her to be here. She had to admit that she was curious about it, too.

She hopped out of her car, grabbed her bag and locked the doors. Consulting the ticket Logan had given her, she made her way to the appropriate gate.

The SDPD had a section of reserved seats. Logan had told her that she should watch for Rick Vasquez and he'd introduce her to the others present. He'd explained that Rick usually competed, too, but his longtime canine partner, Sniff—another championship title holder—had recently retired. Rick's new partner—Nitro, the former explosives detection dog who'd worked the airport—showed great potential, but was still being retrained for narcotics detection. Logan said he believed Rick and Nitro would be serious contenders in next year's competition.

Ariana showed her ticket to the attendant and he directed her to the proper staircase. She stopped at a concession stand to buy a soda before making her way down the stairs. She could see the dogs on the field. As she'd guessed, there were *hundreds*.

Of course, with the SDPD being the host organization, they had their seats closest to the action…and all the dogs.

What on earth had compelled her to come to this event?

The answer was simple. Logan.

Despite everything that was going on, she was in love with him. There *had* to be a logical explanation for what had happened yesterday. For now, he wanted her here for him and she was.

She took a steadying breath, hitched her bag higher up on her shoulder and headed down.

She spotted Rick right away. With his height, dark coloring and rugged appeal, he was hard to miss. There was another tall, athletically built man standing beside him. She'd seen him somewhere before. A cop, too, she surmised.

A number of other people were gathered around them. They appeared to be a close-knit group.

As she neared them, Rick moved to the side and Ariana stopped short. Rick's large form had blocked her view as she was approaching. Now she saw both the redhead and the blonde from The Runway, the night she'd seen Logan there after they'd first had drinks together.

She narrowed her eyes. There was no mistaking the redhead as the one Logan had spun around and kissed. Except she was even more stunning, if that was possible, in the bright light of day. Ariana again had the urge to turn around and leave, and not because of the dogs. She'd thought the redhead had been Becca, but now she knew that wasn't the case. She'd been so wrong about Becca, though. Surely that was the case with the blonde and the redhead, too. Knowing she was being irrational didn't help her overcome the reactions she was experiencing. Looking at the redhead and the blonde, she remembered where she'd seen the other cop. He was with Logan's group at The Runway.

Just then Rick raised a hand in greeting. All the others turned toward her, too.

There was no way to back out now without appearing foolish.

Rick left the group and scaled the steps two at a time until he was standing in front of her.

"Hey, it's great to see you, Ariana. Come meet everyone."

He placed a hand lightly on her elbow and guided her down to where they were gathered.

Ariana felt the redhead, in particular, scrutinize her. She noticed the blonde watching her, too. The two women exchanged a glance, just as Ariana stepped into the box.

Then she saw Logan's sister, Becca, at the far end of the group. Becca's friendly wave and bright smile went a long way to calming her. Becca quickly made her way over to Ariana and gave her a warm hug.

Rick introduced Ariana first to a few other K-9 Unit officers, Cal Palmer—the one she'd recognized from The Runway—Shannon Clemens, whom she of course had met, and their newest recruit from the Harbor Police, Brett Holloway, an officer who'd replace Brody.

"A rather sly move by Logan," Rick said with humor in his voice, "to hire Brett to start with us before the competition, seeing Brett and his canine partner have been Logan and Boomer's stiffest competition the last couple of years.

Since he's just joining us, he doesn't have a dog yet to compete with."

Brett shook Ariana's hand and grinned. "I'll have a whole year to make sure I'm ready to take the title from Jagger next time. It's great to meet you, Ariana. I understand I'll be working with you at the airport."

"Yes...it's nice to meet you, too, and congratulations on the new job. Let me know if you'd like me to arrange a tour of the airport for you." She had only a moment to wonder why Logan hadn't told her there'd be a new K-9 Unit officer working the airport instead of him before Rick continued with the introductions.

Rick turned to the blonde next. "This is Jessica Palmer, Cal's wife," he said, just as Cal slid a protective arm around his wife's shoulder and gently touched her protruding stomach.

She was pregnant, Ariana noted immediately, and that explained who the blonde was.

"Last but by no means least..." Rick motioned to the redhead. Ariana tried to will her palm not to be clammy when she shook hands with the woman. "This," Rick continued, "is my fiancée, Madison Long."

The love and pride was evident in Rick's voice and glowed on his face. He'd put emphasis on the word *fiancée* and went on to explain that they'd just gotten engaged recently.

Ariana hoped her face didn't reflect her embarrassment although the heat that warmed her cheeks suggested otherwise. The night she'd seen Logan pick up the redhead and kiss her, he was probably congratulating her on their engagement.

So much for her brilliant ability to read people. Still, relief flowed through her, along with little pangs of hope and pleasure.

Rick pointed out to Ariana where Logan was on the field. He let out a piercing whistle that made Logan look over at them. When he saw Ariana, he waved to her, but even at a distance she saw an odd expression come over his face. Then he signaled to Rick to come join him. Rick got Ariana settled next to Madison before he hopped over the side of the bleachers and jogged toward Logan.

Ariana stretched her legs out in front of her, took a sip of her drink and watched Logan.

"He's quite a catch," Madison remarked next to her.

"Sorry?"

Madison chuckled, and motioned with her own soda toward Logan, who was running Boomer through some drills with Rick's help. "Your sigh as you were watching him. It told me more than words could. So I said, he—he being Logan—is quite a catch."

Flustered, Ariana glanced toward Rick Vasquez. "I could say the same about your fiancé."

The grin on Madison's face widened. "No question. I'm very lucky to have met him and have him fall in love with me."

"The way he looks at you, I think he considers himself to be very fortunate, too."

Madison's eyes sparkled. "What a nice thing to say! Thank you."

Watching Logan give Rick a one-armed hug, Ariana's warm, misty feeling persisted. She couldn't catch herself in time to avoid another breathy sigh. She laughed. "Listen to me! How silly do I sound? Sighing like a schoolgirl?"

"Not silly at all," Madison assured her.

Ariana glanced over at her.

"Actually, you kind of sounded like someone in love—"

"I didn't say that," Ariana objected quickly.

Madison waved it away. "Okay, let's not split hairs."

"Well..." She didn't know what else to say. She really *was* in love with Logan.

Rick rejoined them shortly before the official start of the event. Ariana watched and cheered with the others, and kept conversations going. Rick and Cal explained most of what was going on to her.

She enjoyed speaking with Jessica and Madison, when they weren't concentrating on the competition, getting to know them, learning how they'd met their significant others.

Ariana felt the cold sweat along her spine, especially when the suspect apprehension trials were on. She watched with a dread she tried to conceal as the dogs were dispatched to chase and apprehend the "suspects" wearing heavily padded guards. Every time they'd get up in good spirits and obviously uninjured, she felt her heart rate settle.

When it was time for the explosives detection dogs to get to work, Ariana and her companions fell silent. Ariana found that she could watch and enjoy the competition, and was surprised that she felt mild apprehension about the dogs rather than her customary paralyzing fear.

The cheers from their group were near deafening when Logan and Boomer placed first in their category for the third year in a row.

She watched Logan leave the field with Boomer. Rick explained that he would put the dog in a pen while they finished watching the other competitions.

When Logan joined them, he got high fives and slaps on the back from the other cops, but Ariana sensed the change in him immediately. Madison started to get up from her seat to let him sit beside Ariana. Before she was up, he placed a hand on her shoulder to keep her where she was and took a seat on the far side of Becca instead.

Logan had to leave them again for the awards ceremony. Ariana watched on the Jumbotron as Logan and Boomer received their first-place ribbon. Rick and Cal whistled loudly while the others cheered. He seemed happy on the podium and she couldn't figure out what had happened to change his demeanor toward her so drastically from the night before. She loved him and was getting tired of the ups and downs. They were going out to dinner with the others to celebrate, but she had to find a moment alone with him, tell him how she felt about him and ask directly what was going on with him.

When the awards presentation was finished, Rick and Cal started to move them out of the stadium with the rest of their group, explaining that because Logan had Boomer with him, he'd meet them outside by their vehicles.

Ariana glanced over her shoulder at the large screen once more and spotted Logan walking away with Boomer. She watched him long enough to notice that his smile was gone, and he walked with his head hung and shoulders slumped. Then the screen flickered and the Jumbotron went black.

Dread settled over Ariana, but she didn't know why.

CHAPTER EIGHTEEN

LOGAN CAUGHT UP to Ariana and the others in his group just as they were exiting the stadium. It was hard for him to keep a distance from Ariana, but he had to.

"So, champ, where do you want to go for dinner?" Cal asked.

"About that. I'm sorry but I won't be able to make it." He glanced at Ariana and could easily see the hurt and disappointment on her face. He hated lying to her, and to his colleagues and friends, but after his meeting with the two federal agents that morning, he had no choice. "I got a call as I was leaving the field. I have to go into the division."

"You've got to be kidding me!" Cal's look was skeptical, and Logan couldn't blame him. Even more concerning—and nearly ripping his heart to shreds—so was Ariana's.

"I'll take the call," Rick suggested. "You should go out and celebrate."

Logan shook his head. "Thanks for the offer, but this one is for me."

"All right. Ariana." Rick turned to her. "Why don't you come with us, and Logan can join us once he's done?"

Logan could read Ariana's face clearly and knew that she wasn't fooled. "Oh…thanks for asking, but I think I'll just go home. Congratulations, Logan."

She said a quick goodbye to everyone else, waved to him and hurried off before anyone could stop her. Logan was sure she was barely holding back tears. He wanted to rush after her and take her into his arms, apologize and tell her he loved her. But after what he'd been told that morning by the federal agents, it wasn't possible.

The feds had busted the members of the smuggling ring in Texas. Their leader was carrying a phone programmed to another mobile phone—stupidly enough containing a number that was listed as San Diego International's head of security.

In combination with the bills of lading found in Ariana's office, she was now the feds' prime suspect.

ARIANA'S HEART WAS truly and completely broken.

Logan called her later that evening. He thanked her for coming all that way to watch him and Boomer compete, and apologized for having canceled their dinner plans on such short notice. She wasn't fooled for an instant and when she repeatedly asked to see him so they could talk things through, he finally confessed that he just wasn't good at relationships and it wasn't possible for there to be anything more than friendship between them. He told her that he'd hired a new K-9 handler for explosives detection—she'd met him at the stadium. As a result, once the current investigation was over, she wouldn't have to see Logan again. He said he hoped she understood and he wished her well.

So, Ariana tried to focus on her job. She spent Sunday analyzing all that had been going on in hopes of finding some answers. She thought about people she'd had confrontations with. Her job wasn't without them. Dave Langdon was a perfect example. But hard as she tried, Ariana couldn't think of a person or situation that could have been serious enough to precipitate the spate of events they were experiencing. She kept circling back to motive and outcome, and none of it made sense.

She couldn't help but wonder and worry where it would all end.

With no other answers coming to her, by midafternoon, she'd drafted up a letter of resignation and sealed it in an envelope addressed to Calvin.

LOGAN WANTED TO hurl his glass against a wall. If he hadn't been in as public a place as the patio of Buster's Beach House Bar, he might have given in to the temptation. He didn't think he'd ever been this miserable or this conflicted in his life. He'd fallen in love and there wasn't a darn thing he could do about it. He hadn't been able to protect Ariana and now he couldn't have a relationship with her because she was a suspect.

"Hey, Cal, aren't you glad we decided to have a drink with our cheerful boss?" Rick said with a laugh as he and Cal walked up to the table where Logan sat, slouched ovcr his beer.

Cal took a seat opposite Logan. "And to think I chose this over the company of my beautiful wife this lovely Sunday afternoon!"

Logan was tempted to retort but realized his friends were right. He'd invited them out—hard as it was to get them away from their significant others lately—and he wasn't much company. He took a long drink and purposefully straightened in his chair and tried for a relaxed look. "Sorry, guys," he mumbled.

"You want to tell us what's bothering you?" Rick asked as he sat between Logan and Cal. "And what all that was about not going out with us for dinner last night?"

Logan thumped his beer bottle on the coaster, signaled for Carly to bring two more beers and leaned on the table with his arms crossed. He stared out at the ocean. It wasn't the sapphire-blue water he was seeing but Ariana's face and the hurt on it when he'd seen her last outside the stadium. "I envy you guys," he said, and glanced over in time to see the quizzical look his friends exchanged.

"Want to elaborate?" Cal asked.

Logan shrugged, then thanked Carly when she placed the two bottles of beer on the table.

"C'mon, Jagger. You invited us out for a beer, not to have us watch you mope in your drink."

Logan's only response was another shrug. All three of them watched a schooner sail past.

"Cal, you remember back when you and Jess were here that time, and I was having dinner inside over there?" Rick said, gesturing with his beer toward the building.

"Yeah. I do. You were just about as grouchy then as our pal Jagger is right now."

"True, and you called me an idiot," Rick responded.

Logan shifted his gaze to Rick but kept silent.

"And with good reason!" Cal replied with a smirk. "You were about to toss away the best thing that had ever happened to you. Not to mention a happy future."

Rick's face sobered. "I'd hurt Madison." His

eyes were downcast. "That whole situation with the Los Zetas cartel targeting me, it had me rattled. In an effort to keep her from getting hurt, I lied to her and ended up hurting her myself."

"If I remember correctly, you broke up with her and in a way that made it impossible for her to question or refuse. You believed you were doing her a favor and she'd get over you in time."

This was the first Logan had heard any of this. He had no idea where the conversation was going. Rick and Madison were as well matched as any two people could be, and they were insanely in love.

Rick's expression was grim, and he stared into his coffee cup. "I wanted to protect her and keep her safe." He shook his head. "I can't begin to picture what my life would be like without her, if you hadn't come along and straightened me out. Made me understand how foolish I was being. I nearly lost Madison because of my misguided desire to protect her from harm."

"So you figured she was in danger because of you and decided to end it with her," Cal summarized. "And you didn't level with her? Give her a choice to weigh in?"

Rick shook his head.

To Logan, the idea of Rick and Madison not being together was...well, unimaginable.

"As I said. Idiot." Cal grinned.

They both stared at Logan. "So we're guessing your mood has to do with Ariana. If you're trying to protect her, keep her from getting hurt, do you really think that's what she wants? Think about what Rick went through with Madison," Cal urged. "Considering Ariana's profession, I'd expect she'd be even more averse to you making decisions on her behalf and trying to shield her from harm."

"You can't make an arbitrary decision about your future together without consulting her, well-intentioned as it might be," Rick continued. "You said that to me, Cal, didn't you? As much as it pains me to admit it, you were right."

"You care about Ariana," Cal added. "That's clear. I'm betting she cares about you, too. Whatever is bothering you, be honest with her. Give her a say…a choice. If you think Ariana could be right for you…talk to her."

Logan had invited his friends out because he wanted to talk to them, but so far they had been doing all the talking. "I'm in love with Ariana," he said abruptly.

"Well, how about that!" Rick exclaimed, and he and Cal did a high five.

"Never thought it would happen to you, Jagger, but boy am I glad it did, and with such an extraordinary woman," Cal added.

Logan took a long drink and glared at his friends.

"Okay, so what aren't you telling us?" Rick asked, his tone serious. "I get the feeling it's not just that you don't *want* to be in love."

"Heck, no," Logan said. "It surprised me, but I liked the idea of being in love with Ariana."

"Then what?" Cal prompted.

"If only my situation was as simple as Rick's. Sorry, pal, no offense meant." He sighed heavily. "As Rick knows, ATF and DEA have been cooperating on the investigation of a smuggling ring operating out of the San Diego airport. They know that there were insiders involved, probably in baggage handling and security."

Rick nodded. "You mentioned to me yesterday when I joined you on the field at Qualcomm that you'd met with the two agents heading up the investigation that morning."

"Yeah. I did." Logan's eyes burned with anger and frustration. "Ariana is now their prime suspect for the operations in San Diego." He got some satisfaction from the immediate and heated response to his statement from both his friends.

"I believe in her innocence, but you both understand that, under the circumstances, a personal relationship is out of the question."

"Man, that's a tough situation to be in," Cal

observed. "You're right that your situation is much more complex than Rick's was."

"All we can hope for is that the investigation wraps up quickly and you can explain it to Ariana. With her training, hopefully she'll understand and forgive."

Logan raised a brow and shook his head.

"Yeah, that would be asking a lot, wouldn't it?" Cal observed.

He'd never have a chance with Ariana. No dating…no marriage…

Logan was just lifting his bottle to his lips when his hand stilled. Had he just thought that? He'd known for some time that he loved Ariana, but the thought of *marrying* her…? He'd never considered marrying anyone.

"Hey, you with us, Jagger?" Cal's voice was cajoling.

Logan glanced at Cal then at Rick. He'd been so absorbed in his own musings, he'd nearly forgotten where he was and that his friends were there with him.

It was obvious he had some serious thinking to do. He saw no easy way to resolve the conflict raging inside him. Wanting…loving Ariana with his entire being, and not being able to do anything about it. Unlike Rick's situation with Madison, *he* couldn't discuss the circumstances with Ariana. There was no easy answer for him.

Logan forced a smile. "Since Rick is our designated driver tonight and he's switching to coffee, Cal, you and I should have another beer."

CHAPTER NINETEEN

"SO WE'RE NO further ahead?" Max asked. He, Ariana and Logan were huddled in Ariana's office after the multiagency security committee meeting. "Dave Langdon was the only person we could come up with, even if the SDPD didn't consider him a viable suspect, but he's got a solid alibi for the time Ariana's office door was rigged with the IED. The whole time we've been suspecting the wrong guy?"

"He was never a serious suspect," Ariana corrected Max. "You're grasping at straws."

"But we had...*have* no one else. We thought it was Dave Langdon, because we knew he had it in for you, not to mention that he's unstable with violent tendencies—now we know that was the reason he was let go from the SDPD. I have to admit my second choice was TSA FSD Stewart. Maybe I just wanted it to be him, because he's so annoying, but he's not plausible as a suspect either."

"There's no question Langdon is resentful and consumed with hate for Ariana," Logan responded, giving Ariana a sympathetic look. Somehow, they had managed to put their personal issues behind them and established an equitable working relationship...at least on the surface. He still believed in her innocence 100 percent, even more so since the feds suspected that the bomb on Ariana's door and the discovery of the bills of lading in her office weren't connected. Sheer luck, they thought. Logan didn't believe it for a second. "Langdon's not our guy, but he's certainly soaking it all in. Seeing the incidents as a demonstration that Ariana was wrong to terminate him."

Max made a snorting sound. "That's his opinion. We had no end of issues with him here, but it was Ariana who had the courage to address his performance head-on." Max gave her an encouraging smile. "George either didn't see it or was too worried about possible repercussions."

"She's a smart lady," Logan agreed, eliciting a frown from Ariana. "But it's impossible for him to be responsible for everything that's been going on here." Logan shook his head. "It's not Langdon."

"So we're no closer to knowing who could be behind all this," Ariana said.

"It would seem," Logan acknowledged reluctantly. He wanted to catch the person responsible. He had a job to do, but he worried about Ariana. He couldn't be in two places at once. If he remained in Ariana's office with her and Max, he couldn't hunt down the person responsible. He was reluctant to leave her, but he had to trust Max and his own SDPD colleagues when he wasn't with her.

Besides, he appreciated that Ariana wanted as little to do with him as possible. After the way he'd behaved, he couldn't blame her.

"I've got to get going. I'm trusting you to keep her safe, Max," he said as he walked out of her office.

ARIANA AND MAX watched Logan leave. "You can go now, too" Ariana said to Max, breaking the silence. "I know you're watching me and so is the cop outside in the hall. Trust me. I'm safe." She gave him an encouraging smile. "I have the two of you, and Boomer swept my office and our entire space. Go do some work, before we drive each other crazy."

She could see his hesitation, but he did as she asked.

Ariana had barely gotten into her paperwork when she heard someone enter her office.

"Could I see you for a minute, Ariana?"

She turned from her computer and glanced at Marlene, Calvin's executive assistant, standing in her doorway. Whatever Calvin wanted now, it wasn't likely to be good for him to send his EA to her personally, instead of a simple call or email. She thought about the resignation letter she'd written on the weekend and had stored in her top drawer. She just hadn't had the courage to hand it in yet.

Then she noticed Marlene's red-rimmed eyes, the puffy circles under them and the crinkled envelope she was clutching in her hands. The always impeccably groomed woman was more than a little tousled this morning.

"Of course. Come in and have a seat. Can I get you a bottle of water?"

"Thanks, and no thanks to the water. I won't take much of your time." Marlene closed the door behind her and settled on the edge of Ariana's chair. She lifted the hand that held the envelope, then rested it back on her lap.

When Marlene didn't say a word, Ariana took the lead. "What's up, Marlene?"

"I… I…" Her eyes filled, and she dropped her head into her hands with a choked sob.

Ariana rose and rushed to Marlene's side, draping an arm around her shoulders. "What is it? Take your time, but tell me what's wrong."

"It…it's… Here," she finally said and handed the envelope to Ariana. Ariana took it, and gave Marlene a questioning look. For a horrible moment it occurred to her that the envelope might contain a letter of termination from Calvin. Yes, she'd been considering quitting, but if she had to leave, she'd prefer it to be her own decision.

Ariana dismissed the idea, although she suspected it had been on Calvin's mind. She and Marlene might always have gotten along well, but they weren't close enough for Marlene to be so upset if Ariana was being fired. And even Calvin wouldn't be so insensitive as to delegate firing her to his assistant.

Unable to speak, Marlene gestured with her hand for Ariana to open the envelope. Ariana moved back behind her desk and sat in her chair. Just in case it *was* a termination letter, she wanted to be sitting down when she read it. She gave Marlene another apprehensive glance—the woman was still crying—before pulling the sheet of paper out of the envelope. Unfolding it, Ariana's heart started hammering like a piston, threatening to crash through her ribs. She held the sheet out to Marlene. "Where did you get this?"

Marlene covered her face with her hands and sobbed harder.

Ariana dropped the sheet of paper on her desk, pushed out of her chair and moved in front of Marlene. She'd had enough. She grabbed Marlene's shoulders and shook her firmly. "Marlene, where did you get it?" she repeated, her voice stronger, carrying authority now rather than shock and dismay.

"It's related, isn't it, to what's been going on?"

Ariana kept herself from turning to glance at the printout of the web page with instructions on how to make a bomb. "It might be, but you have to tell me where you got it."

Marlene swiped at the tears coursing down her cheeks. Ariana reached for a box of tissues she kept on her desk and held it out.

"I… I knew I had to show you when I saw it. It… I've been seeing a man now for almost ten months. It was going really well at first, but then it changed. He seemed preoccupied, not as attentive, late for our dates. Once or twice he forgot all about them." She took a fresh tissue and blew her nose. "So…so, I thought he lost interest in me. That he was seeing someone else. He stayed over last night at my place. This morning—I know this is so wrong and I shouldn't have done it, but I couldn't help it. He was working on his computer first thing and when he went to shower, it hadn't gone into hibernation, so I looked at it. I wanted to see his emails. See if there was any indication that he *was* seeing someone else." She gulped air and mopped at her eyes with the soaked tissue. "So, there was this minimized file, and the file name was...was Bomb Recipe. Because of the file name, I opened it, and..." She motioned with a trembling hand toward the sheet of paper on Ariana's desk. "That was in it. I emailed it to myself and deleted it from the sent and trash folders. When I got to work, I printed it, because I had to show you.

"Is this possible? Is it really that simple to make a bomb? And why would Wayne have it on his computer? What does it mean in terms of what's been going on here?"

All good questions, Ariana acknowledged. And ones she didn't have the answers for. Then one question overrode all the others. "His name is Wayne?"

She nodded. "Yes."

Ariana thought she already knew the answer, but she had to ask. "What's his last name, Marlene?"

Marlene lowered her eyes and started shredding the damp tissue in her hand. "I know we're not supposed to date other employees, but it just happened. We went out for a drink after the company barbecue and—"

Ariana feared she knew the answer. She cut Marlene off regardless. "His name?"

"Wayne Gallagher."

Ariana tried to keep her breathing steady. She asked Marlene some more questions. She told her she'd notify the police and they'd probably want to talk to her. After getting her confirmation that she didn't think Wayne was aware of what she'd done, despite his IT skills, Ariana firmly cautioned Marlene not to speak to him. Ariana wanted to make sure Marlene didn't act in a way that might cause him to become suspicious or, more importantly, put Marlene at risk with a dangerous man.

She understood that Marlene felt guilty about her possible role in the occurrences at the airport, and humiliated and heartbroken to realize that someone she loved could do what Wayne apparently had been doing. Considering Marlene's emotional state, Ariana suggested the best course of action would be for her to take the day off and avoid seeing him or talking to him until the police were informed and had a game plan.

Ariana closed the door behind Marlene and leaned back against it. She took a moment—only a moment—to try to make sense of what it all meant.

She called Logan and asked if he was able to meet with her as soon as possible. He'd left the airport but said he'd be there as quickly as he could.

True to his word, he was sitting in her office in under an hour.

"I have our first solid lead," Ariana began

and handed him the sheet of paper she'd gotten from Marlene.

Deep lines formed between his brows and at the corners of his mouth as he read. When he finished, he handed the paper back and stared at her. "Where did you get this?"

"Calvin's executive assistant brought it to me." She told him the boyfriend's name and that he was employed at the airport.

"So what does Gallagher do?"

"He's a senior systems analyst for our IT department. I've been told he's our very best. That means he knows our IT, including our security and access control systems."

"That explains a lot. Anything else she told you that might be relevant?"

"No. That covers it. She was very distraught and I didn't want her to inadvertently alert him. I suggested she go home and asked her not to communicate with Wayne, at least until I could inform you, and you could decide on a course of action."

"Smart moves all around. You did well. I'll have him run. See what we come up with, but I'm betting nothing will pop."

"Do you want to speak to Marlene?"

"I will, but I want to speak with you first. What is your connection to Gallagher?"

She shook her head. "I don't have one. Other

than contacts I've had with him regarding IT-related matters, most recently to do with the duplication of my card and the investigation into how the false notification about the active shooter got sent with my passcode… He's an IT expert. He might very well be responsible for those things, too. Am I right?"

"That's what came to my mind."

"But why? What did I do to him?" Her voice was high-pitched and not quite steady.

"Ariana, take a deep breath. Are you okay?"

When she didn't answer, he pulled a chair up in front of her, so they were eye to eye, and took her hands in his. "You're *not* responsible," he repeated emphatically. "You can't take it upon yourself."

He held her gaze until she finally nodded her head. He gave her hand an encouraging squeeze. "I'll move on this quickly. Yes, I'll need to speak to Marlene. Does anyone else know about this yet?"

"No."

"Her boss?"

Ariana grimaced. "I told her not to tell Calvin, but she's loyal to him. I'm hoping not."

"Okay, let's trust that's the case, and let's keep it that way for now."

Logan rose and moved to her, holding a hand out. Ariana appreciated the offer of comfort, but she shook her head. With the way things were between them, she had no right to lean on him or expect his sympathy, nor did he have a right to offer it. "No, please."

She saw a flicker in his eyes, but it was gone as quickly as it had appeared.

After Logan left, Ariana took a while to evaluate this new development. She had no idea why Wayne Gallagher had done what he'd done or why he'd been targeting her. She wanted to do her own digging into Wayne's background, but she'd turned the matter over to Logan and the police. It was inappropriate and potentially dangerous for her to pursue it. Even worse, she didn't want to inadvertently alert Wayne that they were on to him, in case her digging sent up a flag somehow.

She'd leave it to Logan and trust him to do the right thing, but it was tough when she was this involved and connected.

CHAPTER TWENTY

ONE THING ARIANA could do was use the airport's systems and keep an eye out for Wayne. When Logan, with backup, had gone to Wayne's office they'd been told he wasn't in. He hadn't called. He simply didn't show up that morning.

What they did know was that he was somewhere in the airport, because he'd used his access card to get into a secure area. Logan and the other officers were trying to locate him. Meanwhile, Ariana diligently reviewed video footage.

When Max called to say they had something—he thought they'd spotted Wayne Gallagher on camera—she contacted Logan and they both joined her in her office.

"Oh, my God," Ariana murmured as she watched the security camera footage Max directed her to.

Logan glanced over at her. She was sure her face was pale from the look he gave her.

Her eyes met his briefly, before focusing on the monitor again. "That's him. Wayne Gallagher. Even with the jacket and his hood up I recognize him." She'd known what he looked like, but she also studied his security ID picture at length.

Max leaned in. "I think he has a gun. See the way he's holding his hand on his right hand side?"

Logan agreed with him and typed up a short text, sending notice to his team to mobilize, then stared at the screen again. "It looks like he's on to us. He must've figured out what Marlene did. Where do you think he's going?"

Ariana frowned as she rewound the video clip then fast-forwarded it again. "He's in Terminal 2. In a service area. Secure." She watched silently for a few seconds. "My best guess is he's heading for the international baggage handling area." She glanced at Max.

"I think so, too."

"Then I'd better get moving," Logan said.

"You can't go alone. You can't get in there without security access, which I can provide. This is my airport," she reminded him. "I'm going with you."

"No, you're not," Logan objected. "And don't argue. The guy's got it in for you for whatever reason. If he does suspect we're on to him, he'll be desperate. No way do I want you there, in harm's way, especially if he has a gun."

Ariana signaled for Max to leave them. She crossed her arms. This was *her* airport. It was her reputation. She bit back a sharp retort, as she knew that would only make Logan dig his heels in. Instead, she counted to five in her head—there wasn't enough time for ten—and placed a hand on his forearm. "Logan, you can't shield me from this. It's my job. If it was anyone but me, you wouldn't be doing this. You wouldn't be standing in front of that person." She put her fingertips on his mouth when he started to speak. The shock of the contact, when they'd been so formal with each other lately, caused them both to step back.

"Logan, look at me. Whatever else, I need you to trust me…and let me do my job. No one on our security team knows that space better than I do. I was involved in the design and layout of the scanning equipment. The installation is brand-new. The SDPD cops assigned to us don't know it at all."

He took more than a count to five, she was sure, but his posture, the softening of the lines of his face, told her he'd understood. She knew she was getting through to him and gave him a final nudge.

"You need me…"

She saw a tenderness in his eyes that had been absent, and it nearly broke her.

"Ariana, so help me, if you get hurt..."

"I won't." She wanted to touch him, but she had no right.

He raised a hand. Let it drop. "We've wasted enough time. Let's get going. You can fill me in on the risks we face in that area on the way, and what other critical areas he might be able to access from there." Logan handed her a body armor vest. "I don't plan to take you in. I'll have other cops with me. But I also don't want to take any chances, so put that on."

Ariana did as he asked.

He instructed Boomer to heel, and they headed out of her office at a run. "How long will it take to get there, and where should I instruct the others to meet us?"

"Fifteen minutes. Maybe a little less. We'll take a shuttle and once we're in Terminal 2, a cart." She told him to have the others meet them at the baggage sorting area.

"Tell me what we can expect," Logan said as they moved at a quick jog, Boomer loping at his side.

"It's a large area, but there's not a lot of open space. It's tightly filled with the conveyor belts—nearly three miles of them—all the sorting and security scanning equipment. There's a lot of metal," she stated, knowing that could be dangerous if firearms became involved.

"Help me understand the risk to the public. Where's the area situated? If he's got explosives with him, which is likely, what would it mean if he was able to detonate an IED in there?"

Ariana tried to catch her breath. She was fit, but the near run and talking at the same time were taking a toll.

"It's okay. Inhale deeply a few times before you answer. The weight of the vest is tough if you're not used to it."

As he'd been on many occasions before, Logan seemed to be entirely in tune with her. She hadn't considered the twenty to thirty extra pounds she was carrying.

"Okay. Okay. The baggage sorting area is situated mostly under service space. It's below grade for the most part. There's a concrete slab above it. A structural slab. But it also extends to the check-in area in the terminal, where the bags originate, and to the loading area, where the bags get put on the trucks that take them to the flights." Ariana stopped, placed a hand on her belly as she bent over to catch her breath. "Oh, my God! If he knows what he's doing, he could put explosives in luggage bound for different international destinations." She straightened, grabbing Logan's arms. "He could ground all flights. If the planes took off, not just here but at the destination airports, too—if he wanted to kill people, he could detonate the explosives in flight."

Logan glanced at her. "Can someone do that? Can they pick bags destined for different locations, pull them out of the system and tamper with them?"

"Yes, it's possible if he knows what he's doing. And Wayne does. The sorting and screening is automated for the most part. If he wants to target the larger, international flights… We handle a significant number of flights at any given time." She didn't want to think of it. "Even if he were to randomly select bags, he could wreak havoc."

"We still have no idea what his plan is or why. Without motive, we have no idea if he'd do something like that, but let's not take chances. Can the system be shut down? Paused?"

"Yes. Yes, it can."

"Then do it. Are you okay to go? We need to move."

"Yeah." They picked up their pace again and Ariana pulled out her phone as she ran. "Max," she said when he answered his phone. "Evacuate Terminal 2 and shut down the baggage handling system as soon as you can. Hold all flights that are currently preparing for departure from Terminal 2 and meet me at door A-173 to the baggage handling area."

With Max's confirmation that he'd take care of everything she'd asked, she put away her phone and picked up speed, as she knew Logan was moderating his pace to match hers.

They were the first to arrive at the entrance to the baggage handling area. Her phone rang as they reached the door. She listened to Max's update. She turned to Logan after she disconnected.

"Okay, the bags won't be loaded on flights, but for some reason they've been unable to shut down the system. They're going to try the emergency override, but that'll take time. The system will be operational when we go in. Meaning the conveyors will all be moving and the screening equipment will be functioning. That'll make it more difficult for us...and for him."

Logan nodded.

"What do we do know?" Ariana asked as she tried to keep her breathing deep and slow.

Logan glanced around and she followed suit. There were no police, no security personnel in place. Boomer was visibly agitated. He lunged at the door repeatedly with short, sharp barks. Ariana realized that with all the excitement, she'd almost forgotten entirely about Boomer being with them, but the aggressive behavior he was now displaying rattled her nerves.

"Boomer and I go in," Logan stated.

Deep in her own thoughts, she'd forgotten about her question. "Sorry. What?"

"We're going into the luggage sorting area. We don't want to give him time to set explosives. We want to be on his tail if we can."

"You need me because of the equipment," she reminded him.

He stared at her for a few moments. "You agree to do exactly as I say?"

"Okay," she said.

Logan radioed his team and Ariana took the opportunity to call Max again. She instructed him to wait and let the other police officers in when they arrived. Propping the door open was not an option, as they couldn't risk passengers wandering in.

"Stay low. Stay silent," Logan instructed her. "Boomer is an explosives dog, not search and rescue, but he'll follow Gallagher if he's got explosives on him, whether dust or actual IEDs." He grabbed her arms firmly, placed his mouth roughly over hers. "Sorry, I needed that," he said, but he didn't appear apologetic in the least. "And for God's sake, stay behind me, please."

Breathless from the kiss as much as the running, Ariana nodded mutely. She used her card to open the access door, and they went in as Logan drew his weapon.

"Stay low. Stay behind me," he repeated in a

whisper, then he instructed Boomer. The dog lurched forward, but Logan kept him on his leash and at a moderate pace. With all the conveyors and equipment, if he let Boomer loose, he'd disappear and they'd have no idea where he was. They both stopped as they heard rattling ahead and to their left. Ariana's phone vibrated, and she had a whispered conversation. Holstering it again, she tapped Logan on the shoulder. "They can't get in," she told him.

Logan turned probing eyes on her. "What do you mean they can't get in? We're trapped in here? I need the other officers with me."

"Max is there. So is your team. They can't open the door."

"Max doesn't have security access?"

She nodded furiously. "Of course he does." They both remained motionless again as they heard more clattering. Ariana thought it sounded as if Wayne had tripped over something. "Same as me," she said. "But his card's not working."

"Can they break the door down?"

"I don't know. It's metal. Heavy gauge. This area is high security."

He exhaled. "Can we open it from this side?"

"I think so."

"I don't want to separate from you, but I need to go after him. Go back. Open the door, if you can, but then stay outside with Max. Don't stay in here or try to catch up with me. Please don't argue with me on this."

Ariana realized there was no point disagreeing, and it would cost them time they didn't have to spare. She gave him a quick overview of the configuration of the space. "Okay. Stay safe," she begged. Despite how much he'd hurt her, she still loved him and didn't want him injured.

"I will."

Ariana watched for a second as he ran off, Boomer on his leash, Logan's weapon was in his hand. She sprinted back to the door, only fifty yards or so behind her.

She scrambled to open it, but it wouldn't budge. She tried again, throwing all her weight into it, with no success. She pulled out her phone, called Max. "I can't open it from this side either. It must be in lockdown. I don't have anything to force it. You need to do it from your side. If the cops can't get it, I have to see if I can help Logan." She disconnected before Max could object, and with Logan's admonition ignored, headed off at a run again.

When she heard a gunshot, she ducked instinctively even though it sounded far away. The sound of the bullet ricocheting chilled her right down to her bones. The soft thud that followed terrified her. She wanted to cry out to Logan, but he couldn't respond for risk of giving his location away and it would only serve to draw attention to her. If she was to be of any help to him, she'd have to stay silent and hidden.

Fresh gunfire, whether it was Logan or Wayne shooting, meant that Logan was alive. She continued to run, crouched low to the ground, trying to shelter herself behind the equipment.

Gunshots continued to echo around Ariana, causing her to take cover. Although Logan was armed, Ariana was not, and the many metal surfaces in the confined space could cause bullets to ricochet in erratic ways, making gunfire highly unpredictable and dangerous. She supposed Wayne was either unaware or uncaring of this, as the shots kept ringing out.

She could now hear the sound of booted feet on cement and metal. Two sets at a rapid pace. When she heard a short bark, she glanced up. Boomer was on a conveyor belt above her head. In the wake of the gunfire, Logan must have released the leash. If they'd been right that Wayne was planting explosives in bags, Boomer would have tracked one that Wayne had already tampered with.

But the dog was caught. His leash was wedged in the conveyor propulsion mechanism, pulling Boomer along. The dog was straining against it, but was being dragged relentlessly toward the scanning machine. After clearing the scanner, Ariana knew the conveyor picked up speed as the bags were sorted for their flights. Depending on the flight, the conveyer also made some sharp turns. Bags with unreadable checked luggage codes were tossed into a holding area for manual sorting. If Boomer made it through the scanner unharmed, he'd be treated like a bag with an invalid tag and sent down a steep incline with a drop at the end.

If Boomer made it that far, and his leash hadn't dislodged…well, beyond that point, the conveyer was not designed to carry bags. It had a near-vertical return. She didn't want to think about it.

Without giving it much thought, she stripped off the body armor vest and then her jacket, tossing both on the floor. Releasing her ponytail, she used the elastic to secure her hair into a tight knot at the nape of her neck. If either her jacket or her hair got caught, she'd be no better off than Boomer and of no use to him.

Ruthlessly blocking her own fear, she rose and climbed up on the conveyor that Boomer was on. Moving as fast as she could while keeping low to avoid overhead obstructions, she ran to the dog.

The dog knew he was stuck and in trouble,

and it showed in his agitation. Ariana was well aware that fear could make dogs unpredictable.

Her heart hammered in her chest and her hands were slick with perspiration by the time she was a couple of arm's lengths away from him. Worse, the dog was now only a few yards from the dark, gaping opening into the X-ray machine. Once he was in there, her chance to save him would be lost. She felt the fear creeping into her bones and muscles, threating to paralyze her. She heard the dog whimper. She held her arms out in front of her and tried desperately to not let her voice quaver.

"I'm here to help, okay, Boomer? Good boy," she amended with a prayer as she moved forward, unclipping his leash with her right hand while grabbing his collar with her left, and pulling him toward her.

Not a moment too soon. The leash was pulled into the security scanner, the loose end flailing and hitting the metal walls of the device with loud clanging noises. Ariana pulled Boomer with her away from thc scanner and, releasing him, jumped down from the belt. She landed hard on one knee, and a sharp pain radiated up her leg. She called, "Jump, here, Boomer!" hoping the dog would follow. If he didn't, there was nothing further she could do to save him.

She was relieved to see Boomer, just inches

away from the machine again, shuffle in place and leap.

Ignoring the sting in her knee, she rose and grabbed Boomer's collar again. She didn't want him rushing to where Logan was. She knew police dogs were trained for handler protection in addition to their primary responsibility. She realized that if Boomer was allowed to act on instinct, he'd rush Wayne to protect Logan. He wouldn't have a chance. He'd be shot and it wouldn't help Logan, who she trusted was alive and hopefully uninjured, based on the gunshots that continued to reverberate around her.

There was a loud grinding of gears and she saw the conveyor slow and come to a halt. At least they'd been able to override the system and shut it down. But they hadn't penetrated the door yet. That meant Logan continued to be on his own.

She couldn't be of any help either, if she was holding on to the dog's collar. She glanced around for any item she could use to secure Boomer without risk of harm, or at least use as a leash. When her phone vibrated, it gave her an idea. She pulled her belt off as she answered the call.

"Max, what's going on? Any progress gaining entry at door A-173 or any of the others?" she whispered while pulling her belt off and looping it around Boomer's collar.

"No." She could hear the frustration and worry in his voice. "We've tried the cargo doors, too. No luck with any of them. They're locked down tight and we can't break through the programming."

"Can you take the—" Ariana stopped in midsentence when more shots rang out. They sounded closer. She'd nearly forgotten about Boomer until he tensed and she felt the tug on the belt.

"What was that?" Max asked. "Gunshots?"

"Yeah," Ariana said, keeping her voice low. "I have to go. Break down the doors, if you can. Get in here, if you have to drive a truck through the loading dock door, but get us help." She disconnected without waiting for an answer.

She was at a loss for what to do. If she tied Boomer off somewhere, she bet he'd get loose. If he didn't before Wayne got to him…

Logan had told her to stay back and stay out of the way. As futile as that madc her feel, she understood why. Logan was playing cat and mouse with Wayne. If she got in the way, she'd be a liability for Logan and a possible hostage for Wayne. She didn't have a gun, so at a distance she'd be of no use at all. Keeping herself and Boomer out of the way and safe was her smartest course of action, she rationalized, but it stung to feel so powerless.

She heard another round of shots, more running feet and what sounded like a hard landing on a metal surface. She backed up to the conveyor behind her. At least it remained stationary. With the system down, the rattle in the screening equipment startled her and she spun around and stood back as Wayne shot out and slid down the conveyor belt, gun in hand. He got his balance and stood, feet braced and shoulder-width apart with the large metal box of the scanner behind him.

Boomer growled and strained at her side, the force causing the leather of her belt to dig into her palm. If she let him go, it would mean the end for him. Even so she said a silent prayer that Wayne wouldn't just shoot him for the sheer noise he was making. When her eyes locked with Wayne's, it chilled her to the core, but she understood he wasn't bothered by the dog. He was entirely focused on her.

"Well, well, well, Ariana Atkins. You couldn't just leave matters alone, could you?"

"I don't understand. Leave what alone?"

He motioned dismissively with his gun. "Maybe you really are as slow as George Dennison thought."

Ariana's palm felt slick on her belt. "George?

I don't understand," she repeated in a steady voice.

Wayne laughed, harsh and loud, and hopped of the conveyor. "You ruined it all! Do you have any idea how much money we were making here, until you came along and started tightening your procedures and improving the security systems? George handpicked you, because he figured you'd be nice and compliant and leave things the way he had them. He couldn't keep working forever, but he wanted the fees to keep flowing for him, for Aaron and me. That meant we needed someone to head up security who wouldn't take too close a look at what we were doing."

Things were starting to fall in place for Ariana. Whatever had happened, it was illegal and George had been part of it. George! The man she'd trusted and thought of as a mentor. His betrayal hurt deeply, but she didn't have time to worry about it.

She heard no other sound and had no idea where Logan was, if he was alive or dead. That terrified her. She prayed he was okay. She felt a modicum of relief, because Wayne had lowered the gun slightly. She hoped her skills to read people would help her now. To be able to keep Wayne talking long enough for someone to help her...and Logan.

Ariana could see that whatever was driving Wayne was a cancer inside him. He was not in his right mind. Something had twisted him.

"Why have you been doing what you have, then? Playing with us, rather than just killing me right away?"

"Oh, I had no intention of killing you. That wasn't the plan. The goal was to either get you to quit or have Murdoch fire you for incompetence. When that didn't happen and the feds started to get uncomfortably close to catching us, I thought I'd implicate you, seeing it's all your fault that we've run into the problems we have."

Ariana felt a sliver of hope. "Then you've accomplished that. I've written up my resignation. It's in my office. I just haven't had a chance to present it to Calvin yet. Put the gun down," she pleaded. "Come with me to my office and I'll show you. You can give it to Calvin, if you want."

"No. I'm in too deep now. I can't pay my debts. Our smuggling operation is virtually out of business because of *your* tightened procedures. George is gone, and now it's only Aaron and me." Wayne was waving his gun around. "We can't meet our commitment to the cartels for the firepower they need. And it's not just about the money. You don't break a promise to those people. The feds have caught our colleagues in Texas, so it's only a matter of time before they come for us. Enough of this!" he bellowed.

He pointed the gun with a rock-steady hand directly at her head.

Ariana wanted to squeeze her eyes shut so she wouldn't see him pull the trigger, but before he had a chance, a blur of motion distracted her. She heard two shots fired almost simultaneously, and she dropped down instinctively, wrapping herself around Boomer to restrain and protect him.

Logan landed in a heap in front of her, blood seeping from his left arm.

"Oh, God. Oh, my God," Ariana whispered and spared a quick glance at Wayne. He, too, was on the floor and motionless, with an apparent chest wound. His gun had flown out of his hand. She scrabbled up, letting Boomer go. As much as she wanted to check on Logan's condition first, she needed to ascertain Wayne's state and ensure he couldn't get his gun. Boomer immediately ran to Logan.

She kicked Wayne's gun away and toward Logan, while she felt for a pulse. He was still breathing.

"Is he alive?" Logan asked, pushing himself up.

"Yes." She flipped Wayne over, uncaring of the loud groan. Pulling a flex cuff out of her pants pocket, she secured his hands behind his back, getting a small sense of satisfaction from hearing him grunt again, even though she tried to be gentle when she moved his arms behind his back to secure them.

Confident that Wayne could no longer hurt them, she scuttled over to Logan, who'd risen to a sitting position, primarily to avoid the exuberant licking Boomer was administering. Kneeling in front of him, Ariana cupped his face with her palms. "Are you okay? I mean are you injured anywhere other than your arm?"

"Just that and my head." He reached up, likely checking for blood, but thankfully his hand came away dry. "When Gallagher shot at me, I fell back against a conveyor track. I must have knocked myself out." She nudged away his other hand that had been covering his wound in an effort to stem the flow of blood so she could inspect it. "But that one hurts a lot."

Noticing her jacket on the floor not far away, she scrambled over to get it, to use it for a tourniquet. They both froze when they heard a loud crashing sound.

Logan tensed. "What the heck was that?"

It took Ariana a minute, but she knew. "A vehicle breaking through the loading dock doors."

Logan relaxed, and Ariana quickly tied her thin jacket around his arm. She called out so they could find them. Knowing they'd have moments at best before Logan would be whisked away to the hospital, she clasped his face between her palms and stared into his eyes. "You saved me. You got hurt but you saved me." She pressed her lips to his hurriedly. "Whatever was or wasn't between us, I owe you my life. Thank you."

"For a kiss from you, I'd like to say anytime, but this does hurt. Besides, we're even." He glanced at Boomer. "If I'm correct about what happened here, you saved my dog."

Ariana looked at Boomer, too, and briefly explained what she'd done. "So, I guess I did, yes."

Logan placed his good hand on her shoulder. "Knowing your history, that's a remarkable act of bravery."

The vehicle could be heard approaching as close as it could get, and then they heard running feet.

"Did you hear what Wayne said about the smuggling?"

Logan nodded. "Yes."

Ariana stared at him in disbelief. "You knew and you didn't say anything to me?"

"I couldn't. You were a suspect."

"What?"

"Yeah. They had evidence that the airport's chief security officer was involved. A number programed on a phone they confiscated, the keying of the baggage storage room to your master but not Max's, and other bits of information. Now we know it was the *former* chief security officer, Dennison. We have Gallagher. We're getting Aaron Wilkes, and Dennison will soon be in custody, too. We've got them," Logan said. "You don't have to worry anymore." His eyes were fathomless. "Things will go back to normal for you now."

They could see the team running toward them now. The hurt and disappointment caused by George's betrayal sliced through her again, but it didn't match the pain caused by losing what could have been between Logan and her.

"Goodbye, Logan, and take care of yourself," Ariana said, before she rose and walked toward Max.

LOGAN WAS MORE than happy to turn Gallagher over to members of his team for booking. He was equally relieved to have Rick and Nitro on the scene to check the bags to ascertain that Gallagher hadn't done what they'd feared and placed explosives in any of them.

It was obvious now that Gallagher had taken over from Dennison to run the on-site smuggling operations after Dennison's retirement. With the cartels not getting the firearms he'd promised them, he would have known it was more than loss of revenue; his life was at risk. Before Logan handed Gallagher over, he told Logan that at first, he'd just wanted to be rid of Ariana, with hopes of everything going back to normal if she was gone. For a period, he'd hoped that Dave Langdon might have gotten the position. That would have meant the smuggling operations could have continued unfettered, not because he was involved in the ring, but simply because he would have been lax.

As Logan watched Ariana walk away with Max and some of the others, again clearly in charge, the pain in his chest overshadowed that in his arm.

He loved her. She'd handled herself well. She hadn't fallen apart at the sight of guns or blood. But he'd destroyed whatever chance they could have had together through no choice of his own. Although his belief in her had never wavered, he could not pursue a personal relationship with her, nor could he have told her about the smuggling ring investigation when she was a suspect. How ironic that when he'd finally found love, forces conspired to keep them apart.

The pain intensified and he nearly shouted after her. Instead, he let Carl Rossi help him to the vehicle so he could be transported to the hospital. He prayed that the painkillers they'd give him would at least dim the excruciating ache in his heart.

Even as they drove off, he couldn't take his eyes off Ariana. He kept his gaze on her until she walked out of his sight and…now that he'd hired another handler to deal with the airport… out of his life.

CHAPTER TWENTY-ONE

ARIANA STRODE INTO the Security and Asset Protection office area. Cyn immediately pushed out of her chair and rushed over to her. She clasped Ariana's arms and peered into her eyes.

"Are you okay?" Cyn asked.

No, she wasn't okay and probably wouldn't be for a long, long time. Ariana understood that Cyn's concern was about the trauma she'd been through helping to apprehend Wayne Gallagher and discovering that she'd been a suspect in a major smuggling operation. All weekend she'd stayed inside her apartment, barely eating or sleeping. She was deeply shaken by what had happened, yes, but that wasn't what bothered her the most. She would never have guessed that loving someone could hurt so much, if that love was not returned. It didn't surprise Ariana that Cyn would be worried about her. In the year they'd worked together, this was the first time Ariana had arrived at the office after Cyn, with the exception of when she'd had off-site meetings.

She surprised herself by rubbing a hand over Cyn's in a comforting gesture. "I'll be fine. Thanks."

Based on the expression on Cyn's face, she hadn't convinced her.

"Okay," Cyn said skeptically. "I'll get you a coffee." She hesitated a moment. "You really don't look well. If you're not up to work today, you could go back home. There's nothing today that I can't reschedule."

"Thanks again, but I really need to be here." For her sanity, if nothing else. The last thing she wanted to do was to continue to sit at home in her apartment with nothing to do but think about Logan.

Ariana was just starting up her laptop when Cyn walked into her office, a mug of steaming coffee in her hand. She placed the mug on a coaster and handed Ariana an envelope. "This arrived for you."

The last time Ariana had received an unexpected plain white envelope was *not* a good experience. Turning it over, she noted with mild relief that this one had her name typed on the front with the SDPD logo on the top left. It was marked private and confidential. "Any idea what this is…or who brought it?" she asked hopefully, thinking of Logan.

Cyn shook her head, her bright gold hair

bouncing around her face. "I have no idea. It was dropped off by an SDPD officer I hadn't seen before just before I poured your coffee."

"Okay. Thanks." Ariana didn't know what to make of it. Could it be from Logan? Her heart rate accelerated, but her elation was short-lived. No, he wouldn't use official SDPD stationery or have someone else deliver it, if he was sending her a personal message.

Ariana waited for Cyn to leave before slicing the envelope open.

The note was on official SDPD letterhead and carried the seal of the chief of police. She scanned the letter and slumped back in her chair.

Then she read it again, to convince herself it was real.

> The San Diego Police Department and I, personally, are grateful to you for your selfless act on behalf of one of our dedicated public servants.
>
> We cannot adequately express our gratitude to you for your heroic conduct in saving the life of Police Service Dog Boomer.
>
> As a token of our appreciation, we would like to bestow you our medal of valor. The honor of your presence is requested at our awards ceremony this month to give me the

pleasure of presenting the medal to you in person, along with my heartfelt appreciation for saving the life of one of our finest.
Police Chief Marcia Cohen.

It was all there, in black and white. Ariana was getting a medal of valor from the police force that had deemed her unfit to serve. She let out a breath, followed by a nervous laugh. She was excited…until she read the honor roll at the bottom of the page and realized that Logan was also up for a commendation for his actions.

After having kept it together—barely—when she'd said goodbye to him at the airport, she'd have to face him once more. Panic swelled in her chest. Would she be able to do it again?

She glanced at the date and time of the event. Should she decline the presentation, make some excuse that she had a prior commitment?

That would be plain stupid and cowardly. She had to go.

She had to suck it up and face Logan. How could she not accept such a huge honor in person? In a way, it made up for her rejection by the force…to be recognized by the chief of police for the department she'd wanted to work for. If her goal had been to make a difference, it seemed that all these years later she had.

The ceremony was only a few days away.

She'd have to steel herself against seeing Logan. She'd be polite. She'd be pleasant.

She'd keep her distance as much as possible.

She didn't think she could stand much more.

THE DAY OF the ceremony arrived quickly. Ariana was glad for it.

She was excited and honored to receive the recognition, and knowing that she'd saved the life of a police service dog rather than that of a human officer didn't trivialize it for her. She knew how closely bonded the K-9 handlers were with their dogs, and she appreciated the important and dangerous job the dogs performed.

Still, she just wanted the event to be over.

As much as she was apprehensive about seeing Logan, to her surprise she no longer had such reservations about seeing Boomer. It astonished but also gratified her to realize that she hadn't been frightened, even when she was essentially lying on top of the dog, shielding him. At least something good had come of it, if she was over her phobia.

Ariana contemplated wearing a dress for the occasion—something celebratory, and maybe just wanting to let Logan see her in a way he never had before. That was wrong, too. She thought about her suits, and decided on the rich, royal blue one that complemented her skin tone and eyes. The severely tailored jacket showed off her slim figure, and the pleated, flirty A-line skirt that went with it was all feminine, a style she didn't often go for.

It mattered how she looked, and it had nothing to do with the expected presence of the media.

She'd first coiled her hair in a bun, but at the last minute decided to undo it and leave it down. That was vanity, as well, she had to admit. She *wanted* Logan to see her at her best. As childish as it seemed, she wanted him to see what he'd missed out on. She applied eye shadow, liner, mascara, blush and a light coat of lip gloss. She slipped into high-heeled shoes, another rarity for her.

Staring into the mirror, she was pleased with her appearance.

"Hey, Sabrina, what do you think?" she asked when the cat walked in. Ariana scratched Sabrina behind her ears and took the low purr as a sign of approval. Let Logan eat his heart out, she thought.

She could have been picked up by a uniformed officer, but she'd declined. As much as it would've added to the thrill, it would've prevented a quick-and-easy escape in her own vehicle. If her emotions got the best of her and she had to leave in a hurry, she didn't want to risk breaking down in front of a stranger—not to mention a person whom Logan would probably know. She anticipated that she might have to make a fast exit. If she couldn't *think* of Logan without being overwhelmed, what would happen when she *saw* him?

And she did, as soon as she entered the banquet hall where the awards ceremony was being held. Her eyes were drawn to him immediately through the crowded room. She'd never seen him in his full dress uniform, which he was wearing today.

Why did he have to look so darn good in it? Boomer was by his side, wearing his police collar and badge, and a spiffy little vest. He was being decorated today, as well.

Concentrate. Concentrate on why you're here, she ordered herself.

Logan must have seen her, too. With Boomer trotting beside him, he was making his way toward her.

He stopped inches in front of her, and she felt as if his eyes were boring right into her.

"Ariana. You're…stunning," he said after a moment's hesitation.

Certain she was blushing, she bent down to greet Boomer. It amazed her that she didn't feel the least bit apprehensive petting the dog, or even when he licked her hand.

When she straightened again, she preoccupied herself with a small piece of lint she'd noticed on the sleeve of her jacket.

Logan held a hand out toward her. "Ariana, I—"

"May I have your attention, please!" Whatever Logan might have been about to say was interrupted when a woman dressed in civilian clothes called for the attendees' attention, asked them to be seated and introduced Chief of Police Cohen. Both she and Logan turned to face the podium.

The chief took the stage and went through the preliminaries. Ariana was acutely aware of Logan standing only inches away from her, where they'd been asked to wait until they were introduced. She prayed they'd get on with the ceremony soon as she didn't know how long she could stand there and not humiliate herself by throwing herself into his arms.

When Ariana's name was called, she nearly sprinted up to the podium, only to be horrified to hear that the medal would be presented to her jointly by the chief and Boomer's handler, Captain Logan O'Connor. She forced the smile to remain on her face.

Logan and Boomer mounted the podium. She had no idea what the chief or Logan were saying. She found she was having trouble breathing let alone hearing over the roar of blood rushing in her ears. All she could think of was escaping, going home and burying her head under her pillow.

The thunderous round of applause was her cue that she could make her way off the podium, and she took the opportunity to do so quickly.

She wished she could've enjoyed the proceedings and taken pride in the honor she was given, but she was too broken up about seeing Logan again. She had every intention of rushing out of the auditorium, but a firm hand on her arm forestalled her.

"Where are you going in such a hurry?" Calvin Murdoch, her CEO, demanded.

Ariana hadn't realized he'd been there. Calvin had said nothing to her about attending. Of course, she'd been so fixated on Logan, she'd neglected to look around to see who else she might know in the crowd.

"I… I have an appointment. I don't want to be late."

"An appointment? On a Saturday? And when you're getting one of the highest forms of recognition the SDPD offers to civilians?" He shook his head. "Surely you can spare a little more time. Molly's here," he said. "She mentioned that there are a number of reporters wanting interviews with you. It's an opportunity for you to get us some positive coverage. To start rebuilding the reputation of the airport."

Releasing his hold on her arm, Calvin waved to someone behind her to join them. Ariana glanced back. Her desire to flee returned with a vengeance.

Logan, with Boomer heeling by his side, was walking toward her and Calvin.

Ariana was searching for a way to avoid him, but Calvin broke into her thoughts.

"I owe you an apology." When she shifted her startled gaze to Calvin, his eyes were on her and his lips were compressed into a grim line. "I doubted you. I shouldn't have, but I did. The board was putting so much pressure on me with what was going on. When that spineless incompetent Angus Stewart from the TSA started to insinuate that you weren't up for the job, it gave me a way out. It only added fuel to the fire when George approached me, expressing his concerns about you." Calvin's laugh was harsh, but he held her gaze. "To think I trusted him over you. I'm sincerely sorry.

"It's not the type of leader I am. At least not the type I want to be. I sacrificed you to take some of the burden off me. You are one of my key team members and deep down I knew you were managing as well as anyone could under the circumstances, but…"

He shrugged. "I was wrong." He gestured toward the direction from which Logan was approaching. "And Captain O'Connor stood up for you. Each and every time your competence was challenged by anyone—Angus or a member of the board—O'Connor never wavered. He was in your court, solid and constant… I should have listened." Ariana heard footsteps and clicking nails on hardwood directly behind her.

Ariana now knew that Logan had been working with the Drug Enforcement Administration and the Bureau of Alcohol, Tobacco, Firearms and Explosives to break up the smuggling ring. Of course he couldn't see her nor could he tell her what was happening while she was a suspect. What Calvin had revealed was more for her to digest. Contrary to what she'd believed, Logan had *not* been working to undermine her. He'd *supported* her. According to what Calvin had said, Logan might well have been her only supporter… and perhaps responsible for her *not* losing her job.

She struggled to keep the shock from showing on her face as she turned and her eyes locked with Logan's.

Her reservations…her conflicts with Logan had been misplaced. No wonder she couldn't make sense of why he'd want to undermine her…because he hadn't been. She'd been so wrong and so unfair in judging him. She'd been wrong with her mind, but not her heart.

When she'd chastised herself for loving a man who'd treat her the way she believed he had, her heart had been unwavering and recognized what her mind had not.

Her heart had been steady and true.

She *loved* him and it appeared that there was no reason for her not to have.

Although the realization caused her heart to soar, the sensation was short-lived.

To love and not have that love returned was worse than not to love at all, wasn't it? Would she be able to live with the emptiness and ache that caused? Or was it possible that he did want her? If they could just start over…

"ARIANA," LOGAN SAID when he reached them, and held a hand out to Calvin. "Mr. Murdoch."

Logan was proud of the recognition Ariana was receiving. Truth be told, he'd been instrumental in making it happen. He'd put in the recommendation for her saving Boomer. More than that. He'd lobbied vehemently for it and made the case personally to Chief Cohen. Ariana deserved the commendation as much as anyone.

What he hadn't counted on was that simply seeing her again nearly brought him to his knees.

He *loved* her. There was no question in his mind.

In that instant of looking into her eyes, a flood of images flashed through his mind. Of his mother, broken and forlorn after the death of his father. Of his parents, him and Becca in a happier time. His mother had had a good life. She hadn't always been the way he remembered her near the end. She'd loved and laughed and raised two kids. Somewhere along the way the fear had begun to consume her, but that didn't detract from a lifetime of happiness and love.

He thought of Cal and Jessica, their two little girls and their joy about adding a new baby to the family. Of Rick and Madison, and how Madison had complete trust in Rick regardless of the perils of his job. And of Ariana, so calm and composed when they were hunting down Gallagher, and the risk she took, despite her fear of dogs, to save Boomer.

He'd loved his mother and would forever, but maybe her reaction wasn't universal. Maybe in his memory it had become exaggerated. Maybe things could be different with Ariana.

Was it right for him to deny himself and—looking deep in Ariana's eyes and recognizing the depth of her feelings for him—deny her a lifetime of love?

If she'd still have him.

Calvin said something that Logan had missed. He tried to pick up the conversation without having to admit he hadn't been paying attention because he'd been daydreaming. About Ariana.

"...wanted to thank you for all that you did

for us, apprehending Gallagher and, working with the federal agencies, putting an end to the smuggling." He extended a hand again and Logan shook it. "On a personal note, thank you for standing up for Ariana. I know I should've been the one to do it. I failed her. You didn't. I respect that type of integrity."

Calvin released Logan's hand and shook Ariana's. "Congratulations and well deserved," he said to Ariana, before walking away.

Logan turned to Ariana. Her eyes were huge and round, her mouth slightly open. All he could think of was taking her into his arms and kissing her.

"You supported me. You stood up for me…" Her voice was a soft whisper.

"I don't know why you believed I wouldn't. You're good at what you do. Very good. I respect that."

"The way you acted…" He recognized the bewilderment on her face as much as her struggle to comprehend. She glanced at all the people around them. She must have realized this was not the time or the place for her to try to understand what had happened. He stepped in, close enough he could see the thin black rim around her light blue irises. He'd been so wrong, too, he realized.

Ariana was strong and steady. She valued the

work he did, had in fact aspired to do the same. It didn't take away from his mother or his love for her, but Ariana was a very different person. She *respected* rather than feared what he did.

He shook his head to clear the haze he'd allowed to exist there and impair his thinking for far too long. He reached toward Ariana's hand, but didn't dare take it into his, as much as he wanted to. Not here. Not now.

He feared her rejection. Believed he deserved it.

Instead, he brushed his hand over the back of hers. It would have to last him until they could be alone. Until he could explain, and hope… *hope* they could have a new start. "We need to talk, Ariana…"

"Okay," she said, her voice so eager that it gave him courage.

When she started to move in the direction of the exit, he laid a hand on her shoulder. "No. Not now." He wanted to grin when he saw the disappointment on her face. He smiled. "This is your moment. Enjoy it. Take it all in. Do the interviews Calvin wants you to do." When she hesitated, he did take her hand into his briefly and squeezed. "I'll wait for you. I'll be right here."

She sighed his name, and he could no longer resist. He didn't care who was watching. He cupped the back of her head gently. Briefly, light as a feather, he brushed his lips across hers. "We'll talk when you're done, but know that I love you."

He saw a shimmer of moisture in her eyes, and a faint smile on her lips. "Oh, Logan, I love you, too."

Now he grinned. "We have a lot to talk about. Go!" He gave her a gentle nudge in the direction of the airport's vice president of communications and the reporters clustered around her. Chief Cohen was there, too. Logan knew there'd be pictures of Ariana and the chief in the papers and newscasts. He knew Ariana well enough that it would mean a lot to her. She'd earned it.

He watched as she walked up to the group, shook hands, smiled, spoke into microphones and posed for pictures. Logan was immensely proud of her. He knew he'd not only found his lifelong love, but an equal partner, a woman both spirited and capable. He saw her shake her head decisively at a statement someone made. She was determined and principled, too. He chuckled to himself as he contemplated life with Ariana. It wouldn't always be easy, and it would never be boring. That was okay with him.

It would be a true partnership, an intellectual challenge, built on unwavering love and devotion.

He kept his eyes on her as she wrapped up the interviews. When she started to move with her confident, practical stride toward him, he noticed a sexy, teasing smile, and something deeper and more serious—a promise, perhaps—in the depth of her eyes.

He knew he'd have to convince her to marry him.

And soon.

Boomer let out an impatient whine. Logan placed his hand on the dog's head to settle him. He could relate to Boomer. He was feeling impatient, too. He didn't want to waste another moment without Ariana, knowing how much he loved, adored and respected her.

When she stepped up to him and into his arms, her eyes closed and she brushed her lips across his.

"It hasn't been easy or smooth, but I'm so glad I found you," he murmured. Then he said again the words he'd been wanting to say to her so badly and for so long. "I love you."

She smiled up at him. "I love you, too, and *I'm* so very fortunate to have found *you*," she replied, before he lowered his lips to hers.

* * * * *